Another minister attacked. Get home ASAP.

As Bryce looked over at her phone, she watched his expression go from neutral to grim.

"You got the same message?" she asked.

"Yes. Time to roll, partner."

They made quick excuses to their tablemates and worked their way out of the ballroom.

"He didn't wait long," Zora said. "It's not even officially the fourth Sunday of Advent."

"No."

"He's probably going to try something at the Children's Pageant on Christmas Eve. That's the big showstopper, isn't it?"

"You could be right. No matter what, you're not doing this alone, Zora. That's one thing about local law enforcement you should understand—no one's a loner. We're a team."

"So you've mentioned. It was like that in the navy. I get it."

"Good." From the grim determination in his tone, she knew he'd single-handedly do whatever he had to do in order to protect her.

Dear Reader,

Welcome to Silver Valley, Pennsylvania! Silver Valley is the fictional setting for the Silver Valley P.D. series, but is based on the Cumberland and Susquehanna Valleys. Since moving here several years ago, I've discovered an area rich in natural beauty, historical significance and warm citizens. It's a place I'm proud to be a part of. I knew I had to bring this setting to my writing, and when the characters started showing up in my head (a writer's affliction) I followed their lead to create the SVPD series.

When I reached out to the superintendent of police, Dick Hammon, not only did he return my call but he took me on several research trips and introduced me to people critical to maintaining the safety of our township and county. I've done a lot of exciting things in my navy past, but riding in an unmarked police car to the county prison made this writer's day.

If you've read my Whidbey Island series for Harlequin Superromance, you will find the same sense of community here, as well as many military veterans and other ties to the military, including a supersecret shadow government agency. I hope you'll enjoy the suspense and sexual tension in each story as the heroes and heroines fight to keep Silver Valley safe for all.

I hope you enjoy meeting the SVPD and the Trail Hikers, and I look forward to sharing this journey with you.

Peace,

Geri Krotow

PS: I love connecting with my readers! Please join the fun by signing up for my newsletter at my website, finding me on Facebook at my author page and adding to the storyboards for the Silver Valley series on Pinterest.

HER CHRISTMAS PROTECTOR

Geri Krotow

HARLEQUIN® ROMANTIC SUSPENSE

Recycling programs
for this product may
not exist in your area.

ISBN-13: 978-0-373-27943-2

Her Christmas Protector

This edition published by arrangement with Harlequin Books S.A.

For questions and comments about the quality of this book, please contact us at CustomerService@Harlequin.com.

® and TM are trademarks of Harlequin Enterprises Limited or its corporate affiliates. Trademarks indicated with ® are registered in the United States Patent and Trademark Office, the Canadian Intellectual Property Office and in other countries.

Printed in U.S.A.

www.Harlequin.com

Former naval intelligence officer and US Naval Academy graduate **Geri Krotow** draws inspiration from the global situations she's experienced. Geri loves to hear from her readers. You can email her via her website and blog, gerikrotow.com.

Books by Geri Krotow

Harlequin Romantic Suspense

Silver Valley P.D.

Her Christmas Protector

Harlequin Superromance

What Family Means
Sasha's Dad

Whidbey Island

Navy Rules
Navy Orders
Navy Rescue
Navy Christmas
Navy Justice

Harlequin Anthology

Coming Home for Christmas
Navy Joy

Harlequin Everlasting Love

A Rendezvous to Remember

Visit the Author Profile page at Harlequin.com for more titles.

Dedication:

For my mother, Susan. My gratitude for the love
of reading you gave me is surpassed only by
how much I miss you.

Acknowledgments:

A sincere thank-you to Richard Hammon, retired
superintendent of police for Silver Spring
Township, for your distinguished service and for
introducing me to so many wonderful community
servants who keep us all safe each day.
Thanks to Ron Turo, Cumberland Valley public
juvenile defender, for your invaluable insight.
Thank you to Dr. Lisa Davis, who helped me keep
my medical details credible.

Thank you to Paula Eykelhof, editor extraordinaire,
for supporting my romantic suspense muse,
and to Patience Bloom for welcoming me to the
Romantic Suspense team with such enthusiasm.

Chapter 1

Detective Bryce Campbell climbed out of his aging Ford Mustang and walked across the Silver Valley Police Department's graveled lot to the waiting unmarked cruiser. Its taillights glowed like two red Christmas tree bulbs in the darkness. Both of the officers assigned to him for this patrol were in the car, and he made out a third, smaller head in the backseat of the sedan.

A third person?

He opened the back passenger's door and slid into the car. Slim hands rested on slim thighs in utilitarian khakis.

A woman.

"Evening."

No response from the stranger.

"We never get enough of you, Detective Campbell." Officer Julian Samuel—Jules to the force—spoke from the driver's seat. He never wasted a chance to send a zinger at Bryce. They'd been up for promotion at the same time, and Bryce had not only received the advancement, he'd been assigned as one of three detectives on Silver Valley's force.

He ignored Jules. "How are you doing, Nik?"

"I'll be better when we catch the killer." Officer Nika Pasczenko's voice purred from the passenger's seat in front of Bryce. Although he couldn't see her in the dark interior, Bryce knew the first-generation Polish-American woman wore no makeup to emphasize her model-quality beauty. Not on the job. She'd been a godsend to Silver Valley, as her natural talent with languages, including Spanish and Russian, had helped them break into the drug and crime rings that were ever-expanding into their central Pennsylvania town from New York City, Philadelphia and Baltimore.

"And you're…?" Bryce didn't want the mystery rider to feel left out.

"Colleen Hammermill. I'm the volunteer chaplain tonight."

He made out shoulder-length hair, probably dark as it wasn't catching any of the ambient light in the car, and a throaty voice that sounded vaguely familiar.

"Bryce Campbell. Have we met?"

The leather seat creaked as she shifted.

"No."

Liar.

She was a rookie, too, at whatever she was trying to pull off. That tell with her body language could cost an officer his or her life.

"Are you a minister?"

"Yes, but I'm not assigned to a local church at the moment. I'm ecumenical and float from congregation to congregation as needed to give the local pastors a break."

He knew every volunteer chaplain, made up of local ministers, counselors and psychologists. They rode with the officers on a rotating basis and sat in the backseat as they encouraged the officers to open up about what dedicated law enforcement agents usually avoided—their emotions. Sometimes the volunteer chaplains were present during a crime or right after, and often proved excellent witnesses. No matter their background, they were all required to be certified counselors. If they thought an officer might be in emotional or mental difficulty, they were free to inform the superintendent of police.

Bryce had ridden with all of the chaplains, or so he thought.

He'd never met Colleen Hammermill.

His phone buzzed in his front pocket and he pulled it out.

Superintendent of police Colt Todd.

Now what?

"Campbell."

"Bryce, I assume you're in the cruiser and have met the new chaplain?"

"Yes, sir. But I don't…"

"No, she's not on the permanent roster, and yes, she's temporary. No questions. Just…"

"Sir?"

"Watch her six for me, will you?" Superintendent Todd's voice was gruff. That wasn't unusual, but his more personal request to watch Colleen's back, using the military term both Todd and Bryce knew well, certainly was. Superintendent Todd's request was clear—he needed him to protect the mystery ride along.

"Yes, sir."

Bryce ended the call and stared at the phone's screen for a full beat.

Just who the hell was Chaplain Colleen Hammermill?

Zora Krasny wanted to kick herself for even thinking about squirming when Bryce Campbell slid in beside her. She'd be able to do that later, after this mission was complete. The fact that he'd acted as if he was suspicious of her, as though he knew she was giving him a fake name, as if he might find her familiar, made her want to bolt.

But they had a mission to accomplish.

Zora unobtrusively stretched her shoulders under her body armor. While her Kevlar vest was like an old friend and still fit her perfectly, she needed to get used to it again. She rarely needed bulletproof gear in her new job. She'd resigned her navy commission and ended her seven-year naval intelligence officer career three years ago. After six months of downtime she agreed to go to work for the Trail Hikers on an as-needed basis while she completed her civilian counseling degree program.

She'd been sporadically employed for the past two years by the Trail Hikers, a secret government shadow agency that existed to aid local and federal law enforcement with particularly difficult cases. Cases that needed more financial backing or expertise than was provided in the everyday operating budgets of regular law enforcement.

The training she'd received from the Trail Hikers had far surpassed her military schooling and she relished the new tactics she'd learned. The only reason she felt any jitters at all was that Bryce Campbell was sitting next to her.

So far the Trail Hikers had only sent her into the field on basic missions. Decoy, undercover distraction, tailing a suspect. Nice breaks from her schoolwork and new, permanent counseling position in the Silver Valley community. The Trail Hikers took care of clearing her counseling schedule whenever they needed her, as they paid for her answering service. She'd worked hard to get her psychology degree and knew that assisting clients through their tough times was one of her passions, as she'd had help in her darkest hours. When she'd had to start over because of the criminal actions of others.

Justice was another passion.

This was the first time the Trail Hikers had assigned her to track with the intent to ensnare a criminal. The fact that it was in her hometown made it that much more personal, more imperative to her that she get the suspect.

The Female Preacher Killer, as the FBI and local law enforcement agencies—LEA—referred to the murderer, was blamed for two murders and three near misses in central Pennsylvania. The second killing had occurred in Silver Valley Township two months ago, and the Trail Hikers and every other LEA in Silver Valley wanted to catch the killer before they found another murdered minister.

The last victim had been one of Zora's clients, a Methodist minister who'd come to counseling to work through issues from her childhood. Like the first victim, she'd been found dead in her driveway. The near misses had been more recent, female ministers shot at as they'd left their respective church services. Two had sustained significant but not life-threatening injuries, while the third had been grazed on her temple by the killer's bullet. Like her childhood best friend—Bryce Campbell, sitting next to her—this case was too close to home for Zora's liking.

She hadn't run into Bryce Campbell in the entire time she'd been back home, not while living as herself nor as Reverend Colleen Hammermill. When she left the navy she'd moved back to Silver Valley, but to a different part of the sprawling suburb of Harrisburg than where she'd grown up since age twelve. With a population of twenty thousand, it wasn't extraordinary that she hadn't run into him yet. She hadn't sought out any of her former high school classmates or friends.

Why did she have to bump into him tonight, when her undercover disguise was vital to the operation's success?

"You nervous about doing this with that lunatic out there, Chaplain?" Bryce's voice betrayed no suspicion of her. He was a pro.

"No. I've got the best protection in Silver Valley, right?" She smiled but inwardly winced. Lying came too easily to her. The officers in the front seats thought she was a real chaplain, needing protection from the man or woman who'd been making female ministers a target for the past year.

No one in SVPD knew about the Trail Hikers, except for one man. The man who ran the entire force, Superintendent Colt Todd.

Officer Samuel pulled out of the SVPD lot and toward the main artery of the surrounding area. Zora cast a quick look at Bryce. His profile was more attractive than she'd remembered. Fifteen years had passed since they'd graduated from Silver Valley High School, fifteen years since she'd canceled their date for the senior prom and effectively ended their childhood bond.

It was more than that.

She'd given him a week's warning that she wasn't going to prom with him. Guilt still prodded at the mental floodgate that kept her memories of the boy who had been her best friend compartmentalized.

He wasn't the boy she'd known anymore, though. His profile was etched with the years that had passed.

Her mother had tried to catch her up on Bryce and other classmates but Zora had asked her to stop. Truth was she had no intention of looking up Bryce or any past Silver Valley acquaintances.

She should have checked the SVPD roster and told Superintendent Todd to assign a different detective to tonight's mission, or she'd have to go back to the Trail Hikers and let one of the other women on the team fill in.

Too late now.

The bright lights of the football stadium, so large it rivaled many college fields, made the night sky glow even though they were a full mile away from their target area. It was a prime spot to lure out the killer. It had been announced for weeks that a female minister would give the invocation for the community's holiday festival, and an exposition football game was part of the celebration. Zora, in her cover as a female minister, was to play the killer's victim of choice.

Adrenaline surged through her system and she curled her toes, trying to stay grounded. She really wanted to get this bastard.

Officer Samuel spoke to her from the front seat. "Chaplain, we'll continue as planned. You take your time walking around the concessions, around the bleachers where the fans are seated. We have officers all over the place—that stadium is on a virtual lockdown. Everyone attending the game has gone through a metal detector.

When they call you out on the field for the invocation, go up and say the prayer. As soon as the marching band finishes the national anthem, leave the field and immediately go around the back of the main school building. We'll be waiting for you in the teachers' parking lot and we'll bring you back to the station. You're safe with us."

Zora nodded, sensing Bryce's attention on her as he finished speaking.

"Right. I'm not worried about my safety with you backing me up. I trust you. Besides, it would be pure stupidity for the killer to try something in such a public place." But she hoped her words proved wrong. She hoped the psycho who thought picking off women of the cloth was some kind of sport took the bait. The killer was sloppy—he'd attempted to kill three women, and of the two he did manage to kill, one had only died because she had been on a blood thinner. She'd bled out from what otherwise would have been a survivable wound.

The officers in front murmured their agreement. Bryce remained silent.

Did he recognize her voice?

Impossible. She'd never come back since she'd left for the naval academy, save for short holiday visits to see Mom and Dad. They were adoptive parents in name only—they'd loved her through her hardest years.

From what her mom had told her, Zora knew Bryce's parents had moved to a fifty-five-plus community a few years ago. The house with the top window she'd stared at for so many dark summer nights had been sold to a new family at least a decade ago.

Even if he *was* available, she'd be the last person he'd ever want to befriend. Not after how she'd betrayed him, betrayed the deep friendship they'd shared.

You betrayed yourself most of all.

She tried to force back the unwanted memories of the way she'd closed herself off, even six years after moving to Silver Valley. She'd been placed in the home next to Bryce's as part of the Witness Security Program when she was twelve years old.

But she'd never told him about her life before Silver Valley, or where she was from.

Snap out of it.

Mission focus was essential. With any luck, there'd be a serial killer with a weapon aimed at her in the next fifteen minutes. SVPD would apprehend the psycho and Silver Valley would be safe again.

Zora watched the stadium lights grow from a soft glow to the harsh glare of hundreds of incandescent lights. The rumble of the crowd's cheers penetrated the unmarked car's tinted windows.

She pretended to stretch and allowed her fingers to lightly brush her weapon under the roomy Silver Valley High School jacket she wore over her bulletproof vest. She hoped she'd never need to use the pistol; her job was to attract the criminal's attention, giving the local and federal agents that were part of this operation something to work with. A suspect.

"Here you go, Chaplain." Officer Samuel opened her door.

"Thanks, officers."

Before she eased her way out of the car she allowed herself a quick look at Bryce.

The stadium lights illuminated the car and his eyes glowed with intensity. How had she forgotten how bright his blue-gray eyes were?

You haven't forgotten one thing about him.

"When you get back, let's see if we can't figure out how we know each other, Chaplain Hammermill."

She laughed. "I don't think…"

"Save it for some other chump. Is that a wig you're wearing, or have you dyed your hair? And those black-rimmed glasses—pure Halloween. Next time, don't be so obvious." His voice was low, precluding Officers Samuel and Pasczenko from hearing his words.

Zora ignored the sick drop of her stomach and got out of the car.

Combined aromas of hot popcorn, funnel cakes and hot chocolate triggered memories Zora would rather forget. The first couple of years after she'd been placed in witness protection and moved to central Pennsylvania, far away from her abusive "family"—aka the cult her mother had joined—had been rough. Growing up on a compound in upstate New York had made her people smart. She knew when a man looked at her if he was genuinely interested in her or only wanted to satisfy his lust. It had taught her to trust no one and make friends only if she needed something from the other person.

What it hadn't taught her was that truly good people existed in the world, that not all teenage girls were waiting for their sacrificial bonds of matrimony to honor the Family Father, that not all boys grew up to be misogynistic monsters.

Misogynist. She'd first learned the word in eleventh grade, in Ms. Perkins's English literature class.

The entire True Believers cult she'd been forced into at age seven was disbanded now, two decades later. Because of her testimony. The little girl who'd wanted freedom from the madness more than she'd wanted to live.

"Reverend Hammermill?" A slim woman in a sport jacket emblazoned with the high school logo smiled at her.

"Principal Essis. Nice to meet you." Zora held her hand out to the middle-aged woman, who grasped it firmly.

"Thanks so much for coming out and saying the invocation for tonight's game." The principal's gaze was frank and assessing.

"It's an honor."

"You're probably safer here than anywhere at the moment. I want my students to be kept safe." The principal's voice conveyed her frustration. The school district had paid for metal detectors and extra security at the entrance to the stadium. Zora was grateful for the precaution.

"As do I." She wanted to add that she'd had Principal Essis as a math teacher in ninth grade, but that would have to wait for another time, when Zora wasn't undercover.

The low, steady rhythm of the marching band's drums vibrated in the air.

"If you'll follow me, I'll take you out to the podium."

Zora walked behind Principal Essis. They were escorted around the metal detectors to the area below the stands. Zora barely felt the press of her weapon in the small of her back, under the school jacket, but her fingers were ready to reach for it at the first sign of the gig going bad.

Once out on the field, Zora stood in front of the marching band and faced the home crowd. It had grown from the time she'd been a student, and for a moment she was struck by the enormity of her mission.

Find the Female Preacher Killer. Draw him out.

The band played "America the Beautiful." Zora used the time to take stock of her surroundings.

"Silver Valley High School, welcome to the opening game of the season! Welcome alumni, community members and students. We have Reverend Hammermill with us to start off our great night with the invocation. Please stand."

The band quieted and Zora took the microphone.

"Let us give thanks…" Zora recited the ecumenical vanilla prayer she'd memorized last night. A part of her, deep inside, balked at portraying a woman of the cloth. She'd lived a life far from the world of church meetings and Bible studies. Yet she meant each word when she'd come up with the prayer.

Her memorization allowed her to do her job as a Trail Hikers agent. She scanned the crowd for anyone appearing different from the ordinary winter festival-goer or football fan.

A sea of the Silver Valley Hawks' royal blue school color faced her, most of the faces pointed in her direction. She wasn't interested in the crowd, but the fringes. A killer would need a quick escape, and the tall bleachers prevented that for most of the ticket holders.

A line of concession vendors, with boxes strapped around their necks and resting on their waists, stood near the entrance to the field. They were all dressed for the chilly weather and all had the same box—white with the school logo on it. All wore matching school-themed knit ski caps with huge pom-poms on top.

Except for one.

"May we play honestly and win graciously…"

Male, average height and build, baseball cap. To her far right at the edge of the bleachers. With sunglasses—totally disguised.

"Thank you for our school…"

He reached over his shoulders and behind his head. With both hands.

Zora reached behind and under her jacket, her SIG Sauer's handle firmly in her grasp.

"Thank you also for our teachers…" She had to draw out the prayer, to keep the crowd in its place, so that the undercover and regular LEAs could protect everyone.

The Hawk County sheriff's snipers would've had this guy in their sights by then. If they didn't, she'd take him out.

The "vendor" pulled his hands up from behind his back, holding a long dark object. If it was a rifle, she had seconds to neutralize him.

"Amen." Total silence surrounded her and Zora waited for the crowd's response.

"Amen. Go Hawks!" At least the roar of the crowd would drown out the sound of gunfire.

The vendor held the long item in his arms, his face on Zora. He flashed a wide grin that Zora knew was meant for her.

The first strains of the national anthem began to a crowd that soon began to sing along to the school's marching band.

He was waiting for her to tip off that she wasn't a chaplain.

She could outwait with the best of them. But not when other lives were at stake.

If he planned to try to kill her here in front of all of these civilians, including many children, it was out of pattern for him. He had no decent escape route.

Her hand steadied as she pressed against her back, her weapon ready to fire. She watched as he pulled his weapon. The minute he revealed it, she or a county sher-iff's sniper were in the clear to take him out.

The vendor shot first.

He opened a golf umbrella.

Relief flooded through Zora, followed by red-hot anger. That was no vendor. She was sure he'd meant to make her believe he had a weapon.

"Thank you, Chaplain." Principal Essis stood in front of her, blocking the vendor from her sight. She reached out her hand.

Zora blinked. She released her weapon and grasped the principal's hand.

"You're welcome."

She walked off the field as the band started an upbeat number, revving the crowd for the kickoff. As she headed straight for the spot where the man with the golf umbrella had stood only seconds before she knew what she'd find.

He was gone.

She searched the crowd for SVPD and her gaze landed on Bryce. He was walking toward her, his mouth in a grim line.

"Did you see him?"

"Who?"

"The man with the umbrella." She filled him in on what she'd witnessed, frustrated that he hadn't seen it, too. To her surprise Bryce called in her description to SVPD on his cell phone as soon as she finished speaking.

"Thanks for taking me seriously."

"Why wouldn't I?"

She couldn't tell him she'd been in the navy and had, as a woman, had to fight for credibility with each new command, each new tour. Apparently SVPD took it for granted that if you were assigned to work with them, you'd earned it.

"No reason. Just…thanks." She walked toward the waiting SVPD vehicle, aware of Bryce's silent presence next to her. One thing hadn't changed in fifteen years— she still had a sixth sense where Bryce was concerned.

Chapter 2

"He wasn't just a vendor with an umbrella, I'm certain." Zora spoke in the privacy of her car as she drove home, her mission to draw out the killer over. For today.

"I'm not doubting what you saw, Zora, but it doesn't fit this criminal's profile." Claudia Michaels, retired US Marine Corps general and CEO of the Trail Hikers, sighed audibly over the secure cellular connection. "This is supposed to be one of our easier missions. I wouldn't have risked you blowing your cover otherwise. Not this close to where you live."

"We'll get him. It's not over." The same foreboding that had struck her on the football field made her grip the steering wheel tighter. "But I may have blown my cover all by myself."

"Go ahead." Claudia's voice remained level but Zora knew her boss was gritting her teeth—the secrecy of the Trail Hikers was paramount to its success.

"The detective assigned to the case—Bryce Campbell—was my neighbor growing up. He may have recognized me. If he didn't, he'll figure it out. He's a smart man."

"That's not a problem. Detective Campbell has a stellar reputation and he'll follow Superintendent Todd's orders. I'll double-check to make sure."

Bryce must be one hell of a detective if Claudia was aware of him—he was SVPD, not fed or ex-military, as far as Zora knew.

"Are you going to tell me he's a Trail Hiker, too?"

Claudia sighed.

"You know I can't tell you who's on our team until you need to work with them."

"I do." The Trail Hikers worked on a strict need-to-know basis. Zora had come to recognize familiar faces at the agency's headquarters in Silver Valley but never pursued finding out who they were. There'd been no need to.

She'd know if she'd seen Bryce, however.

"I'm sorry I wasn't more careful with my disguise."

"Go back to your civilian job, Zora, and we'll be in touch soon."

"Roger."

Claudia ended the connection and Zora shut off her Bluetooth. The ugly brunette wig itched and she wanted a hot shower, a chilled glass of chardonnay and a couple hours with her favorite author's latest novel before bed. Maybe she'd spend the whole weekend reading. She had a full day of clients on Monday in what she considered her *real* job—family counseling. Claudia referred to it as her "civilian job" because it allowed Zora to live a normal life while taking on missions as needed for the Trail Hikers.

Counseling was her vocation now. But when the client she'd been seeing since she'd started her practice had been murdered two weeks ago, simply because she was a woman and a Protestant minister, Zora had known she had to take the mission. Louise had been seeing her for over a year and had been the kind of woman Zora hoped to become. Wise. Compassionate. Generous.

Her killer could not go unpunished.

Forcing herself to ease her grip on the wheel, Zora looked out over the dark and quiet farm fields that surrounded the property she'd chosen to make home two years ago. The area had promised safety, a place to stop running. The farmhouse had fit her desire for a slower pace of life, a respite from the grind that a military career demanded.

Bryce's presence, his stare, had unnerved her earlier. Of course she'd recognized him immediately—he'd been the only boy she'd ever let get close to her when she'd moved to Silver Valley as a twelve-year-old. Make that the only person, save her adoptive parents.

Her *real* parents.

And then she'd let Bryce down, broken their childhood friendship in the worst way. She'd left Silver Valley and never spoke to him again. Complete silence, no explanations. It'd been too risky to let him into her life completely. She'd believed she was protecting him from the worst parts of herself. She'd entered the naval academy without a backward glance at Silver Valley or Bryce.

Until tonight. He'd matured, grown handsome as she'd known he would. Seeing him again made her wonder why she'd been so awful to him, why she hadn't at least written to him over the years and apologized for her behavior. It always came back to the fact that she'd never explained why she'd left the way she had. Revealing her reasons would mean revealing her past. And that would be too painful, too complicated.

By his reaction tonight she knew he still remembered her on some level. He might not have figured out it was her under the wig and bulky bulletproof vest, but she had no doubt that he would, eventually.

He'd remember.

Bryce had always figured out what was bothering her, how to make her laugh on an otherwise dreary winter day during high school exam week. He'd been the best friend a girl like her could have hoped for—funny, kind and respectful. He'd never made her feel he wanted to be any more than friends even when the sexual pressures of their teenage years had confronted them on a daily basis.

The headlights swept her long driveway as she drove up to her old, small farmhouse. She noted that her front porch light was out. She hadn't had to change a bulb since she'd moved here, and seeing the darkness of the porch gave her the creeps. She parked and opted to walk around the well-lit right side of her house to use the back entrance. She had no close neighbors so she didn't have to worry about explaining her wig. It was one of the many advantages of buying a home outside of a conventional development.

The back of the house was dark, too, and she waved her arm high to activate the motion detector light.

Nothing happened. No light.

Butternut's sharp bark from within the house made her stop in her tracks. The German shepherd never barked when she came home. And those weren't playful barks—Butternut was trying to warn her.

A twig snapped in the inky night in front of her an

instant before something slammed into her chest, throwing her backward into darkness.

Bryce ran the rest of the way up the dirt driveway to the farmhouse. His gut had told him tonight wasn't going to go smoothly, and it wasn't only because he suspected Colleen Hammermill wasn't who she said she was.

He'd heard gunshots while he was on duty exactly four times in his ten years with the SVPD. Two were when hunters had been in an off-limits area and one was when he'd fired his own weapon to take out a convenience store robber who'd shot a cashier and then pointed his gun at Bryce.

The fourth was ten seconds ago, in the dark fields surrounding the farmhouse he'd followed Colleen Hammermill to. Superintendent Todd had given him her address when he'd texted him after the ceremony.

"Need backup, Cherry Creek and Skyline Drive. The old Shropesbury farm."

He shoved his phone back into his chest pocket and kept running, weapon drawn. He'd explain to his boss later why he'd made the decision to follow the "chaplain" home.

The house was dark but the side of the structure was lit as a dog barked incessantly, probably inside. He scanned the surroundings as he approached but found no one near the house. No one running away, either.

A still figure lying on the ground came into view as he crested the top of the drive. Sirens grew closer but they weren't here yet. He did a rapid check of the shrubs and trees around the house for an assailant.

Once he was satisfied there wasn't a shooter in the immediate vicinity, he went to help the chaplain. Backup would scour the woods around the farm later. She was conscious but looked confused as she struggled to sit up.

"Hang on, are you hit?"

A pale, feminine hand brushed her chest at heart level. "My vest…"

"I've got it." He lifted her school jacket up, revealing a tight-fitting T-shirt underneath. It was stretched over a bulletproof vest.

Holy shit. No way was this woman only a minister.

The glint of metal peeked from a hole in the shirt. The shooter had aimed for her heart.

"You're okay. You still have your Kevlar on. Good going." He eased her back and was relieved she didn't fight him. She had to be on the verge of being in shock and the EMTs couldn't get here soon enough as far as he was concerned.

As he laid her back, her red hair caught his eye, right at her temples. Where her wig was sliding off.

Her *wig*.

He removed it the rest of the way. Thick, lustrous red hair spilled into his hands.

"Zora." He breathed out her name before he could stop himself.

"Bryce, I'm undercover."

"For who?"

She closed her eyes, shielding him from the pale green irises he remembered too well.

She stayed silent, but was still breathing.

Did the shooter want "Colleen the chaplain" dead, or the girl—no, woman—he'd once dreamed of spending the rest of his life with?

"You don't need to know what she was doing, Bryce. All you need to know is that she helped us draw out the Female Preacher Killer. Unfortunately, we didn't catch him." Superintendent Colt Todd spoke matter-of-factly, refusing to answer Bryce's questions.

"We're still not certain if it's a he or she, and I disagree, Superintendent Todd. This is my assignment and that was my patrol last night. I have a right to know who's working with me."

"You know as well as I do that there are some cases we need a little extra help on, Bryce. And I appreciate that you kept your eye on the chaplain."

"On Zora Krasny, you mean." He'd gotten something out of her after she'd been examined at least. Her curt answers to his questions hadn't eased his mind over who she was working for, however. She'd admitted she was a licensed counselor, not a minister, and had lived in Silver Valley for almost two years.

And had never contacted him or any of their high school acquaintances.

Whatever.

"Yes, Zora Krasny. Any reason why you've taken such an interest, other than for your operational needs, Bryce?"

"Yes, sir. We went to Silver Valley High School together."

Superintendent Todd's eyes narrowed and Bryce realized he'd never seen the superintendent taken aback by anything. He'd surprised him with that one, though.

"Is that so?"

"Yes." He shrugged. "She went to the naval academy, I went to Penn State, and I never heard from her again."

"Sounds like a broken-heart issue. Not my problem, Bryce."

"No, sir. We still have a killer out there." He said that

as much to remind himself. Zora's presence was distracting to say the least.

Damn it.

"Yes, and I fully trust you're going to flush him out, Bryce. We came close last night."

"We did. Zora told me she caught a good glimpse of a male vendor at the game who she believes was suspicious."

"Any chance whoever shot her saw her wig come off?"

"No, sir. I only noticed it because she was lying on the ground."

"I don't like that she was ambushed at her house."

Bryce didn't, either. Especially since he'd followed her home, and hadn't noticed any other vehicles tailing and none in the surrounding area. That meant the shooter had been waiting at her house before they got there, and that the shooter most likely wasn't the same person they'd tracked at the football game. But they couldn't even be certain of that. Anyone who knew the local farm roads could have beaten the SVPD units to the scene.

Whoever the shooter was, he knew where Zora lived. Whether he thought she was Colleen Hammermill the minister or not was irrelevant.

Zora was in danger.

"What do you mean I can't work out for a couple of weeks?" Zora hated how weak and squeaky her voice came out. She felt stronger than that, save for the pain that radiated through her rib cage. Whatever medication the doctors had prescribed last night hadn't been strong enough. She'd barely slept during her mandatory overnight stay for observation at Silver Valley Regional Hospital.

"You took a bullet to your chest, Zora. Your heart stopped momentarily from the blow—if you hadn't had your vest on we wouldn't be enjoying this conversation, and you wouldn't have another workout to look forward to, ever." Dr. Mark Lassiter eyed her over his reading glasses, his expression uncompromising. They'd met when she did her hospital rotation as part of her counseling degree and struck up a decent rapport—enough that he'd asked her out on a date. She'd politely refused. Luckily, he hadn't harbored any ill feelings about it.

She'd had top-notch care at the Harrisburg area's new hospital, which sat on a sprawling medical campus known for its trauma expertise.

"I'm grateful to be here." She winced as she struggled to stand. "I don't mean to be a pain in the ass."

Mark's hand touched her shoulder and she sat back down.

"Trust me, in a few weeks you'll be back in your yoga classes or whatever you're so fired up about missing. But for now you need to rest."

"Fine. And yoga's not as easy as you think, by the way." Since she'd left the navy she'd found a lot of joy in yoga, as it balanced her more than her running routine did.

Mark smiled.

"I'm in a power yoga class and I know what a good workout it is." He held up his hand. "And guess what? You'll be relieved to know I moved on—I'm engaged."

"Mark, that's wonderful! I'm so happy for you. Really." Pain twisted through her torso as she took too deep a breath in her exuberance.

"Thank you."

"This is going to hurt when the drugs wear off, isn't it?

That's what you're not telling me. I won't *want* to work out for a while, will I?"

"It'll be uncomfortable, yes. About the time your bruise turns yellow, you'll be ready to ease back into your fitness routine."

Mark turned at a sharp knock right before Bryce walked through the hospital room door.

"Detective. Just in time."

"In time for what?" Zora asked. "Wait—no. I don't need any more help." No way was Bryce going to help her home. He'd seen enough of her vulnerability in the past twenty-four hours.

"Trust me, I don't want to be the one to take you home but it's Silver Valley PD policy—we take care of our own. You took a bullet from a criminal in our territory. That makes you one of us. I'm grateful you agreed to the bulletproof vest before you said the invocation last night."

Nice save, Bryce. He left nothing undone. Mark wouldn't suspect what she did in her hours away from counseling. To him, she'd been a lucky victim, not a willing participant in the effort to take down a murderer.

"That was a good call on your part, Bryce." Mark looked at his watch, then back at Zora. "I'll leave you now—remember what I said. No cheating."

"Got it."

Mark left the room and Zora's skin prickled at her excruciating awareness of Bryce's proximity.

It had to be the narcotics. They'd wear off as soon as he got her home.

"You look like hell." His gaze assessed her with practiced attention to detail.

"Why, thank you. You're as charming as I remember."

"And you're as untrustable as ever."

"That's not even a word. You mean *unreliable*."

"No, I meant it the way I said it. I don't trust you any more than I did when you stood me up."

"Really? We're going to discuss something as silly as a prom, something that happened fifteen years ago?"

"No, we're not. And if it wasn't so important, why do you remember exactly how long it's been?"

She *wouldn't* let him make her feel pretty, despite the way he was looking at her.

Nor would she let him make her feel desirable.

"Let it go, Bryce."

"Ready to go home?" A nursing assistant pushed a wheelchair into the room and stopped at the bed. She looked at Zora, then Bryce.

Bryce didn't budge.

"Here, let me get you into the chair," the assistant said.

"I've got her."

"My parents..."

"Were notified last night. I called them myself. Your mother is at your house waiting for you. I spoke to her earlier."

Strong, steady hands grasped her forearms and her vision was filled with a white dress shirt, red tie and Bryce's chest. It wasn't the thin, teenage physique she remembered. Because she did remember every last thing about Bryce.

He smelled more mature, too. More sexy, as his cologne or soap was spicy and hinted at the power that his muscles demonstrated. She didn't consider herself a petite woman by any means, but he moved her easily.

"I've got you. Take it nice and slow." His voice, God, his voice! Deep, gravelly and all adult, yet still achingly familiar.

She'd missed him. She'd missed *them*. The bond they'd shared for the better part of six years, through their worst growing pains and hormonal fluctuations. They'd each dated others, but only fleetingly. Mere experimentation.

Nothing had come close to the chemistry and friendship that had grown between them.

You were kids. You were a lost girl. It's history.

"I'm not an invalid." Still, she leaned into him—it was that or risk crying out in pain and humiliating herself in front of both him and the aide.

"There you go. Nice and easy."

He held her the entire way down to the chair, and made sure she was settled as comfortably as possible.

Blue-gray eyes were level with hers.

"You okay?"

"Yes." She nodded to emphasize that he wasn't affecting her, wasn't doing anything but helping her get into the blasted wheelchair.

"You're a real pro there, sir. You do this before?" The nurse's aide all but drooled at Bryce. Zora damned the chair for not being powered. Zipping out of the room and back into her life without Bryce was beyond tempting. Of course, she'd have to run over Bryce to escape since he was standing in front of her.

"A few times." Bryce left Zora's vision and she was being propelled through the door, down the hall to the elevators.

As the aide chatted up Bryce, Zora allowed her mind to wander. Her first concern was her mother's safety. Mom would be safe staying with her, since Zora had Butternut as an early-warning detector, and of course, her weapons. They were in a hidden storage compartment— she usually only kept one pistol accessible and used whatever the Trail Hikers issued for a particular mission, if any. Before the football game last night she'd signed out a few different weapons, just in case they didn't draw out the killer in a predictable fashion.

She'd never expected to be targeted on her own property. Not without noticing a tail. Bryce had been behind her but not close enough that she could see him. The killer had beaten him to the house.

"Wait here while I get the car." Bryce left her at the hospital's portico. His butt was too cute, and it annoyed her to admit she was enjoying the view.

"He's such a sweet guy. You're lucky."

Zora grunted and tried to clear her dry throat. It was like talking through cobwebs and exacerbated her nausea.

Pain meds—not her favorites.

"He's a colleague."

"None of *my* colleagues look at me like he looks at you. I'd say he's interested."

Zora craned her neck to look at the aide's name tag. Upon closer inspection, the woman was much younger than she realized. The drugs were really playing with her reasoning. It wasn't Bryce.

"Nice to meet you, Heidi Kurtz."

"Same here, ma'am."

"You really like your job, don't you?"

"I do. And I'm taking classes at HACC to get my RN. Only two more semesters to go." Heidi referred to Harrisburg Area Community College.

"That's the ticket, Heidi. Go after your dreams."

"Is being a police officer your dream?"

"Oh, I'm not…" She was a beat too slow but at least Zora's brain caught up to her mouth before she blabbed anything Heidi didn't need to know. "Yes, I've always wanted to help protect people."

"The whole staff was abuzz about your injury. We don't get a lot of gunshot wounds this side of the river."

"They get plenty in the city." Harrisburg had one of the highest crime rates per capita in the United States. At least her mind hadn't seized completely.

"Yeah, that's where I used to live. I went to elementary school in Dauphin County."

"What brought you to the West Shore?" Keeping the aide talking about herself would prevent her from asking any questions Zora wasn't prepared to answer.

Like why she'd taken a bullet to her chest.

"My grandparents. My father was never around and my mother's been in and out of rehab, so they raised me."

"Good on you for going after what you want. Your grandparents sound like good people."

"They're the best."

The quiet engine of a luxury SUV hummed under the portico as Bryce parked his vehicle in front of Zora. It boasted a cheery Christmas wreath on its grille, complete with a red bow.

"Here's your ride," Heidi said.

Bryce was out of the driver's seat and at her side before she could even try to stand.

"Here, give me your bag." He took the small duffel and placed it on the backseat before he opened the passenger's door and turned back to her.

"Thank you, Heidi. You've been most helpful."

"No problem. It's my job."

Zora didn't have to look to see the blush she was certain was blazing on Heidi's cheeks. How could any young woman be immune to the high-voltage smile Bryce flashed at her?

"Okay, warrior woman, time to roll."

Warrior woman?

"I'm not a warrior."

"Save your energy for getting up into the seat." His breath caressed her face as he leaned toward her and lifted her out of the chair.

A groan escaped her before she could check it. Damn the drugs and her resulting lack of control!

"Sorry. I know this hurts like hell, but it's quicker and easier on you. I don't think you're up to climbing steps yet."

The impulse to argue with him vanished at his words and she allowed herself to relax against his broad chest. She hadn't been held for so long, and certainly not by a man she had such a complicated history with. Besides, she was blaming any foolish surrender on the drugs.

He placed her onto the leather seat as if he was putting an intricate ship into a glass bottle. She giggled.

"What's so funny?"

"I always laugh when I'm in pain. And it's kind of silly how nicely you're treating me."

His gaze steadied on her. No drugs could keep the warmth of his nearness from creating a coil of tension in her midsection.

"It's my job."

He stared at her for a moment before he clicked the seat belt in place and closed the passenger door, leaving her to shiver without his body heat.

Chapter 3

She thought he was *silly*?

Bryce took a moment to breathe and think before he got back into the driver's seat. Damn it but he'd wanted to kiss her. And it had been less than twenty-four hours since he'd laid eyes on her again. Maybe it was like they say addiction is—progressive. A drug addict can be straight for two decades but if they pick up again they're right back where they were when they quit, and they spiral out of control almost immediately.

He certainly understood what "out of control" meant when it came to his feelings for Zora.

You weren't addicted to her. You loved her.

He'd been a boy, for God's sake.

As he settled into the front seat he was immediately impressed by her scent. Under the hospital starchy-clean smell she was still pure Zora. Not floral like the women he'd dated, but spicy, musky.

Pure sex.

"Thank you for taking me home. Please tell Superintendent Todd that I'm okay, and appreciate the support."

"Save the canned gratitude for your navy life, Zora. We don't do the fluffy feel-good words here. We're taking care of you because you're part of our team. You were hurt while working with us."

"Not technically. In fact, if you weren't there, I might still be lying on the ground. Why *were* you there, Bryce?"

Her expression was softer than the grim face she'd put on for him last night and he hoped it was a sign that she wasn't in as much pain. The drugs certainly weren't affecting her logic or memory.

"A hunch. I felt something was off and thought it'd be a good idea to follow you to your place. After I found out it was you, I wondered why you didn't go back to your old house."

"Where Mom and Dad live? No. I bought my own house a couple of years ago. They don't need their thirty-three-year-old daughter living at home with them."

"I never heard you'd moved back."

"There was no reason you should have."

"It's not that big a place, Zora. You haven't touched base with anyone from high school, have you?"

"Why would I? You were my best…" She abruptly stopped speaking. Just like she'd abruptly ended their relationship all those years ago.

It had been a lot of years. He thought it was nothing more than an adolescent memory. But seeing her last night, finding something inexplicably familiar about her, and then his reaction when she'd been shot…

"What made you decide to go into law enforcement?"

"Who says I'm in law enforcement?" She had the gall to play him, after he'd seen her in action last night.

"You're not on any force locally from what I can tell, and I've found your counseling credentials are all up-to-date. But you weren't acting like any counselor I've ever met last night."

"Who says I'm not a chaplain?"

"That you're not a minister? Oh, I don't know, Zora. That god-awful wig? Your Kevlar vest? Your loaded weapon?"

"I'm a counselor. That's what I got out of the navy for."

"And yet you were playing undercover agent last night."

"You know what you saw. I can't comment on it, Bryce. You have to understand that. You've been in this kind of life long enough."

Yes, he had been.

"So why did you get a degree in counseling? What's the attraction there?"

"Life. Wanting to help people trying to improve their circumstances."

Her voice quavered and he noted the pinch lines around her lips.

"We'll have you home soon, Zora."

He navigated the winding, narrow road that lifted them above Silver Valley into the foothills of the Appalachian Mountains. Leaves glinting with gold flecks remained on a few branches, but most were bare. The ride was as smooth as ever to him but he knew each tiny turn and bump was excruciating to Zora. Bruised ribs were like that.

"Nice ride you have here, Campbell."

"It's my parents'. You wouldn't be as comfortable in my old Ford."

"The Mustang you drove last night." She hadn't missed a thing.

"Didn't you want to stay in the navy for the full twenty?"

"No. Not after the war, after so many moves. It was time to settle down, and I wanted to find something that would allow me to help people more directly. You know, go from the global perspective to the everyday world."

"No, I don't know. You probably got to make a big difference as a naval officer. Is Silver Valley going to be enough for you?"

"More than." She almost laughed. He suspected her ribs hurt so much she'd stopped herself. He didn't want to examine why the fact that she seemed so pleased to be settled down in Silver Valley appealed to him.

"Then why did you agree to do the ride along last night?"

Silence. He shot a glance at her and she stared straight ahead, her lips pursed in determination or pain, he wasn't sure.

"Not talking, Zora?"

"I can't, Bryce."

She wasn't the first unknown player who'd shown up during an op to help them bring down a bad guy. That was what bothered Bryce. He'd been a police officer for over a decade, the past five years on the Silver Valley force as a detective. And still, Superintendent Todd wasn't willing to cut Bryce in on the source of these "part-time" operatives.

"What made you become a detective?"

"Life." He snorted. "I studied criminal justice in college, then did a stint in the marines. After I got out I decided to come back home. I toyed with law school, but my first love is law enforcement. And there's nowhere else I'd want to live."

Did she hear the recrimination in his voice? His resentment that she'd been able to leave Silver Valley without a backward glance? And come back with apparently no regrets?

"I didn't realize you were a vet, too. The marines… you probably saw a lot in a short time."

"More than I care to ever see again, yes," he said. "Unfortunately, it can be a war zone here, too, depending on the timing of a heroin shipment and the availability of officers to combat the dealers. Still, I do love Silver Valley."

"You always did. Love it here." Images of them hiking for hours on the Appalachian Trail, or spending time down at Spring Creek, floated across her memory. It had been simpler before they'd each gone on to become the adults that sat in this car.

Not going there.

"You once did, too."

"I've missed Silver Valley since I left." Her words were succinct, quiet in the closed car.

"You have an odd way of showing it."

"Not everyone has as clean a slate as you do, Bryce."

Anger at himself made him want to pull over and call in someone else to finish driving her home. What the heck was he thinking, going all nuts on her when she'd suffered such a grave injury? It wasn't physically grave—her bruises would heal—but psychologically, mentally, it didn't get much worse than surviving an attempted murder.

She would be dead if not for her preparedness and Kevlar vest.

"I don't know what you mean by a 'clean slate.' Is my life simple? Yes, for the most part. I'm happy here. It's my hometown. But I've had my share of challenges. It's life, Zora. Life happens."

"You sound like you've had some challenges since… since…"

"Since you left?"

"I'm fine, Mom. I just need a day or two to catch my breath."

"She needs to take it easy for at least a week." Bryce spoke from across the room, at the dining table where he and Anna Krasny sat, assessing her health as if she weren't within earshot. Zora couldn't have sat at the table if she'd wanted to. She rested against several pillows on her overstuffed chair-and-a-half.

"Zora, you're not fine. Not when some crazy person shot at you last night!" Anna would take out the assailant herself, given the chance. Zora loved her mother's fierce protective streak. "There are at least two police cars parked on your street," Anna went on. "If SVPD thinks you need protection, you must be in danger."

"Mom, stop."

Silence blanketed the room but Zora felt her mother's anxiety. The unspoken fear.

They've come back for you. For revenge.

"It was taken care of years ago, Mom."

"They didn't catch everyone, Zora. And you know some of their prison sentences are up…"

Yes, she knew.

"May I ask what you're talking about?" Bryce.

"Surely you told him, Zora, didn't you? In high school? You were best friends—I assumed, I mean…" Her mom was flustered and Zora wanted to punch Bryce. Not for any particular reason, just because he was there and it was easier to be pissed off at him than have to deal with the reality of her situation.

That someone who had nothing to do with the Female Preacher Killer had shot her.

"Told me what, Zora?" Bryce modulated his voice like the professional he was. Cool, clean, with no hint of the anger Zora knew he must be feeling. She doubted he knew about the Trail Hikers, and the fact that she wasn't willing to tell him anything didn't help.

"Nothing. Mom's just overreacting. You're watching too much *NCIS* again, Mom."

Anna got the hint and sipped her coffee, but worry was etched in the tired lines around her eyes.

Zora tried to shoot Bryce a "shut the hell up" look but judging from his unwavering stare, it wasn't going to work. Not permanently anyway.

"We haven't had time to catch up, but now that I know Zora's back we'll have plenty of time to talk. Right, Zora?" he said.

A spark lit in her mother's eyes and Zora wished she had a little more energy. Not a lot, just enough to slap that grin off Bryce's too-handsome face.

He knew she was concerned about her mother, knew she wasn't going to do anything to upset her.

Butternut laid her head on Zora's lap, her tail thumping on the wide-plank pine flooring.

"You're such a lady, Butternut, girl." She stroked the shepherd's long pointy ears and marveled for the millionth time since she'd rescued her at how intuitive Butternut was.

"It's impressive how she doesn't even try to jump on you." Bryce walked across the room and sat on the small sofa across from her. Butternut's gaze followed him but otherwise she made no movement toward Bryce.

"She's always been empathic. I picked her out of a litter of five at the animal shelter. They were rescued from a puppy mill." Puppy mills were a dark side of their bucolic surroundings in central Pennsylvania. "I wish I could have taken all of her brothers and sisters, but she was the one who showed the most interest in me."

Bryce stretched his long legs in front of him and leaned back into the sofa.

"You must have a lot of paperwork from last night." She stroked Butternut and kept her focus on the dog. Looking at Bryce required more emotional stamina than her injury and pain meds afforded her at the moment.

"No, the officers on the scene recorded everything. I finished my report while you were still in the ER."

Of course he had.

"Any idea who the shooter was?"

"No. We didn't come up with anything from the description you gave us of the suspicious vendor, unfortunately."

"He wasn't a normal spectator." She'd bet he was definitely involved, even if only posing as a decoy to see how the law enforcement agents would act last night.

"Maybe not, but he didn't show a weapon. He could be any crackpot."

"Zora, I'll be in the guest room. Bryce, call me when you leave, will you?" Anna wasn't interested in police business.

"Mom, you don't have to leave."

"No, I do. I need a quick catnap, and you need to have some privacy to discuss your work." Anna left the room, taking her mug with her.

Bryce waited until they heard the guest bedroom door click shut before he looked at Zora again.

"Last chance," he said. "Want to give me a clue as to who you think wants you dead?"

He knew he was pressing it to expect Zora to spill her guts so soon after the shooting. But a killer was on the loose—Zora's aching chest had to take a backseat.

"How can we be sure it wasn't the same guy I saw at the football game?"

"We can't. But neither you nor I saw anyone tailing you back here. The fact that you were shot, when you live here as Zora and not Chaplain Hammermill, tells me it could be more personal." He knew not to ask her who she worked for and why she'd been the one sent to pose as a female minister. Superintendent Todd had been explicit in his orders for Bryce to mind his own business.

"No one wants to kill me. The only work I've ever done has been with the navy, and that's nothing that would bring a killer to Silver Valley."

"What about your work downrange, during the war?"

She shook her head and opened her mouth to reply, then winced.

"Sorry. I keep forgetting that I need to breathe shallowly."

"No, you need to take deep breaths so that you don't get pneumonia."

"What, are you a medical professional, too? My tours to Iraq and Afghanistan had me mostly behind the scenes, providing intelligence."

He tried not to glare at her.

Not that she wasn't beautiful to watch. If he hadn't known her before, he would have described her as a red-headed Sofia Vergara, although even slimmer. But he saw beyond her physical features to the sharp intelligence behind her eyes, the keen wit that had drawn him to her during his own nerd days. They'd been perfect as friends. Neither of them had particularly cared about hanging out with other teenagers, not when the talk revolved around the opposite sex, booze and, too often, drugs. They were both academics at heart. He'd studied biology with a vengeance, convinced he was going to discover a cure for cancer. The same cancer that had taken his little sister when she was a toddler and left his family forever changed.

Zora had mirrored his studious nature. She was passionate to the point of obsession about anything that had to do with science, particularly astronomy and physics.

"I didn't go into medicine, in case you haven't figured that out yet," he said.

"What made you change your mind? I thought you'd be a top research doctor by now."

"I didn't have the brains for the chemistry. Organic chemistry was a killer. But I loved the lab work that parlayed into forensics. I majored in criminal justice."

She nodded.

"That makes sense."

"What about you, Zora? You were going to be an astronomer like Jodie Foster's character in *Contact*." They'd watched the movie together one autumn night, forgoing their homecoming dance. He'd imagined being her best friend for life. More, if she'd let him.

Instead, they had barely made it through senior year.

"I wanted to go far away. The navy made sense to me. I found out about the academy at the last minute—I didn't get in right away, remember? I was put on a wait list."

"You left two days after you found out. That's what your mother told me."

"About that…I'm sorry, Bryce. We were kids, and I realize you probably don't even remember much about it, but the way I left—it was chicken shit."

"Yes, it was. And no apology necessary. You're right. We're different people now. Certified grown-ups. That was a lifetime ago."

Zora thought that living back in town for two years meant she'd dealt with all of her memories arriving in Silver Valley as a little girl. At first coming back home to where she'd found shelter after leaving the cult had stirred up all kinds of memories, and she'd been able to utilize her counseling classes and training to work through them. Even her memories of Bryce—she hadn't needed to see him to exorcise his ghost from her mind.

Yet since last night, it was as though he'd never left her life. As if they could go back to being friends again.

"I'm taking too much of your time, Bryce. You're free to go, you know."

"Showing me the door already?" His grin was easy but it didn't reach his eyes, which looked wary.

"I'm safe, Bryce. Buttercup is the best security system out there. And as you know, I'm armed."

"And on pain meds, nursing bruised ribs and sore muscles."

"There's that."

"We're going to place surveillance on your house starting when I leave today."

"That's not necessary."

"Superintendent Todd and I beg to differ."

"You don't think the shooter will come back here, do you?"

"Actually, no, I don't. If it was the man you saw at the game, he'll be too afraid to get caught. He'll see the patrol car—we're not going to do anything covert here. And if he still wants to target female ministers, he'll do anything to stay out of jail."

"I should have taken him out last night."

"At the game? Get real. You never saw a weapon."

"No, but you have to trust me—I saw him ready to pull it on me. But it was as if he was testing, to see…"

"To see if you were for real." Bryce ran his fingers over his chin. "I think we messed up with that op, Zora. It was too coincidental for the holiday festival to have an invocation that was publicly announced and advertised for the entire week before. We were too obvious."

"I agree. When I heard the local rock station announce the prayer and moment of silence was going to be dedicated to the two slain ministers, I hoped the killer was stupid."

"He—or she—obviously isn't."

"No."

"I hate to put you on the spot again, Zora, but I'd really like to know what you were doing in the patrol car last night. Why you, why now?"

"I've told you—I can't tell you."

She hated not being able to open up to him, especially in light of how shabbily she'd treated him in the past. No matter what his words said, she felt his judgment with each glance he shot her.

And she found her attraction to him was real and adult. Nothing like the schoolgirl crush she'd had on him throughout high school. Back then she'd buried it, not wanting anything to threaten their friendship. After the daily terror of living in a religious cult, she'd needed stability and calm, relationships without drama.

Besides her adoptive parents, Bryce had been part of that safety net.

"Fine. I'll talk to Superintendent Holt about it. In the meantime, it looks as though we'll be working together for a bit longer, until we nab the killer. And if you work with me, you have to accept that I'm not going to let you put yourself in harm's way unnecessarily."

"And you need to know that while I may not have the same level of experience that you do, I have the training I need to handle myself. I won't let you down, Bryce."

He got to his feet.

"I'm sure you won't. Rest up and I'll see you tomorrow morning."

He walked to the bottom of the stairs and called for her mother.

She hoped they'd catch the killer soon. Holding back her feelings for Bryce wasn't going to be easy.

Chapter 4

"You did the right thing, Zora. It's not your job to inform Detective Bryce Campbell or anyone about your background. If you feel a need to tell him about your past, that's your call. I don't see how it has any relevance to the current mission, however." Claudia looked out over the farmland surrounding Zora's home as she spoke. She'd come out to see Zora on a Sunday morning, underscoring Claudia's dedication to her role as head of the Trail Hikers. Anna had excused herself to go for a walk around the property, giving them privacy. Zora was grateful for the patrol cars Bryce had ordered to specific points around her place, so that her mother could walk in peace.

"I appreciate that you came to visit, Claudia. As you can see, I'm okay."

"You could have been killed! That's not something I'll ever take lightly." Claudia's eyes sparked with anger and concern as she faced Zora.

She was a formidable woman, Claudia.

Her sable chin-length bob was thick and shot through with streaks of silver. On anyone else the gray would be aging but Claudia could have a second career as a cover model. She certainly didn't look like the chief of operations for a government shadow agency, apart from her exceptional height and obviously pristine physical condition.

"No, ma'am."

"Cool it on the *ma'am*. I told you, I'm Claudia, you're Zora. We're all on a first-name basis no matter how long we've been with the Trail Hikers. This isn't a ranked organization, nor is it military. It's barely government." Claudia grinned and Zora caught a glimpse of the woman she must have been years ago, before the responsibilities of the Marine Corps and now Trail Hikers weighed on her.

"Sorry—it's a reflex." Zora suspected that Claudia had participated in her share of covert ops before she'd become a high-ranking military official but wasn't about to ask.

"I know." Claudia tapped her foot impatiently. "Just as it's reflexive for me to want to nail the scum who shot you, preferably between the eyes."

"That's not very PC, Claudia." Political correctness wasn't something Zora missed from her military days.

"I see your pain meds won't be needed much longer."

They both laughed.

Claudia sat on the ottoman across from Zora. Claudia had insisted Zora stay on the couch through their meeting.

"I'm relieved that you're doing so well. I must admit, I had my doubts when I first spoke to your attending doctor."

"He was rather old-school. Plus he has no idea what we do, what we're trained for."

"But he is a doctor and you have to listen to him. I need you to heal quickly enough to be of help to the op." Claudia's no-nonsense expression was back.

"Yes, ma—Claudia."

Claudia patted her knee.

"That's my gal. Now, let's try to figure out how the man you saw on the football field could have made it here in time to be waiting for you when you drove up."

"If he knew that I lived here ahead of time, then he knew I was undercover. That means there's someone on the inside of the Trail Hikers who's leaked the information, doesn't it?"

"No, impossible. All of us have the highest level of clearance not only by government standards but by our standards. There is someone at the SVPD who knows about us, of course. Theoretically it's possible that he leaked it…or that someone overheard him talking to me. But I doubt it."

"How do you know it's not him?"

Claudia answered with one decisive shake of her head.

"It's not him. Our contact at SVPD is a virtual vault when it comes to operational security."

"You're that sure, huh?" Zora had a hard time believing anyone could be trusted completely. She'd held clearances and guarded national secrets for her entire career. Even the best of agents made mistakes, left files in the wrong place, spoke about something they shouldn't have in an unsecured area.

"Let's focus on the region around the farmhouse." Claudia pulled a tablet out of her designer leather tote and tapped polished fingernails on the surface. A satellite image of Zora's property appeared, taken in the spring, judging from the heavy foliage on the oak trees that peppered her yard.

"The timing doesn't match, Claudia. Even with driving back to the station and getting into my car, it would take me only five or seven minutes longer than if I'd driven straight from the high school. Which we're presuming the shooter did, if it's the same guy?"

Claudia sat, her chin resting on her hand as she leaned over the tablet from the corner of the ottoman.

"It's far-reaching but indeed possible. If he was driving a four-wheel-drive vehicle, he could have made it via these three farm roads." Claudia used her cursor to mark the route. "He would have had to hide his car in the woods here or here." She circled the copse of trees nearest to Zora's house, and one a mile or so away.

"Bryce tried to pursue him and had the area blocked off within minutes of me going down. I find it hard to believe that no one saw anything at all while the shooter escaped. Don't you find it odd, too?"

"I do. Unless the shooter lives around here."

Zora sat up straight and immediately regretted it as a sharp stab of pain bit through her rib cage.

"Easy, Zora."

"I'll relax once we have the bastard. I know all of my surrounding neighbors. None of them look like the man I saw at the football game."

"Like you, he could have been wearing some kind of disguise."

"Has anyone done a profile on the residents?" Zora had a sinking feeling in her stomach. It was sickening to think one of the neighbors that she trusted to get her mail or watch Buttercup could be a killer.

Claudia swiped her tablet a few times until a spreadsheet of the Trail Hikers' findings on her neighbors appeared.

"That's fast work."

"It's what we get paid for." Claudia handed the tablet to Zora and leaned back. "Robert Blumenthal, the Trail Hiker you met during your initial read-in, did the work."

"It's impeccable." She'd expect no less from the agent who had, in two days, briefed her into the Trail Hikers and taught her their history, mission and capabilities. On top of that Rob had certified that she was proficient in a variety of weapons as well as hand-to-hand combat.

The Trail Hikers had to be dependable. It was part of what made Zora agree to sign on for a five-year stint. The other part had been that she knew she was going to miss the navy in terms of being operationally relevant. As much as she loved counseling and the people she helped, nothing compared to helping local and national LEA take down the bad guys in the most expeditious manner possible.

"Looks as if my neighbors are all trustworthy, thank God."

"Which leaves the shooter on the loose."

"Sit down with your father and eat your borscht, Zora." Anna motioned at the spot near her father, Adam. Zora's Ukrainian immigrant parents had given her a love for authentic Ukrainian cuisine as well a new name when they adopted her. They were as American as anyone but when it came to food, no one made a meaner borscht than Anna.

"I can't thank you enough for setting up the tree for me, you two. I don't know when I'd have gotten it off the back porch." They'd cut down two trees last weekend and Zora had brought the smaller noble fir to her home, leaving it on the back porch to settle in a bucket of water.

Adam and Anna had set it up while she napped, and they had all decorated it together. It lit up the front room, its glow visible from the table where they ate.

"Your mother tells me you're involved with more of your detective work, Zora." Adam's gravelly voice was in stark contrast to his fit form. Seen from behind, he looked thirty years younger than his true age.

"It's not *my* work, Dad, it's with a private agency. They were looking for someone with my background for some local work." She'd given them minimal information on her work with the Trail Hikers and they hadn't pressed it, accepting that it was similar to the type of work she'd done in the navy. She hadn't been able to talk about that, either.

"Counseling's not enough?" Anna slid into the chair opposite Zora, next to Adam.

"Yes, it's more than enough. But it's good for me to still give back in some way."

"You owe nothing to no one." Adam spooned the hot red broth and appeared calm but Zora knew better. Under his steady exterior was a bear that, once disturbed, could be formidable. And when it came to his only child, Adam was overprotective and immovable.

"Dad, it's not as if anyone is forcing me to do this. I want to. And I don't want to talk about it right now."

"We're talking about it because we love you, Zora." Anna spoke quietly from her seat, her bright blue eyes reflecting her concern.

And the same stubborn attitude as her husband.

"I know, Mom, and I appreciate that. I wouldn't be here without either of you."

"You'd be here, *lubovichka*, just with another family. We're blessed that we got the pick of the litter." Adam laughed at the family inside joke. They'd done all they could to draw Zora from the hardened shell she'd arrived with when the social worker had dropped her off in Silver Valley. Zora didn't remember those days clearly, only that she'd taken months to learn to cry again, to allow her heart to open and pour forth incredible sorrow and grief over what she'd experienced in the True Believers cult. The trauma and emotional abuse she'd been subject to with the cooperation of her biological mother...

She shuddered.

"What? What did I say, Zora?" Adam's bushy silver brows meshed into one.

"Nothing, Dad. I'm just thinking of how grateful I am that you both took me in."

"We didn't take you in like you were some bum off the streets. We adopted you." Anna's voice wrapped around Zora's heart like a hand-knit alpaca throw.

"We would have taken her in if she were a bum, too. Enough of this." Adam pointed a salad fork at Zora. "You need to relax. You did your navy time, and you don't have to do anything that's so dangerous anymore."

Working for the Trail Hikers was far more dangerous on a day-to-day basis than her navy job had been, but she wasn't going to volunteer that to her parents. They'd been through enough, worried plenty about her over the years. Not to mention their own struggles before and after they immigrated to America.

"Dad, I'm not doing anything I don't want to do. And my counseling is starting to take off."

"Until your client was murdered." Anna spoke as simply as if she'd said it was getting chilly outside. Zora loved the practicality of her parents, who had escaped the former Soviet Union as soon as the Berlin Wall's collapse had allowed them to. They, too, had seen a lot in their lifetimes when they were still so young. Learning to speak English without much of an accent was the least of their accomplishments.

Zora didn't believe in coincidence, and the fact that Adam and Anna had become her adoptive parents remained a miracle in her estimation.

"Have they found this Female Preacher Killer, Zora?" Adam buttered a piece of the bread Anna had baked.

"No, not that I know of." Her parents didn't know she was working the very same case.

"We're worried, Zora, that maybe who shot you is somehow connected to what you left behind in New York all those years ago."

"New York is a crazy place!" Anna chimed in.

"It's a very large state, Mom. And the city is only part of it. I never lived anywhere near the city." She turned back to her dad. "No one from that cult knows where I went. My name, my entire identity, was changed. You know that, Dad. How could they find me? Besides, so many of them are gone, either dead or in prison."

"Some of their prison sentences are up." Anna voiced the concern she'd mentioned yesterday in front of Bryce.

"I know—you pointed that out yesterday in front of an SVPD detective who knows nothing about it, Mom."

"Don't give me that stern tone, Zora. I'm your mother. And Bryce is like my own son. I certainly fed him as much as you while you were growing up."

"He's a detective now and he doesn't know anything about my past. He doesn't need to."

"How was I supposed to know you never told him?"

"Mom, I was in the Witness Security Program. None of us were supposed to talk about what we'd been through, ever. You know that. You never mentioned it to his mother, did you?"

"No, of course not. Your soup's getting cold, honey." In typical Anna fashion, her mother deflected Zora's ire and sidestepped her own culpability.

"I noticed a police car at the end of your drive when I came in." Adam carefully buttered a second slice of the pumpernickel bread, the creamy spread in direct contrast with the rich dark brown grain.

Anna reached out quicker than a viper and slapped Adam's hand. "Your cholesterol!"

Adam grunted.

"They're giving me a little extra security, just in case that random shooter thinks of coming back. But he won't. It was a chance in a million."

Adam grunted again and Anna crossed herself three times in Orthodox Russian fashion. She'd remained faithful to her beliefs throughout the communist era and occasionally visited an Eastern Orthodox church two hours away in Washington, DC, but they attended a local Roman Catholic church normally, where Zora had gone with them.

"It's not that dire, Mom. You can relax already."

"I'll relax when I'm dead."

"Mom, you know I hate it when you say that."

Anna shrugged. "It's true, right?"

"Enough dark talk. When are you going back to work, Zora?" Adam stood up from the table and started to make tea for all of them.

"I'll start seeing clients again next week. I thought I'd go out on my own tomorrow." She'd already cleared her client schedule for a week, as Mark had directed her at the hospital.

"Are you sure?" Anna had been at Zora's side for the past several days, not wanting Zora to lift or strain herself in any way.

"Yes, Mom. You should go home, too. I'm doing fine. I showered on my own today."

"You did."

"And I have Butternut." She also had several types of weapons available to protect herself from any intruder. Another fact her parents never needed to know about.

Butternut's tail thumped on the kitchen floor as she sat in her usual dinner spot, far enough away from the dining table so that she wouldn't get reprimanded for begging, but close enough to dive in if any crumbs fell from the table.

"She's a good girl, aren't you, baby?" Anna stood up and placed her soup bowl, still half-full of broth and bits of beef, on the floor in front of the shepherd.

"Mom, I told you to please not feed her people food." Zora's tone sounded lame even to her. As if she was going to get up and stop Butternut from enjoying the yummy snack—not.

They all watched Butternut devour the treat with her incredibly long, almost clownish tongue.

"That dog has the life!" Adam chuckled as he brought the mugs of steaming tea to the table. "When we were kids, dogs were lucky to live a few years. This dog will outlive us all."

"It's not the USSR, Dad." Zora still liked teasing her parents, even though she was immensely proud of them for the pioneering spirits they possessed. Not a day went by that she didn't send up a prayer of gratitude that they'd made it to the States and had been available to nurture her when she'd needed it the most.

She felt a wave of nostalgia and she wanted to blame her healing body, or the coziness of being together with her parents over a bowl of borscht, or setting up the Christmas tree.

But she knew none of that was the reason for her sense of loss. It was the realization of how the time since she'd left Silver Valley could have been spent.

With Bryce.

"This isn't as straightforward as I'd like it to be." Superintendent Todd stood behind his desk with his hands on his hips, a look of frustration stamped on his face.

"Sir, I went over all of the people in the immediate vicinity of Ms. Krasny's house and they've all come out clean."

"Which leads me to believe that whoever shot her could have been our man. It may have been the man she saw at the football field."

"I still don't know how we let him slip away." Bryce's gut twisted in knots and he regretted the near miss at the football game. If Zora's observations were accurate, and he had no reason to think they weren't, they'd come very close to nabbing the killer at the game.

"There's something you need to be aware of, Bryce." At Superintendent Todd's somber tone, Bryce felt the hairs on the nape of his neck stand up. Colt Todd was the furthest possible thing from a trauma-drama type. Never an alarmist, he approached operations methodically. This was perhaps his strongest character trait and the one that had gotten him hired as Silver Valley's police superintendent.

"Sir?"

"As you've probably figured out, we occasionally have part-time agents of a sort who help us out with particularly difficult cases, or cases that involve federal jurisdiction."

"Like Zora Krasny." Posing as a minister.

"Right." Superintendent Todd looked as though he was hesitant about what he had to say. Bryce had never seen Todd appear anything but confident.

"You've caught their attention, Bryce."

"Whose attention, sir?"

"The agency I'm talking about. Hell, they're not even an agency. It's a contract group, for want of a better term. You need to meet with their CEO later today."

Bryce felt an automatic resistance to having these sorts of decisions made for him and tried to hide the anger in his voice.

"I have a job, sir. It's here at SVPD."

"And that won't change. But I can't be the only one to interface with them—if something were to happen to me, or if they needed to pull in a local officer, you're the best candidate for the job. Just go meet them and decide after that, okay?" Superintendent Todd pulled out his wallet and drew out a business card.

"Go to this address. There's an intercom at the door. They'll buzz you in, same as our security here."

"And if I'm not interested?"

"Tell them." Superintendent Todd had his "you're dismissed" expression in place and Bryce knew better than to refuse. Todd was one of the most fair-minded men he knew—he had to have good reason to send Bryce to this mystery organization.

Besides, Bryce didn't mind finding out about the organization Zora *really* worked for.

Zora had been eager to get out of the farmhouse and away from her mother's scrutiny, but twenty minutes into her field trip to Walmart she was winded, sweaty and annoyed.

Her irritation was at herself for allowing a lone shooter to get close enough to hit her, and on her own property to boot. As much as her past with the True Believers was over, she more than anyone should have known to put a decent security system around and in her home when she purchased it two years ago.

There were members of the True Believers who'd probably give their eyeteeth to find her after all these years and make her life miserable, if not snuff it out completely.

Familiar anger left her hands shaking as she walked up and down the holiday aisles, reaching out to touch an ornament here and there. She'd been twelve, damn it, and the abuse had started years before that. Being primed to become a "true disciple" of Leonard Wise, the sick bastard who'd convinced over a thousand people that he alone knew the meaning of life and had direct contact with God. He'd preached that all of his descendants would inherit his God-given abilities, too. Hence the need for so many of his own offspring.

By as many young women—"god mothers" as he'd referred to them—as possible.

She'd been one of the lucky ones. She'd gotten out at age twelve, before he'd had a chance to touch her. Her biological mother had told her over and over how lucky she was that "the Master" had chosen Zora as one of his mothers for the True Believers' children. Her mother had never wanted to believe that meant Zora would be molested by the man. Truth was, he molested all the girls once they reached seventeen. They'd be impregnated by him and a few select male disciples as mothers to his future minions. This way he skirted the law on the legal age of consent.

If not for the newspapers she'd read in the grocery store they'd visited on random Saturdays, she'd never have realized that the world wasn't meant to be such a scary place. That real families who loved and nurtured their children did exist. That Leonard Wise was a criminal.

"Can I help you find something, ma'am?" A young clerk smiled at her and Zora willed her grimace to relax. Since taking her counseling courses she'd figured out she still suffered from PTSD, a remnant of a childhood under constant duress.

"No, thank you, I'm just browsing."

"Let me know if I can help you."

"Will do."

The young man walked away and relief that it had only been a store clerk, not one of the True Believers, made her shoulders relax, as if they'd been carrying a huge burden.

There are no more True Believers. You're safe.

Of course there would always be bad guys, just not the kind who wanted to entrap her for the rest of her life.

Her PTSD had kept her from choosing to serve on board a ship as a full-time career. The thought of being confined to a ship in the middle of the huge ocean could bring on a panic attack without warning. So she'd picked Intelligence, knowing her shipboard time would be limited, if not completely avoided. As it was she'd had to serve on board an aircraft carrier for two years, but only three months of the tour was exclusively on the ship since it had been in the yards for a refitting. She'd lucked out.

"I want some candy, Mommy!" A tiny girl harangued her mother from her precarious seat in a shopping cart, throwing skeins of yarn from the cart into the aisle.

"That's not very nice. You know the rules—no candy in the morning, Becky. And if you make a mess of the nice yarn we picked out, there won't be anything to make pom-poms with." The mother looked like Zora felt—weary.

Had her biological mother ever taken her out for a normal mother-daughter shopping trip? Or had it all been as she remembered and centered on their "community"?

Cursing her trip down memory lane and knowing she had minutes until the exhaustion from her healing body would catch up to her, she made a beeline for the grocery section. Mom had said she needed eggs and milk. Zora preferred almond milk to cows', so she'd need to get a carton of each if she didn't want to listen to her mother's explanations of why Zora should drink cows' milk to ensure she got enough protein and calcium. She'd tell Anna that the almond milk was a treat, for special concoctions like her homemade hot cocoa. It was a bold-faced lie, though, as Zora rarely drank dairy milk if she could help it. She caught a movement out of the corner of her eye. Whether it was the color of the woman's scarf, her uniquely styled hair or the silhouette she made in her long, dowdy skirt and plaid blouse, topped with an unbuttoned, very basic wool coat, Zora didn't know. But something forced her gaze to the strange woman who stood at the end of the aisle Zora pushed her cart in. The woman who stood there and watched every move Zora made.

As if she knew her.

Recognition bolted Zora to the spot.

The woman had the same green eyes as Zora. The same wide mouth. The same red hair, only streaked with gray, and pulled into a tight bun that made the woman look far older than she should, that emphasized the long lines that splayed from her eyes and again from her nose to her lips.

Deep wrinkles—the kind that either a long life or a hard life brought.

Lines a woman who'd lost her only daughter would have.

Panic pressed into Zora's lungs, and bright spots floated across her vision. Her hands clutched her shopping cart.

No. Breathe, damn it.

She closed her eyes and breathed, using every yoga technique she could muster in the middle of the busy store.

When she opened her eyes, the woman was gone.

But she hadn't been a figment of her imagination. Zora knew the woman too well.

Edith Simms. Her biological mother.

Chapter 5

"I'm sorry to come unannounced but I need to speak with Claudia." Zora had to tell someone what she'd seen at Walmart and it wasn't Bryce or anyone at the SVPD who needed to know that Anna seemed to be right—the True Believers had somehow found her.

"She's in a meeting." Lara, the young receptionist who Zora suspected did more than administrative work, looked at her monitor. "She might have a few minutes when they break, but I'll have to ask her."

"That's fine, I'll wait."

Zora turned to take a seat in the small waiting area when she heard the door behind Lara's desk open.

"Zora, what's going on?"

"Claudia, I'm so sorry to barge in like this." Zora realized in that instant that she must look a sight in her loose flannel pants and oversize hooded sweatshirt. She'd dressed as comfortably as possible to go out, wanting to appear like any other shopper on a cold autumn day in Silver Valley.

"It's actually perfect timing. Come on in."

She didn't have time to wonder what made the timing perfect as she followed her boss into the spacious room that was the heart of the Trail Hikers organization. At least, the center of all operations that didn't have to be monitored from the bunker deep in the Appalachian Mountains, which Zora had only visited once, during her training.

"Have a seat, Zora. I trust you're already acquainted?" Claudia motioned to the man who sat in one of the tall wingback chairs in front of her black lacquer executive desk.

He unfolded himself from the chair and his expression wasn't as surprised as Zora knew hers was.

"Bryce."

"Zora."

Claudia laughed at how they spoke in unison and gave them no time to speak further.

"Sit down, both of you. This saves me from having to tell each of you separately that you're going to work on the Female Preacher Killer case together."

"We are? But I'm just helping out as needed. That's what I thought anyway." Zora didn't want Claudia to think she was shirking, but having to work with Bryce around the clock wasn't what she'd signed up for.

"You were, but it's clear that at least one shooter is out there, on the loose, and he knows where you live. He might even know that you're not Chaplain Colleen Hammermill, but Zora Krasny, former naval intelligence officer. Since you're a counselor, you may come close enough to being a minister in his eyes. And anyone who doesn't think women should be in the pulpit probably isn't thrilled about them being in uniform, either."

"And since I'm a live target, it makes sense that you'd need me to stay on the case."

"Right. As for Bryce—we've just begun the process of indoctrinating him into the Trail Hikers. We needed another point of contact at SVPD besides Superintendent Colt Todd, and Bryce is a perfect fit."

"I don't see how Detective Campbell and me working together will make a difference—the entire SVPD and surrounding law enforcement has been looking for the killer for over a month. Aren't we all working together?"

"Of course, but it's not getting wrapped up as quickly as we'd hoped." Claudia nodded at Bryce. "Bryce's work at both murder scenes was impeccable. There's no doubt that both ministers were killed by the same weapon, presumably fired by the same suspect."

"He's going to strike again, most likely in the next several days, as the local churches gear up for the end of Advent and Christmas festivities." Bryce spoke quickly and without looking at Zora.

He acted as if he barely knew her.

"The churches need to stop their activities until we catch him." Zora spoke from her experience as a naval officer.

"This isn't a base or a ship, Zora. We can't ask an entire community to put a lockdown on Christmas. Plus, their spiritual beliefs won't stand for it. The congregations won't allow a criminal to stop their faith practices."

"They will if they understand we're dealing with a cold-blooded killer."

"They already know that. Two female ministers are dead. To date we've been able to keep the most telling details out of the press, but it's only a matter of time before something leaks and the killer is able to get ahead of us." Bryce looked at her this time, his expression serious. "The public knows the killer is after female ministers, but none of the crime scene details have been leaked."

"Yet." Claudia turned to Zora. "It's a matter of time, and once that happens, we'll have to consider the possibility of a copycat."

"What do you need me to do?"

"We need you to continue as Reverend Colleen Hammermill, and to work with a local church as their 'interim' pastor. You'll fill in for their regular minister, who will tell her congregation that her mother has taken ill in another state and needs her."

"Won't that be rather obvious to the killer?"

"Not necessarily. Ministers are people, too, and their families get sick. They'll be more focused on another female minister taking her place. You."

Zora ran over the figures she'd read. "We have as many as fifteen female ministers and two rabbis in a one-hundred-mile radius of Silver Valley. How will you pick which church to put me in?"

"So far, the shooter has only hit the smallest of the congregations shepherded by a female minister. He hasn't targeted the temples and Hanukkah is almost over. I think, and the evidence points to, the killer wanting a big finale—a Christmas service of one type or another. It's possible he targeted smaller churches to start with because there'd be fewer witnesses if he was seen."

"And fewer families to affect." Zora spoke her thought aloud. Claudia and Bryce stared at her.

"Think about it. If the killer wants to make a big statement, they're not going to go after a big church to start with—they'd have too much of a pushback from law enforcement and the public, not to mention church members who would voluntarily rally to protect other ministers in the area."

"Right—and that goes along with my theory that whoever this is wants to make a big splash." Bryce rubbed the back of his neck. "But the big splash might very well mean Christmas, and at a very large, very public church."

"Silver Valley Community Church." Zora almost whispered the words. Silver Valley Community Church boasted a congregation of over two thousand who all met in one large theater-like building in the center of town. They'd hired a female pastor a year earlier, before the killings began.

"Exactly." Claudia confirmed Zora's fear.

"Do you really think the killer would try to take out the new pastor in front of her congregation?" Zora knew the other two ministers had been murdered as they walked to their cars after church functions.

Claudia pursed her lips and shook her head once.

"No. I think the killer will want to take out that new pastor in front of an audience of over thirty-five hundred. That's what the congregation swells to during the Christmas pageants and services."

"No." Zora's response was pure reflex. She knew evil existed, and that it sometimes came to nice places like Silver Valley. The reality of it was still overwhelming.

"I need you to fill in for Pastor Katherine Pearson. She's already been read into the op and is going to go to California to look after her ailing mother. We've had the church secretary send out a mass email with a personal letter from Pastor Pearson, announcing you as her replacement."

"Nothing like getting her as far away from here as possible."

"Right. And getting you in as bait, fully visible." Claudia was on a roll. "You won't be alone—you're going to have a partner to help you with this, Zora."

"Oh?"

Bryce cleared his throat. "Allow me to introduce myself. I'm your fiancé."

Zora's chest started to do its panic-attack dance again and she rested her head against the back of the wing chair. "You're kidding."

Claudia walked around to the front of her desk and stood in front of Zora and Bryce.

"This is no joking matter, Zora. We've got to save Christmas for Silver Valley."

"What did you come in here to talk to me about, Zora?" Claudia looked at her across the expanse of her shiny black desk. Bryce had left to make sure Pastor Pearson's travel plans were confirmed within the next few hours.

"It's going to seem crazy, but it may have relevance."

"Go ahead."

"You know that I was in a religious cult as a child?"

Claudia nodded. "Yes, you told us when we hired you, and I've read the reports and case files that I was able to get hold of."

Which meant she knew everything. Zora didn't need to ask. She knew firsthand the resources of the Trail Hikers were far-reaching and she didn't doubt that Claudia had seen some of the original police files on the cult.

"I have to tell you, Zora, your testimony was the most courageous thing I've ever read. To be able to speak so clearly and succinctly about what you'd witnessed was remarkable. And you were only twelve."

"Yes, but that was over twenty years ago. Most of the prisoner terms handed down to the cult's members are now up."

"Including the leader, Leonard Wise."

"Yes."

"What are you trying to tell me, Zora?"

"I saw my mother—my biological mother—in Walmart earlier. Edith Simms. That's why I came here, why I look like I do. I went to get out of the house, to get used to going out and about again."

"Zora, you've been through a lot, you're on pain meds…"

"I stopped them as soon as I got home. I wouldn't risk driving under their influence, and besides, I hate the fuzzy-headed feeling they give me. I'm not crazy, Claudia. It was her."

"I'll run some checks and see where she was last living. She never went to jail, did she?"

"You read the reports. She rolled over and told the authorities enough to stay free."

"But she'd never know where you went, who you became."

"No, that was her punishment, I guess."

"And you've never tried to contact her since then?"

"No. Absolutely not." Not directly anyway, but she wasn't willing to tell Claudia that. "When I first came to my parents here, it was hard. I felt guilty for all of the trouble I'd caused my mother and my friends in the community. But it faded as I got counseling and grew stronger as an individual."

"Is that why you decided to get your counseling degree?"

"Partly, yes." Zora shook her head. "But this isn't why I'm here—if my mother is here, and she recognized me like I recognized her, this could mean they've found me. The True Believers who are still free, and the ones who are getting out of jail now, may have come to get their revenge. I can't put my parents or anyone else at risk with this."

"One thing at a time. First, it's unlikely that was your mother, no matter how sure you feel. Second, if it was her, she may not have recognized you. Third, even if it was her and she knew you, it doesn't mean any other cult members are in Silver Valley. She could be on her own now."

"But why here, why now? It's possible that whoever shot me in my driveway isn't the Female Preacher Killer. It could be one of the True Believers."

"Let me worry about that. Meanwhile, go home and get ready for life as a minister during the busiest time of the year. One more thing, Zora—have you ever mentioned your past to Bryce?"

"No. All he knows is that Anna and Adam adopted me when I was twelve. I've never told anyone else about my past, except for a child psychologist whom I met with for the first several years after I moved here. They were all approved by WSP."

"You may need to cut him in on it, at some point."

"I don't see how it's relevant to this case."

"It's not, but I think it's good to know as much about your partner as possible. No secrets between partners is a credo I stand by. You have to be able to trust each other implicitly."

"We've known each other since we were quite young."

"But there's been a huge gap in your acquaintance, correct?"

"Yes. I don't even have a Facebook account, and if I had, joining the Trail Hikers would have meant canceling it anyway."

"You're free to keep up your regular civilian routine, Zora. Your role at the Trail Hikers and our mission is to keep things running safely and without the threat of imminent danger to innocent civilians. You'll never work under anything but an assumed name for us. Your private life remains that. Private."

"I know." Claudia had quoted the contract she'd signed with the government shadow agency almost verbatim. The spirit of the words, however, was different. Sometimes fulfilling your mission meant sacrificing everything.

Including the people and things you held most dear, like your family. But she hadn't expected that her work with the Trail Hikers would ever expose them to danger.

"Mom, I'm fine, promise. I'll call you in the morning to let you know how I'm doing. Right now all I want to do is heat up the yummy roasted chicken you left me and relax with Butternut in front of a decent movie."

"Okay, sweetheart. Talk to you in the morning." Anna had her purse in hand along with a huge tote bag, her idea of a suitcase. Zora's heart felt so raw looking at the woman who'd raised her without question, with total unconditional love. She wanted to hug Anna and never let go, never stop thanking her.

"Bye, Mom!"

"Bye." Anna hoisted herself into the Ford F-150 she'd insisted she needed to "haul things for church and my friends." Zora couldn't stop smiling as she watched her, no matter how grim the case she was now involved with.

No matter that she was "engaged" to Bryce.

She gave herself a minute to enjoy the stillness of the house. Finally, after days with either or both of her parents and a steady stream of visitors, she had some peace and quiet.

Butternut let out a sharp bark and trotted to the front door.

Zora groaned. No way, not now.

She ignored the tiny flips in her stomach when she recognized the profile of the man on her porch. She'd left the main door open. Now she unlocked the glass storm door.

"Hi, Bryce. What's going on?"

"Nothing at the moment. Can I come in?"

"Of course."

Anxiety endangered her hard-won calm. How had she gone from a part-time Trail Hikers operative on the side to full-fledged undercover agent in just a few days?

Bryce tilted his head as he gave her a once-over.

"Are you okay? You look a little stressed."

"I'm fine. Have you eaten?" She ushered him through the hallway, past the living room and back to the kitchen, determined to eat a full meal before she had another deep conversation about the case with anyone. Claudia's words had stuck with her all afternoon and she felt as if she'd been away from home for days instead of a few hours.

"No, but I didn't stop by for you to feed me. I thought we could order in Chinese, my treat."

"I thought I should avoid extra visitors to the house while I'm working undercover here in Silver Valley."

"I think takeout from the Iron Wok is safe enough.

We'll keep the security detail on your property for the foreseeable future."

"Normally I'd take you up on your kind offer, since their bean-curd stir-fry is my absolute favorite. But my mother left me a full dinner." She opened the refrigerator and wasn't surprised to see enough food to feed four people. "Look at that. It's as if she expected I'd have company."

"I may have told her I'd keep a close eye on you." His casual stance in her kitchen, combined with how handsome he looked in casual civilian clothes, made it too easy to think they could patch up whatever relationship they'd had all those years ago. Or maybe even start a new one.

"You have to be careful saying things like that to my mother. She's so eager for grandchildren she'll make you your favorite foods and bring them over on a daily basis."

She probably should have blushed at what she'd said, once she realized how it sounded, but Bryce had seen her take a bullet and he'd been the one to make sure the shooter didn't have a chance to hit her again in a more vulnerable place. He deserved some honesty from her.

And she liked the sound of his laughter. Butternut did, too. She gently put her paws on Bryce's chest and stretched out to her formidable length.

"Butternut, down!"

"She's okay." Bryce scratched her behind her ears, cooing to the dog like he'd done with their family pets when they'd both been teenagers. "But you'd better listen to your mother and get down for now, girl." The German shepherd complied but remained at Bryce's feet, staring at him with her most imploring expression.

"You've got a friend for life." She put the glass dish

with the chicken and rice in the microwave before she turned back to Bryce.

"You didn't come here to only eat, though, did you?"

"No, not really. We need to get know each other better than we do, Zora."

"You know more about me than a lot of people I've worked with before."

"I know about who you *were*—I know virtually nothing of who you are today. And you know nothing about me."

The look in his eyes sent a shiver of anticipation down her spine. But she'd be damned if she let him know it. She wrapped her arms around herself.

"It's getting chilly in here. I'll go start a fire." Anything to distract her from her body's reaction to Bryce.

Bryce hesitated, and she was afraid he'd say something about the blatant chemistry between them.

"Why don't you let me do that? I know you can handle it, but you should go easy on your ribs. Save your strength for when we're chasing down the bad guy." He didn't give her a chance to reply as he turned and walked into the larger area of the living room where the original farmhouse fireplace remained.

"Your chimney and flue are clean?" He started to stack logs from the basket into the pit, placing kindling underneath the larger, white-barked logs she and her father had split this autumn.

"Yes. I use it pretty regularly during the winter."

"Did you do all the renovation on this place? It seems so modern, yet still looks like a nineteenth-century home."

She laughed. "No, I'm not a fixer-upper, not by a long shot. The house was renovated by the previous owners, but then they got a job offer in California. They were eager to sell and I lucked out. I own all the property surrounding the house, and quite a bit down the road. I rent out the extra farmland whenever I can."

"So you don't need the money from the Trail Hikers."

Obviously he'd been offered his contract. The Trail Hikers paid generously, because they felt they were hiring the best of the best. They also expected more.

"I don't need the money, no, but my parents can use a little extra to make their retirement easier. I'm not doing it for the paycheck. My counseling work pays a decent wage. But it's nice to be able to sock some extra away for them. They've done so much for me."

Still kneeling next to the flickering flames, he looked at her with blatant curiosity.

"They did more than adopt you, didn't they? They kept you safe from something bigger. Something more than being orphaned at twelve."

"Yes." After not talking about her past for so long, she found it ironic that she had to deal with it twice in the same day.

Three times, counting seeing your mother.

"Are you ready to tell me about it, or am I hoping for too much?"

Chapter 6

"Why don't we eat here, where it's warmer? I can bring our food out on a tray." Zora's hands were on her hips as she stood in front of him. As if she was prepared to do battle.

At least she hadn't refused to share her past with him outright, so perhaps he was making some headway with her.

"Fine with me."

He watched her as she turned and went back into the kitchen where the microwave was beeping. She'd matured into a beautiful woman. No longer the gangly, geeky teen whom he'd realized too late he cared for more than just a next-door neighbor. The blossoming figure he remembered from senior year had developed into the sexy figure Zora had now, whether in yoga pants or a hospital gown.

As he stood to join her and help carry their plates, a movement outside the picture window caught his attention. At the same moment, he received a text from the security detail.

We cleared her. A local florist. Delivery.

A florist? Maybe some belated get-well flowers for Zora. But who knew she'd been hurt except for SVPD and the Trail Hikers and her parents?

"I'll get it." He opened the front door to a woman, bundled for the freezing weather and holding a long box with a huge purple bow on it.

Kayla.

Shit.

"Bryce. Nice to see you. I have this address for a Reverend Colleen Hammermill, but I know Zora lives here. Skyline Drive and Cherry Creek, right?" Kayla looked warily at Bryce. He imagined being stopped by the officers farther down the driveway had thrown her off. While she didn't look as angry with him as she'd been when they'd broken off their relationship six months ago, she wasn't overly friendly, either.

"Colleen Hammermill?" That was Zora's undercover name—how did flowers find their way here?

"Hi, Kayla! I'll take them." Zora had come up next to him and held her hands out for the box.

"Wait! Let me take that." He gave Zora a look that he hoped reflected his concern.

"I know *you're* not a minister." Kayla's comment implied that she knew a racier side of Zora.

Bryce ignored the jealousy that stirred.

Zora laughed and it sounded natural, although he heard a tiny catch in her breath. "Kayla and I know each other from yoga class," she said. "How do *you* know each other?"

"We tried to date. It didn't work out." Was Kayla warning Zora? Damn it. "So you know this minister?"

"Yes, it's my roommate from college. She's staying with me for a few weeks, but she's out at the moment. She'll be excited to get these."

"I have to say it was one of the more romantic orders I've filled since I opened the shop a month ago." Why did Bryce think this was a dig at him, a snipe at how little he'd been available for her during their brief dating period?

"Oh?" Zora played it cool.

"Yes. A man called in the order this morning. It was on my answering machine, and he dropped an envelope off through the front mail slot. It was there when I arrived at the shop. He paid cash, leaving extra for what he said he hoped would be personalized service."

"So that's why you're delivering. I didn't think you usually did all of the driving yourself. Do you happen to remember his name?"

"No name. Just the request and cash for delivery. He left his own note. All I had to do was put the order together."

"Well, thanks so much."

"I'll need your signature." Kayla pulled her glove off with her teeth as she held out a phone with a signature program on the screen.

"Of course."

He waited until he was sure Zora was okay with the transaction. Like the pro she was, Zora handled the whole thing with aplomb.

"Thanks so much, Kayla."

"Sure. And, Bryce, it was nice to see you again." Kayla looked from him to Zora and back, her expression bemused. "I assume you're here for work, right?"

"Actually, yes." Kayla had seen the security detail and she thought Colleen Hammermill was staying here—which she was, in truth. Just not how Kayla thought.

Kayla shook her head. "You'll never change, Bryce. See you!" She smiled at Zora before she turned and descended the porch steps.

Zora closed the door and looked at him, her eyes sparking with humor.

"Let me guess. You and Kayla have something going on, and you broke it off?"

"Had. Emphasis on the past."

"How long ago?"

"A while. It was brief. I'm sure you got her zinger—she was disappointed in my work hours and unavailability to date. She's absolutely right. I wasn't there for her, couldn't be. My work can get pretty intense."

"Like it is now." Her expression softened and he groaned.

"Don't psychoanalyze me, Zora. I'm a detective. Long hours are part of the deal. You've learned that firsthand since being with the Trail Hikers, right?"

"I guess so." Her eyes shifted to the box he held.

"What should we do with it?"

"First, we'll take it to your entryway out back. Then we go from there."

She followed him as he carried the box out to her mudroom and set it down. Butternut's claws clicked on the hardwood and then on the slate-tiled entry floor.

"What do you think it is? We need to call in forensics, don't we?" She held Butternut back, keeping her from getting too close to Bryce and the box.

"Yes, we'll need a full team here. But they'll have to come in waves, so that anyone watching won't suspect what's going on. So you met Kayla through yoga?"

"Yeah, I met her at the local gym when I first moved back. She went to high school with us, a few years behind."

"How *well* do you know her?"

"She's not a criminal, Bryce! You dated her, for heaven's sake."

Anger blurred his focus. He faced her. "We don't know who's a criminal and who's not in a situation like this, Zora. This package is from someone who thinks that you're a minister, and that you live here. We can't rule out anyone, even when we both know them."

"They're probably from the shooter, right?" Zora wasn't backing down.

"Probably. Maybe."

"And they only know me as a dark brunette with a much larger profile. I had an oversize sweatshirt on over my vest, remember? They don't know *me*."

She stood toe-to-toe with him and didn't blink.

"Yes. You're right." He placed his hands in his front pockets before he could do something stupid. Like touch her. "I'm sorry, Zora. We're dealing with a lot of different threads here. You and I have to make sure we're in sync and that our past doesn't interfere with the operation. Even though I know you were in the navy and have military experience I'm still not used to the idea of you being an undercover agent. And now that I know about the Trail Hikers—well, it's been a long few days."

Understanding was reflected in her eyes and he was transported back to long hours spent in either of their bedrooms, doors always left wide-open due to watchful parents, listening to the latest band one of them had discovered. Zora had listened to all his dreams about college, his future. And he'd done the same for her.

She'd never opened up completely, and he'd accepted it. He'd craved her friendship enough to overlook just about anything that bothered him about her.

"It has been a rather shocking reunion, hasn't it?"

Her lips twitched as she spoke and he couldn't help it. His laughter erupted in a burst of relief that she could joke under such dire threats.

"Your humor proves that you're cut out for this kind of work, I'll give you that. I don't even want to comment on how easily you still read me."

She nodded and looked him over in a way he'd never, back when they were in high school, imagined a woman could look at a man.

"You've grown into your job, too, Bryce, from the looks of it. For the record—I can't read you like I used to. We're different, we're not kids. Now, are you going to stand around chatting or are you going to call in your forensics team?"

She didn't want to talk about anything too personal, and he respected her focus on the job.

He scratched his chin.

"Let's wait on that. First, the only person who handled this was Kayla—since we know her and she's a legit florist, we know we're not dealing with an explosive. And only her prints will be on this."

"Except for the note the suspect left for her to include."

He nodded. "Right. Let's get gloves." Zora disappeared and came back with two sets of purple gloves. Once indoctrinated to the Trail Hikers, each agent was issued a standard evidence-collecting kit. It was generic enough that it wouldn't seem suspicious if found by normal civilians.

After they'd each put on latex gloves, he undid the ribbon and took the huge purple bow from the box.

Zora worked beside him, lifting the cover.

White tissue paper.

Under which were a dozen long-stemmed roses. Seemingly innocuous, except for the colors.

He heard her gasp.

"What?"

"The colors—they're the colors of Advent candles."

"Purple, pink and white?"

"Yes."

She nudged him aside and pulled out a small white envelope that was tucked into the stems, whose thorns had been removed.

"Be careful with that."

She had the temerity to glare at him.

"I got decent enough training from the Trail Hikers, don't you think?"

"Right."

He looked over her shoulder and forced himself to ignore her scent, the soft tumble of her red hair. Her gloved fingers quickly opened the note.

The envelope contained a single card with a Christmas emblem on the corner. It looked like something more personal than standard florist stock.

With each candle lit, one less before Christmas.
The last Sunday will have seen the fourth lit.
And by the time white is lit, Christmas will be pure again.

"How many Sundays until Christmas?" he asked Zora as she walked out of the mudroom and into her kitchen. He followed and as she grabbed her calendar, he called his up on his cell.

"One. Because of the way the days fall, we have four Sundays of Advent and then Christmas a few days later—all in December," she murmured as she flipped the page into December. Apparently her schedule was as busy as his as she hadn't touched the paper calendar since October. "The pink candle is for the third Sunday, which we've already had. The white is the one lit on Christmas. At least, that's what I saw last year when I went with a friend to an ecumenical service. My parents celebrate their faith in the more traditionally Catholic way, but the symbolism's all the same."

The wheels in Bryce's head were turning.

"He's already killed two, and you would have been number three."

"But I wasn't—so there could be two more, including me, he wants dead. One for each remaining Sunday of Advent, and then Christmas. And like Claudia thought, he wants to have the last one be a big deal, very public."

"Are you sure about the Advent colors?"

Patience battled with the exasperation in her eyes.

"We'll double-check it, of course, but Anna and Adam raised me Catholic once they adopted me. A lot of Christian denominations use the Advent wreath and candles to signify the approach of Christmas—we always had an interdenominational Advent wreath and candles in the navy chapels and on board ship. The pink candle is for the Sunday that's halfway through Advent. The center candle, if there is one, is white and represents that Christ is born—Christmas."

He stared at the roses. One had been left white, while the others had been hand-dipped into pink and purple dye of some sort. As if the killer had demanded delivery by a certain date and Kayla had to use whatever she had in stock.

"We need to get the note turned in for handwriting analysis after we check for prints. Although it'll take too long to get the results on the handwriting. We need to get him now."

"We'll also analyze whatever note he left with Kayla, in the envelope with the cash."

Zora shook her head. "No, she said he'd left a message on her shop's voice mail."

"Even better. Maybe we can get the call traced."

"Yes, but, Bryce…we can't wait on the results."

"No."

"I mean, are you thinking what I am?"

"That the next, and last, Sunday of Advent is in six days? And Christmas is a few days later?"

"Yes."

They ate the reheated but now cold chicken dinner as they waited for the first officers from the SVPD forensics team to stop buy. While each police officer was trained in forensics, the precinct practiced the common protocol by having its own specialized team consisting of officers who received more in-depth training. They also maintained contact with regional criminal forensics labs that proved vital in time-sensitive cases.

"The FBI will want the information, too. They might

get the evidence correlated more quickly." She hated to mention the feds to Bryce, as she knew it could be a point of contention with local LEA, but Bryce simply shrugged.

"I doubt it. I already emailed our Bureau contact after I called in to the precinct. They have the same access we do."

"As does the Trail Hikers. Should we call Claudia?"

Again, he was ahead of her.

"Already did. I thought you'd have done it since you've been at it longer than me."

"What, the Trail Hikers? Not by much. This is only my fifth or sixth op with them. The other missions involved more of an observational role."

"Which this was supposed to be, more or less."

"Except for playing cheese for the rat at the football game."

"You handled yourself well. You looked every bit the part. I actually wanted to bow my head during your invocation."

She laughed. "Thank you. I'll keep that in mind if the counseling doesn't work out."

Her smile brightened her face and brought out the deep amber flecks in her pale green eyes. His fingers itched to run themselves through her hair, all wavy and wild around her face, neck and shoulders.

He sensed her mirth turning to something deeper. She looked away.

"You asked me about why I came to Silver Valley. The first time." She closed her eyes briefly before bringing her gaze back to his.

"I was abused—you were correct. But it wasn't a simple child abuse case, not that any are. I was an only child, with a single mother. I don't know who my father was, or if my biological mother ever had other children after I left—there's no way to know, not the way we were forced to live."

Her eyes went to the window and she looked as if she was watching an old film. A painful recollection of something she'd worked her entire life to forget.

"You were poor?"

She spoke as if in a trance. As if she hadn't heard his question.

"My earliest memories are of my mother working as a waitress in a restaurant. I hung out in the back of the kitchen, where all the cooks and waitresses took turns holding me and playing with me. I think I was five or six—six, I must have been six, because it was first grade—when the man who'd change everything walked into the restaurant.

"I'd come home after school to the restaurant, where I could do my homework or just play at an empty table until my mother got off her shift. We'd go home and she'd warm up food from the restaurant. Once in a while we went to the grocery store and got fresh food for dinner, but not often.

"The day he came to the restaurant I knew something was going to happen. Something big. Mom acted all excited and when she got off her shift she walked us to the drugstore where she got a new lipstick." Zora paused and smiled as tears filled her eyes. "She'd never spent a dime on herself before. She said things were starting to look up for us. She bought me a coloring book and crayons."

"My next memory is of moving out of the apartment, putting everything I owned into a little duffel bag that one of her customers had given me."

"Didn't you have other family or friends in the area?"

"No. My mother didn't socialize, and she relied heavily on her faith. But it was *her* faith—we didn't go to church, not like I did with Anna and Adam."

"It must have been lonely."

"I didn't know any better. I had the restaurant staff— they were wonderful to me. And I loved school, always did." She looked at him. "You know that much about me, Bryce. I never missed a day of high school except for when I had strep throat our junior year."

He remembered. He'd brought a huge pile of books home to her and collected her assignments from all of the teachers. They'd shared most of the same instructors as they were both in the highest academic classes—honors and advanced placement.

"Go on."

"My mother said we were moving to a bigger, nicer place. With a playground and a new school and television. She wasn't lying—we did move to a huge place. A compound. It was the home of the True Believers."

"Oh, hell."

"You've heard of them, then? Did you ever suspect I'd been part of them?"

"I know of them now, because we studied their takedown ad nauseam in my criminal justice classes. Each course had its own way of looking at it, from profiling religious zealots to group think and mob mentality. Stockholm syndrome plays into it, too, which we studied in criminal psychology."

"Yes. Well, I was the one who got out and reported them. I was only eleven, almost twelve. You met me just a few months after I'd testified."

He fought like hell to keep his hands on the table, to appear comfortable, to not allow her to see how much this shook him.

"I knew I'd be getting my first period soon. That's when you became a 'waiting maiden' for the leader."

"Leonard Wise."

Again, she looked surprised that he knew. She had no idea what surprise was—he was rooted to the spot, realizing that his best childhood friend had been a survivor of that horrible place.

"I couldn't take it."

"How did you get away? Didn't you have to go to homeschool there, too?"

She nodded. "At first, it wasn't set up for all of that. They allowed us to go to public school, so I kept going to my elementary school through second grade. My teacher, Mrs. Powers, pulled me aside one day and asked me how I was doing. She told me that if I ever needed anything all I had to do was ask her."

"Do you think she knew?"

"She knew something. You probably read that a lot of local townspeople had been sucked into the cult. Wise preyed on single mothers especially, and men who were in bad straits. Most often he'd bail them out of jail, pay for attorney fees, to make them beholden to him. The women, he'd seduce."

"But you didn't get help until years later."

"No. I was still so young. At first, it seemed okay. We lived in our own little flat on the second floor of the building where they had worship services. My mother was so nice to me then, and she was always there when I came home from school. But then they started homeschooling, and just like that, I never saw my friends from school again."

She stood up, reaching for his plate. He grasped her hands.

"No, Zora. Sit and talk. I'm listening. I'll clean this up later." The forensics team would arrive in the next thirty minutes and he didn't want her to leave anything out.

He *needed* to know it all.

She sat back down and put her arm on the table, leaning over it.

"If you studied it, you know the rest. I managed to get away from my mother on one of our rare trips to the store, for fabric. I approached the police guard at the front of the store and told them I had to talk to the police. That my mother was hurting me. I was dressed in that god-awful plain long dress that they required, with my hair long and pinned up. We weren't allowed to wash it for weeks on end, and my mother dyed my hair black as she said the red brought out the devil's ways." He saw a shudder rack her slender frame. Not thinking, he was up and around the table in a second. He pulled her out of her chair and hugged her to him.

"You don't have to talk anymore, Zora."

She stiffened but quickly softened and leaned into his arms.

"I'm sorry to be so needy, Bryce. First I get shot and now we have to work together. You don't have to listen to this. You know enough."

"I want to know it all, Zora. If you'll tell me. But only on your terms." He kept her snuggled next to him, massaging her stiff muscles under her sweater. They'd been so young when they'd become friends. There was no way he would have understood her ordeal then. He wondered if she'd ever even understood it herself. Probably not. Some things took adult wisdom to appreciate. Especially the more painful events. If he could make time go backward and steal her from the horror she'd lived through, he would.

Holding her close would have to be enough.

Chapter 7

Zora didn't know the last time a man's touch had felt so good, so right. If she tried hard enough she might remember one or two of the men she'd dated over the years with a special fondness, but none had had a clue about her past, her tortured childhood.

Bryce hadn't known all of it, either, but he'd known *her*.

They'd only been children and he'd accepted her for who she was in the moment, not caring about where she came from. She'd never felt shame with Bryce.

"You are too nice to me, Bryce. Remember how angry you were with me when I canceled our prom date?"

"I'll never forget it. I still went, you know."

"With Jennifer Eastman." Jennifer had been the most popular cheerleader, a bright girl who'd gone on to become a local news station anchor. Zora had envied Jennifer's easygoing way with boys and especially with Bryce.

His chuckle vibrated through his chest and she relished the feeling as her cheek pressed against him.

"I lucked out. No one had asked her because they all assumed she had a date. I didn't know you cared."

"Of course I cared, as much as a seventeen-year-old can. That's why I let you go, Bryce."

He leaned back, still holding her shoulders. It forced her eyes to his.

"Explain, Zora."

She shrugged out of his reach, unable to maintain eye contact.

"It was a teenage crush, Bryce. I figured out I cared for you more than as a friend, but it was the wrong time—I was hoping to get the appointment to the academy within a few weeks' time. I had to focus."

"Did it ever occur to you that you could have talked it out with me?"

She shook her head. "No, not then. I was very driven, in case you don't remember."

"Was?"

"Okay, well, maybe I still am. A bit. But I'm not living out of fear any longer. I'm living the life I choose to live."

"Like becoming a willing target for a psychopath who doesn't think women should be ministers?"

"No different from what you do every day."

"True." He considered her and she found she didn't want to squirm anymore. Instead, she wanted to keep looking in his eyes, where she swore she saw the promise of something she'd never truly had in her life.

Freedom from the past.

"Besides, it's a nice change from what can sometimes be a slow pace, don't you think?"

He shook his head.

"Since I've been with the police department I don't see Silver Valley as a sleepy town anymore. With two interstate highways cutting through town, plus the Pennsylvania Turnpike, we never know who's going to take the Silver Valley exit and wreak havoc."

"It's true. Drugs have torn up this place just as much as they have the big cities. Most of my counseling clients are fighting their own addictions or suffering from the effects of others' addictions. Prescription painkillers and tranquilizers."

"It's not the Silver Valley you and I knew fifteen years ago, that's for sure. But we're still damn lucky—save for the occasional case like this one."

She nodded.

"Yes. I thought my time with the Trail Hikers would be minimal. I expected to travel to other cities as needed. It never occurred to me that we'd have a crazy killer in Silver Valley."

"You get that he's aiming at you, don't you, Zora?"

"Of course I do. Why do you ask?"

He stepped closer. One more step and she'd be back in his arms again.

"We're going for broke here. And I'm not going to let you get hurt if I can at all help it."

"Bryce, you're not my protector. We're partners in this."

"Partners have each other's backs."

"I have yours, too, if that's what you're asking." Did he think she was only out for herself? Then again, why wouldn't he? She'd dropped their friendship too readily all those years ago.

"I'm worried about the tension between us. As much as it will let us play a convincing engaged couple, it could cloud matters when bullets start to fly. And they will, Zora. This killer won't go down without doing everything he can to take you out and to get his sick message across."

"I can handle something as basic as sexual tension, Bryce."

He stepped closer. Toe-to-toe, his eyes sparkled with emotion she didn't want to trust. To believe.

"Can *we*?" His gaze moved to her lips, giving her time and room to take a step back, lean away, hell, duck and run if she so chose.

She met him halfway.

His lips were firm and warm, as she'd expected. What she didn't expect was his hesitation, the pause he allowed even as her lips moved over his.

She pulled back. "Obviously, we can."

His expression gave her a split-second warning before his arms were around her and he drew her body close to his, initiating a kiss that let her know he'd exercised the utmost in self-control until now.

He took charge of the kiss, demanding the most basic and immediate of responses from her. Zora stopped trying to conjure up the images of Bryce as a teen, the boy she'd thought she'd loved.

The man kissing her bore no resemblance to that carefree friend. This was the kiss a man gave a woman he wanted to take to bed.

She clutched his shoulders for balance as he grasped her buttocks and pulled her close.

"I don't want to hurt you—are your ribs okay?" How did he even find words, much less utter them as he continued to kiss her jawline, her throat, the sensitive skin behind her ear?

"Yes."

He stopped.

"Yes, you hurt?"

"No, not at all."

He lowered his head for a lingering kiss that she would have gladly enjoyed for the rest of the night.

Bryce pulled back and swore swiftly and potently.

Zora laughed. "Wow—I haven't heard that combination since I was in the navy."

"The forensics team is here."

Zora released a string of equally salty words as they parted and she smoothed her hair with shaky hands.

Bryce was right. They needed to get a handle on all of this if they were going to do their job right.

Pastor Colleen should have the flowers by now. It'd be hard for her to figure out the message, but that police officer who'd been going to her house would know what it meant.

It meant business. So much was wrong with the world. It used to be perfect here in Silver Valley. Back before all the immigrants started coming in, all the different cultures that weren't happy with good old Pennsylvania Dutch food. No, they wanted to have their fancy rice dishes and exotic vegetables. And that raw fish wrapped in seaweed that they sold in grocery stores.

Then the changes started coming to the churches. It was very unsettling to see that happen, especially in his own church, although things had been changing for a while now in churches that didn't follow the Word as well as his did.

He still wasn't sure how that shot had missed her. It was possible the police made her wear a bulletproof vest because of the other murders but he doubted she'd have been that smart. No, the shot must have gone wide in the dark of night, and she'd fallen to the ground from surprise and pure female weakness. And now the damned Silver Valley police had a car parked out front of her house, so he hadn't been able to drive by again to find out more about how badly she'd been hurt.

He'd come too close to getting caught that night, which would have meant disaster. He had a job to do.

Work to finish. For Mama.

Advent marched on, as did his needs.

He stared at Mama's framed photo. He kept it on the end table where he had a Smith and Wesson pistol in the drawer. Loaded, of course. Why keep a weapon in your house if you weren't prepared to use it?

It wasn't the weapon he'd used to get rid of the girl preachers, though. For that he used his prized hunting rifle.

Mama had taught him well. Sometimes it hurt, the lessons. The whippings. She didn't want him turning into a no-good son of a bitch like his daddy had been.

A bag of furry bones landed in his lap. He slapped the filthy animal off his chair.

"Git, you damn cat!" The old tomcat, Snowball, regained his balance and looked at him with his clouded eyes. The cat was so old, but Mama had loved Snowball so he had to, too.

Just like he had to love the church and the real truth Mama taught him.

He flicked on the television. There was only one station that still had a man for a regular anchor, the only station he could trust.

"Silver Valley Police Department representative Diana Pinker reports that the SVPD is working around the clock to catch the suspect who has killed two female ministers in Silver Valley in the past two weeks. We went out to ask local churches what they think."

The screen flashed to a young male reporter standing in front of Silver Valley Community Church. He sat up and turned up the volume as the reporter shoved his microphone in the faces of startled churchgoers. None of them said much, until the last one. A woman, of course. Women didn't know how to keep their damned mouths shut.

"It's upsetting, with Christmas and all. Our pastor has to go tend to her mother and we're getting a replacement until she comes back. I'm kind of relieved she'll be out of town until this blows over. It's chilling knowing a crazy person with a gun is out there, let me tell you. And I feel for whoever the replacement is."

The shot panned to the reporter, who looked into the camera.

"The replacement pastor is Reverend Colleen Hammermill, we're told. She will be reporting to Silver Valley Community Church this week." He signed off with the news station logo. Stupid reporters—hell, he knew who she was, where she lived, before any of them. He'd already welcomed her with a nice bouquet.

He shut off the TV.

Reverend Colleen Hammermill wouldn't change a thing as far as he was concerned. He'd get his job done.

Zora was impressed with the thoroughness of the forensics team. Seven police officers in total from SVPD, in three shifts, combed her house from where the flowers came in the door to the mudroom. All told it took less than two hours, since they were able to take the flowers and handwritten note with them to determine where various samples needed to go.

"What do we have, Rio?" Bryce addressed a tall, quiet, dark-haired officer whose muscular build had to be the result of hours in the gym.

"Nothing yet, I'm afraid. I'm hoping the handwriting and maybe even the envelope lead us to something."

"The envelope?" Zora knew they didn't get prints with the initial dusting.

"The glue could have acquired a fiber, or a hair or skin cell."

"Enough for DNA?"

"Probably not, but we can always hope." Rio smiled and his white teeth dazzled against his honeyed skin. "I'll check in with you if I find out any more."

Rio Ortego left as silently as he had come into the farmhouse.

Zora turned to ask Bryce how long the tests would take when she looked over his shoulder and spotted a familiar figure walking up the driveway.

"Claudia."

"Claudia?" Bryce turned in the direction Zora was looking. This was the second time Claudia had come to the farmhouse, something Zora suspected was unusual for the Trail Hikers' CEO, whose every minute was scheduled.

It underscored the gravity of the case. Of the urgency the entire town felt.

Everyone wanted to keep Silver Valley as it'd always been. And they wanted to protect Christmas, too.

"I thought this would be more efficient than calling you separately." Claudia nodded at both of them as she leaned down to stroke Butternut. The dog followed her mistress's cues and never barked unless Zora indicated she was stressed about a visitor.

"Come in." Zora motioned toward the hallway. "We're working in the kitchen for the most part." She led them back.

"Ma'am," Bryce greeted her. Zora hid her smile. She knew that Claudia could be a bit intimidating until you got to know her better. Bryce was still a Trail Hikers newbie.

"Claudia, Bryce, it's Claudia."

"Yes, ma'am. Claudia."

"Right. Well, I've got some news on the note."

Bryce and Zora exchanged looks. The Trail Hikers was cutting edge. But to surpass the forensics team at their specialty?

If Claudia read their doubt, she didn't reveal it.

"The note was written on what looks like a holiday notecard. Any florist would have them this time of year, right? But the florist shop owner, Kayla, doesn't stock this particular design, and the killer called in the order. He never actually came into the shop."

"The old-fashioned Santa Claus." Zora had noted it when she pulled the card out of the envelope.

"Right. It's circa 1954, in fact, and they sell them on eBay."

"Do you think 1954 has any significance?"

"It could, if the killer used his own stationery—something he had lying around their house."

"Or he could have ordered it off eBay to stay more anonymous."

Zora didn't think something as simple as a florist's card was going to catch a killer, but her expertise didn't lie with solving crimes. Her talents were in counseling—

listening to her clients and helping them find their way through whatever was keeping them from living a full, satisfying life. Agreeing to join the Trail Hikers had been a natural fit with her military background but she knew she was far from a detective.

Claudia's expression changed in a blink from analyst to team leader.

"You need to show up at the church tomorrow morning, Zora, prepared for a full workday. No one at the church knows you're undercover. Bryce can come in and out, as your fiancé, whenever you need him."

He'd never leave, she was certain. Bryce wasn't someone to use words carelessly. When he told her he'd protect her, he meant it.

"I don't know the first thing about being a minister, in truth. I'm learning as I go."

"You don't have to. Here." Claudia handed her a thick legal-size envelope.

"Reverend Pearson wrote up a turnover at my request. Your complete schedule, along with what she usually does at each event, is included. All you have to do is show up, read some Bible verses and pray. Frankly, we're going to need all the prayer we can garner with what we're facing." Claudia's normally unruffled appearance was shot to hell. Her face was flushed, her hair mussed and her clothes wrinkled. She looked like…

"You've been up all night working this, haven't you?" Zora's guilt was an automatic reaction after years of pulling watch shifts and working late hours and weekends to get to the bottom of a navy intelligence case, or prepare a presentation. You didn't leave a teammate *in extremis*, and that was how she felt she'd treated Claudia.

"It's in my job description." Claudia elegantly shrugged off Zora's observation.

"Call me next time, ma—Claudia."

"Thank you, Bryce, but you both have something more important in front of you. I trust the SVPD security detail will be here for the duration?"

"Yes. And about the church and Zora—Chaplain Hammermill, that is—I'd like to provide her with security. Won't it seem odd if we don't?"

"I've already taken care of it. We'll have Trail Hikers posing as members of the church at each major service. All indications are that the killer will hit during a larger service like the children's Christmas pageant or one of the Christmas services."

The weight of her task settled like an unwanted mantle on Zora's shoulders.

"He's definitely escalating his tactics." Zora thought of the minister who'd escaped with nothing but a scrape on her temple. Talk about a miracle.

"Yes, but he's a bad shot. That's one thing." Bryce was matter-of-fact.

"That leads me to another bit of news." Claudia leaned against the laminate kitchen counter and accepted the coffee Zora handed her. "Thanks." She took a long sip as Zora and Bryce waited for her news.

"The ballistics on the bullet that you were hit with doesn't match the weapon the killer's used to date. You were shot with a handgun and the Female Preacher Killer has been using a hunting rifle."

"Do you think we have two suspects?"

Claudia shook her head. "I don't know. We can't be certain on anything, I'm afraid. The killer could have several weapons he's using."

Zora looked at Claudia before she looked at Bryce again. Their faces were tense with concentration and…

Concern. For her.

"Hey, let it go, will you? I'm exactly who we need to bring the killer, or killers, out into the open. Either way, I'm going to be the best damned reverend Silver Valley has seen at Christmastime. And I have SVPD and the Trail Hikers behind me. It's a win-win."

Neither replied. Stand-up comedy had never been her forte.

Chapter 8

"**R**everend Pearson left you her schedule for the next three months, although we hope she isn't gone that long, of course." Shirley Mae Noll, the Silver Valley Community Church office manager, motioned at the large, detailed desk calendar atop the wide desk in the pastor's office.

"I have her turnover notes, so we should be good." Zora tried not to grimace at how obviously Shirley Mae was pained by the absence of Pastor Pearson.

"Turnover notes?" A wrinkle appeared between Shirley Mae's perfectly plucked brows and the shellacked nails of her right hand rested over her heart.

"Yes, it's a navy expression. Um, my uncle was in the navy." She'd almost blown her cover with one bit of slang.

"Oh, you scared me there for a second! I thought you meant something more permanent. Pastor Pearson is only gone for as long as it takes to make sure her mama's doing okay. You know, it's so strange. Her mother and aunt came to visit her just this summer and her mother looked so young and healthy. I would never have guessed she'd be faced with putting her in a home so soon."

"Excuse me?" A pleasant-looking older man stood at the office door, a large bin on wheels behind him.

"Hi, Ernie! Go on in—I'm just showing our interim the ropes."

The look on Ernie's face was pained.

"Have you heard anything from Reverend Pearson? Is she okay?"

"She's fine, thanks for asking. Her mama needed some tending and she's taken a little time to help. Reverend Hammermill here is filling in for her, and helping us through Christmas. Pastor Hammermill, this is Ernie Casio, our custodian."

"Hello, Ernie." Zora held out her hand.

Ernie raised two gloved hands.

"Sorry, these gloves aren't something you want to touch. Nice to meet you."

"Same here." She moved so that he could pass her and get to the wastebasket in her office.

"Thanks, Ernie. How's that kitty of yours?"

Ernie smiled. "She's as ornery as ever, but healthy."

"Nice to know." Shirley Mae smiled at the janitor before he turned and left their work area. She turned her attention back to Zora.

"Ernie's usually better about getting his work done either very early or later, after we've gone, but sometimes he runs late. I don't give him trouble for it because he's worked here for so long and he's reliable."

Shirley Mae appeared to be an excellent office manager, which Zora was grateful for. But she was also a big talker, and Zora had work to do.

"I understand."

Zora walked around to the back of the expansive desk and took a seat in Katherine Pearson's very comfortable and very modern ergonometric chair. Another thing to like about Silver Valley Community Church.

"What do you think about the killer?" Shirley Mae switched subjects the way the weather changed in central PA.

"I don't let myself think too much about him. We have a full plate between now and Christmas, and we're going to pull it off with as much holiday spirit as we can muster." This undercover minister gig wasn't so bad. Her training in the Trail Hikers had taught her to stay as close to the truth as she could when it came to events and emotions, and lie only about important details.

Like her navy career.

However, she really wanted Shirley Mae to leave her office. Her wig itched and the suit she wore was oversize to accommodate her Kevlar, a safety precaution Claudia had insisted upon. Zora figured she'd lose ten pounds a week from carrying around the vest for so long each day. All she wanted at the moment was to sit still and look over the events she'd be participating in.

"Thank you so much, Shirley Mae. I think I'll dive into these notes and work on the sermon for Sunday. Please shut the door when you leave."

"Oh, okay. Do you want me to hold your calls?"

"No, that's not necessary. Does Pastor Pearson get a lot of calls each day?"

Shirley Mae shook her head, causing her spiral curls to bounce around her face. She was a young woman, full of enthusiasm for her job.

"No, not this early. The long calls and meetings happen more in the afternoons."

"Well, then, I'd better get busy now. Please let me know if I can help you with anything, Shirley Mae. You've been wonderful to show me around and make me feel so welcome."

"Sure thing." Shirley Mae left with a decided flounce but forgot to shut the door. Zora got up, closed it and took the time to close the blinds on the door window, as well.

She needed privacy so that she could at least take off the fake glasses and scratch where the bulletproof vest itched against her skin.

A minister's job was a demanding one, she soon learned. She understood that this time of year would be full of holiday-related events, but the constant, ongoing education that Katherine Pearson engaged in was mind-boggling. She'd attended workshops leading up to the holidays, and already had many scheduled for the new year. Katherine, like Zora, was also a certified counselor, with a psychology degree in addition to her master's of divinity.

No wonder the woman was single and reluctant to leave her church. Zora looked at the screensaver on Katherine's computer—it was a slideshow of photos of her with what Zora assumed were friends and church members.

Katherine Pearson was a beautiful woman in her own right—somewhere in her midthirties with a cute blond pixie cut and sparkling light eyes. Yet in no photo was there a man or woman with her that could be a partner.

Zora got it. Having a serious relationship while working such a fast-paced career was difficult if not impossible.

She ignored the thought that this was what she was facing. A life alone, her career as her only enjoyment.

"Stop it." She clicked the mouse and started to read up on the ins and outs of the children's Christmas pageant, scheduled in a week. Christmas Eve. Hopefully they'd have the killer in hand by then. It was awful enough to worry about another adult being senselessly murdered, but children? Not on her watch.

An hour later a soft knock sounded ahead of the door opening.

"Reverend Hammermill? Your, um, fiancé is here to see you." Shirley Mae looked dazed. And a bit confused. Zora bit her bottom lip to keep from laughing.

"Send him in."

She didn't miss how Shirley Mae looked at Bryce.

"Hi, sweetheart." The endearment caught her by surprise and she wished it didn't elicit a tingling sensation low in her belly.

Careful. It's just a job.

"Hi yourself." She waited for Bryce to shut the door behind him. She was grateful she'd closed the blinds.

"How's it going so far?" His glance took in the office, the walls lined with photos, before resting on her.

Zora laughed.

"I think we've shocked Shirley Mae. She has no idea how I landed a man like you."

Bryce looked at her, blinked, then looked again as if seeing her disguise for the first time.

"I have to say that brown suit and mousy hair isn't your best."

"While you get to wear your…your…" She searched for words other than what she was going to say.

"My plain clothes?"

"Yes." Was she nuts? She'd already let him know she found him attractive; now she was nearly drooling over him. He did look stunning in his formfitting merino sweater and jeans.

"Well, as far as they're all concerned I'm your fiancé, and I work for SVPD. They can think we were attracted to each other because of our similar dedication to duty."

It was smart planning on Claudia's part. There was no reason Reverend Hammermill shouldn't have a fiancé who was in law enforcement. Plus there was a good chance that several people in the church knew Bryce, and his going undercover was improbable without a lot of effort. The FBI profiler connected to the case also felt it might help draw out the killer more quickly—he'd see the SVPD presence as a challenge he wanted to beat.

"Have you heard anything new?"

Bryce shook his head.

"No, nothing. Have you had a chance to meet anyone here besides the office staff?"

"Not yet. But we have our first public appearance coming up. How's your schedule Friday night?"

"Let me see." Bryce pretended to check his phone. "Nope, nothing. Just some big case I'm working on."

"Great. Go rent a tux and pick me up by five thirty on Friday. We have a gala to attend."

"Do we? Where?"

"The Harrisburg Hilton. It's one of the biggest fundraisers of the year for local churches. It'll have a silent auction, corporate sponsors. It's simple—we just have to show up and smile."

"And act as if we're in love."

The warmth she experienced earlier turned into a

white-hot shot of lust that made her wish she was wearing anything but the heavy undercover getup.

At her silence, Bryce walked closer to the desk and leaned over.

"You're blushing, Reverend."

"It's all part of the gig, Bryce."

"Is it?"

She scooted her chair back, putting much needed space between them.

"Of course."

He grinned and with one glance conveyed that he was on to her. He knew she wanted him. And he wasn't afraid to let her see how much he wanted her, too.

"What are you wearing?"

"Wh-what?"

"Tomorrow night, Zora. To the gala. How are you going to cover up your vest?"

"My vest." She took a moment to think. "I'll call Claudia. Chances are she'll agree the risk won't be so great on the other side of the river. The killer's hit all of his targets here in Silver Valley, and there's no indication he's tracking any ministers in Harrisburg."

"Fine, but if you don't wear your vest, then I'm going to be your living vest. I'm not leaving your side."

"You're not my bodyguard, Bryce."

"Not officially, no. But the fiancé of a female minister who's working in a town where two female ministers have been killed? He'd be more than protective of her, especially if he were truly on SVPD. Which I am."

"Yes, you are."

Bryce never leaving her side? It should make her feel

more solid, grounded, able to do her undercover job as well as she possibly could.

And it did. But it also left her hot and bothered.

One thing Zora figured out quickly was that her wig and oversize suit didn't feel so cumbersome when she had her mind on other things—like pretending to be a minister.

"Colleen, your two o'clock is here."

"Fine, send them in."

She figured that as long as she didn't know the church members in her real life, she'd be okay with counseling as Colleen Hammermill. Ministers and counselors often had very similar training.

A pretty woman, who would be beautiful if not for the exhaustion stamped in every line on her thin face, walked in, followed very reluctantly by a preteen girl.

"Thanks for seeing us, Reverend. I would have waited until Reverend Pearson got back but my daughter and I are at odds and we could use some help."

"Of course. Please take a seat."

Once they were seated she got started.

"I'm Colleen, and I want to assure you that besides being a minister I'm a trained counselor. Anything we discuss here is in total confidence, with the exception of child abuse, which I'm required by law to report to the authorities."

"I'm Rebecca Flatwood, and this is my daughter, Jess."

"Nice to meet you both." Her response was met with a grim smile from Rebecca and a roll of the eyes from Jess.

"I'm Jess's only parent as her father took up and left with the whore of a woman who supplied his drugs for him. Meth. Says he's straight for good this time, as if I'd believe him."

"When's the last time you saw him?" She directed her question to Jess, forcing her face to remain neutral even though she inwardly cringed at Rebecca's tone.

"She hardly remembers him, and even if he wanted to see her, I wouldn't let him."

"Jess? How old are you, hon?"

"Twelve going on thirty, or so she thinks." Again, Rebecca answered.

"Rebecca, I need to hear Jess's responses, too."

"Sure." Her insouciant shrug was a clear indication of where Jess's over-the-top dramatics came from.

"Jess?"

"I'm almost twelve. My birthday's next week, but we don't do a big celebration because it's too expensive with Christmas so close. I do remember my dad—he left when I was eight. Sometimes he sends me nice presents."

"Do you email him or text him?"

"Email is for old folks." She met Zora's gaze and must have realized how she sounded. "Sorry. I'm not saying you're old. Yeah, we text sometimes, or do Snapchat."

The Trail Hikers training had included proficiency in all forms of the latest social media, including Snapchat. Zora remembered it as a favorite among teens as it didn't retain the conversations. The adolescents felt freer to write whatever they were really thinking, knowing it wasn't going to be there "forever."

"I hate that damned Snapchat. I can't go back and see what the bastard wrote her."

"Your concern is understandable, Rebecca. Jess, have you ever felt threatened by your father?"

"No, he's always nice to me. Except before he left, when he was high, or right after. He could get mean."

"Is Jess safe now? Are you safe, Rebecca?"

Rebecca snorted.

"Safe? Yeah, we're safe. Struggling to make ends meet, sometimes skipping the doctor if we don't need to go or if I don't have the insurance co-pay, but we're okay."

"So what's brought you in here today?"

"I need to know when Jess talks to her father. And if he's planning to pick her up to go anywhere. She won't tell me, her mother."

"Do you have a court agreement with him?"

"Court stuff costs money. There's no extra money for anything, including the guitar lessons Jess is always harping about. If it wasn't for the church we wouldn't even have a place for Jess to be after school, away from the crazies in our neighborhood."

"I understand."

Rebecca shot her a look that indicated her extreme doubt in Zora's compassion. Like Katherine Pearson, Zora didn't have any children of her own, but she knew more about young girls than Rebecca could guess at.

"You know, I might be able to help you with your music lessons. We have two different contemporary music groups here. And there are plenty of instruments in the band room. I'm sure we can find a guitar to lend you, Jess, and there's bound to be several other teens who'd like to learn. I can put a notice in the church bulletin asking for anyone who has the time to offer beginner lessons."

Jess moved her head in a noncommittal gesture.

"Sure. Whatever."

"Where does her father live?"

"He's in the same trailer park we are, on the outskirts of Silver Valley. He moved back last year, and has been bothering Jess more."

Zora made a mental note to check the church registry for their address. Bryce would have insight on the area, which might be helpful.

"He's not bothering me. He's being a parent." Jess's emphasis on the last syllable of *parent* made it clear she didn't feel Rebecca was being the best at her job.

Rebecca shook her head.

"You don't know what a parent is, missy. Sure, your dad can show up and be the hero now, but where the hell was he when you needed your cavities filled from all that…"

"That's enough for now. Let's focus on why you're here. It sounds to me as if you want Jess to keep you more informed about when she communicates with her father. Jess, I understand that you're getting older and more independent but your mother has your safety in mind. Whether you're talking to your dad or a school friend, your mom needs to know if you're planning to go anywhere, and she has a right to know where you are at all times. Does this make sense to you?"

"Yeah."

"And you realize that your mom can take your phone away if she thinks you're not obeying her rules, right?" Zora made sure to make eye contact with Rebecca, too.

"Yeah."

Zora wished she'd get more than a monosyllabic response from the preteen but at least they were all talking.

"Okay, then. Jess, why don't you go wait in the reception area while your mom and I talk for a bit? Afterward

I'll get that guitar for you, and maybe I can convince you to help out with the Christmas pageant."

"I already am—I'm on the stage crew, helping with the lights."

"Wonderful. I appreciate you sharing your time and talent."

After Jess clicked the door behind her, Zora faced Rebecca with a sternness she didn't feel.

"Are you certain she'll be safe if her father starts spending more time with her?"

"Yes. He'd never hurt her—he loved her as much as a young boy could. That's all he was when we met—a boy. I had to grow up faster, having the baby and all."

"Where do you work, Rebecca?"

"I fill in at a grocery store when they can use me, and now I have a good job at the community college. I work there around my classes. I'm getting certified as a paralegal. I couldn't be away from Jess this long before, and it's taken me until now to save enough to afford a car and the gas to get back and forth."

"You're an amazing woman, Rebecca. I hope you know that. Jess is just being a typical twelve-year-old in many ways. My only concern remains her communication with her father. You'll keep tabs on it?"

"Yes."

"If you have any concerns or feel you need the authorities, don't hesitate. If you won't make the call, I will. It's part of my job."

"I'll do that. And, Reverend Hammermill…thank you. You made such a difference with Jess. She was quiet with you but I know she was listening."

"Anytime."

Chapter 9

As the week passed in a blur Bryce was impressed at how dedicated Zora was to her undercover role, and how much attention she gave to each detail of the upcoming Christmas pageant and Christmas services.

He couldn't help but notice how much he was enjoying his role, too, posing as her husband-to-be. Being able to stop in her office without warning.

Bryce stood in front of Zora's desk for a full minute before she looked up from the laptop she worked on. Shirley Mae had been nowhere in sight so he'd let himself into the minister's office.

"Bryce!"

"Reverend Hammermill." The flirtatious tone of his greeting had the effect he'd hoped it would—she smiled.

Her smile triggered a protective instinct, followed by a blatantly sexual one. He forced his thoughts away from Zora's creamy skin and the pink blush rising up her neck, the same kind of rosy hue he'd love to cause in other ways.

"I didn't hear you come in." She took off the ridiculously huge black-rimmed glasses and massaged her temples. "These don't have real lenses but they're still a pain to look through. They're all scratched, too."

"Want me to find you another pair?"

"No, that's fine. This won't go on forever, right?"

He sat down.

"Not if we can help it."

"Right. I'm glad you stopped by. There's a neighborhood I'd like to know more about, where one of my members lives."

"One of 'your' members?"

"Humor me. It's part of the deal, remember?"

"Go on."

She mentioned the address and he immediately knew the place.

"It's a trailer park on the edge of town. Whoever you were speaking to must be having tough times if they live there." He wasn't going to tell her he'd been tasked to look at the trailer park for other reasons. Not yet.

"They are. Is it safe? There's a preteen girl involved." She wasn't going to spill all she knew, either. They were both bound by the code of their respective professions.

"Honestly? Not so much. But if they keep to themselves, as I'm sure anyone living there must do to survive, they'd be okay."

She sighed.

"I was afraid of that. The mother is working to get them out of there, but it sounds kind of awful."

"Poverty is."

"Yes, and they exemplify the working poor." She frowned.

"You're not going to fix anyone here, Zora. You're not going to be here long enough." He kept his voice low in case anyone walked by the office. They'd think it was simply an engaged couple having a private conversation.

"I know that, trust me. One of the perils of being a counselor is hoping you can change people, or rescue folks from their lives. It doesn't work that way—we all have choices to make, paths to walk. Just one time, though, I wish I could wave a wand and make the journey a little easier for them."

Bryce liked the sense of common purpose they shared.

"In that our two professions are similar."

"At least you get more immediate results."

"A lot of the time, yes. In the midst of a case like this one, not so much."

"So I take it you haven't found anything new?" Her expression, though wary, showed hope that he hated to crush.

"No, nothing. As expected there were no prints on the note with the flowers and the lab hasn't gained any more from your first vest." SVPD had provided her with new Kevlar since they'd had to send off hers for analysis.

"That's disappointing. It's not like the television shows, is it?"

"How so?"

"You don't solve the crime in an hour, with all the latest forensics equipment and law enforcement software in one room."

He laughed and she smiled in return. Her smile was the stuff that inspired classic artists. Genuine, warm and highly kissable.

Down, boy.

"No, I can't say I've ever had that happen. But we're pretty damn good, considering how piecemeal some of the parts are."

"I've been reading up on SVPD and the cases you've handled over the past five years or so. It's getting crazy even here, isn't it? If it's not heroin or meth, it's money laundering, or big-time crime rings sending innocents into the big-box stores in the middle of the night."

"You know about that?" He was once again impressed by her abilities.

She was referring to the high incidence of electronics theft from the stores closest to the interstate, only a mile out of Silver Valley. SVPD worked closely with the treasury department on it, and had been successful at nabbing several perpetrators. But it was an ongoing battle as the crime rings were Jamaican, Russian or Ukrainian run and operated from major hubs that included Philadelphia, Baltimore and New York. SVPD did their part by monitoring events in their jurisdiction and reporting them to Treasury, who worked with the FBI on the bigger picture.

"Yes, I do read the papers, you know. And of course our mutual employer has access to all of the reports. How's SVPD doing with this added burden?"

"We're stretched thin. But one of the other detectives—Rio Ortego—has taken over my other cases for now, allowing me to give *this* my full attention."

He didn't mean to allow his voice to drop on "full attention" and he certainly didn't mean to come off as such a horny bastard. But the heat between them was potent.

Judging by the way Zora bit her lower lip and clasped

her hands as if holding on to a lifeline, she was fighting it, too.

"You feel it as much as I do, don't you?"

"It's the consequence of our shared history and the close confines of this intense case." She looked like an old-time principal with her hands on the desk and her expression serious.

"How many times have you practiced that in front of your bathroom mirror?"

She had the grace to appear speechless.

"You're playing dirty, Detective."

"No, I'm not, but I want to be dirty with you, Reverend."

Her gaze didn't waver from his and he knew that with the tiniest push he'd gladly allow himself to be controlled by his lust for her.

Is it only lust?

"Is that appropriate for this setting?"

He stood and leaned over the desk, putting his face close to hers.

"I left 'appropriate' behind me a long time ago, Zora."

He fought the urge to grab her and crush her lips to his. She had to come to him first. He needed to know that she wanted him as badly as he wanted her.

A fleeting smile crossed her lips and her eyes lowered to his mouth. They were so close he swore he tasted her minty breath, a by-product of her obsession with ginger mints.

"Excuse me, Colleen." Shirley Mae knocked as she spoke, opening the door and clearing her throat. Zora sprang back from the desk, her wheeled chair nearly hitting the wall behind her. Bryce took his time in straightening and looked over his shoulder at the receptionist.

They were supposedly engaged, so he wasn't going to act as if he'd been doing anything but leaning in for a quick kiss.

And he didn't want Shirley Mae to see the front of his trousers. It was enough that Zora knew how hard she'd made him.

"Yes, what is it?" Zora had the gift of quick recovery, he'd give her that.

"Here's the map to the Christmas gala, downtown tomorrow night. You and Detective Campbell need to be there by five thirty."

"Thank you."

As he loaded the garbage into the Dumpster in back of the sprawling complex that was Silver Valley Community Church, Ernie realized how stupid women could be. Not his mother, of course, but women who thought they could take a man's career.

A career that the word of God was pretty clear about.

He'd pretended to be surprised that Reverend Hammermill was at his church when Shirley Mae introduced them earlier. Only a week ago he'd seen her give that awful prayer at the football field. It seemed following her home that night hadn't been necessary after all. Snooping in the office to find her address was easy after-hours.

He'd outsmarted the cops and beaten them to her place by following her home from the police station. She'd never seen him, since he'd taken the farm roads, parallel to her route on the main highway, with his lights off. Once he'd figured out which house she was headed toward, he'd ran the rest of the way with his handgun, ready to shoot her.

It still bothered him that he'd missed her heart.

He thought his flowers would have scared her enough to lie low. He had no idea which congregation she was from originally—she'd just shown up at the football game, and now at Silver Valley Community Church.

He still hoped to take out Reverend Pearson. Until she returned, he'd have to come up with a new plan for his Christmas message to the women in Silver Valley who thought they could wear the holy cloth of God. And anyone who supported women in the holy robes. Robes were meant for men.

The wind grabbed two large corrugated cardboard boxes off the second pallet he'd pulled out and he wound up chasing them across the parking lot. As he flattened the boxes he imagined putting bullets into the hearts of both reverends, Hammermill and Pearson.

At least he wouldn't have to chase Reverend Hammermill down at her house—that dog of hers was a problem, plus the police car was still there when he drove by her house. He was careful not to drive the same car twice; he used his mother's old Buick that he didn't have the heart to get rid of, and the later-model pickup he liked to use when he went hunting. His everyday car was a small sedan.

He took a long drag on the cigarette he enjoyed over his break. He'd have preferred to take out Reverend Pearson at the big Christmas Eve service, but killing Reverend Hammermill would send Silver Valley the message loud and clear.

Women didn't belong in the pulpit.

"Campbell, my office. Rio, go wrap up everything with that florist. And have her call us the minute she gets anything similar to what she delivered to Reverend Hammermill's."

Colt Todd issued orders in rapid fire as he walked in front of Bryce through the police station. He paused to tell the receptionist to get the doughnuts a grateful citizen had dropped off out of his sight "before I eat them."

Colt Todd was on a roll and Bryce wasn't going to argue with him, no matter how pressed for time he was. He had to pick up Zora within the hour, and he still needed to get his tuxedo.

"Shut the door."

"Yes, sir." Bryce complied and turned to face his boss. Well, one of his bosses. Or was Claudia in charge of SVPD, too? Sometimes he wondered about the true role of the Trail Hikers.

"Sit down. Tell me what you've got so far on the Female Preacher Killer, and the trailer park."

Bryce filled him in without delay. "That part about the church family living there—that could open up some leads for us."

"I agree, but I don't want to pursue it until after we get the Female Preacher Killer in custody." Or dead. Bryce couldn't guarantee anything with a psycho—they'd bring him in alive if at all possible, but if he had to be taken out to protect innocents, they would do it. The one part he hated but accepted about his job.

Superintendent Todd ran his hands over his short-cropped silver hair.

"We're out of officers to cover it all. I've had to call in help from two other townships. Next I'll have to put in a request to the county for more bodies."

"Understood."

"How's the new reverend working out?"

Bryce smiled.

"Exactly as you'd expect. You know Zora Krasny—nothing stops her. And she's doing well. The Trail Hikers waste no expense on the best possible training."

"Don't mention them here again, just for security." Superintendent Todd wasn't upset but spoke absently as he tossed a glass paperweight between his hands. "I'd hate to see her hurt by this bastard. It's bad enough that he, or a second assailant, took a shot at her and we couldn't stop it."

"I agree, sir."

Superintendent Todd put the weight down heavily on his worn desktop and leaned on his forearms.

"There's something not right about the trailer park and these murders happening at the same time."

"It could be a coincidence, sir, but Rio's checking on the trailer park. If there's a connection, we'll find it."

"If we have what I suspect we might with the new residents who relocated from that tiny town in New York, all hell's going to break loose here. Silver Valley is not going to tolerate a wacko cult coming into the area."

"We can't do anything until they break the law." Bryce had to keep the voice of reason alive, because Superintendent Todd looked as if he wanted to round up the new inhabitants of the trailer park himself.

"No. That's the tough part, because people the likes of Leonard Wise always break the law again. They can't help themselves." He took a deep breath and let it out as he picked up the paperweight again.

"Claudia told me you're both working at the church for the time being. I didn't formally tell you but any work you do for her organization takes precedence. The way they work is that you'll never work on a case that's not going to help our area. It's win-win."

Superintendent Todd didn't have to say "Trail Hikers." "Yes, sir. It's interesting that Detective Ortego hasn't even asked me why I can't do the cases I've handed him. He's just assuming I'm full-time on the Female Preacher Killer."

"That's good enough. You've always done what's asked of you, too."

"Within reason."

They shared a look of understanding. It was the code among the fellowship of police officers—do what you're told, mind your own business as much as possible and make sure you're keeping the community safe.

"How's your personal life, Campbell?" Colt Todd wasn't a nosy man, but if he felt something might affect any of his team members, he was all over it.

"I'm keeping it separate from work, sir."

"It's not up to me to tell you to stay away from Zora, Bryce. If there's something there, I'll be the first to encourage you to settle your ass down. You need a life partner to ground you—you work too much. But I don't have to remind you that distractions in the middle of this kind of case can be deadly, do I?"

"No, sir. Appreciate your concern." Bryce couldn't tell Superintendent Todd what he didn't know himself—how he really felt about Zora being back in his life.

"Just checking. Keep me in the loop on the whole TH thing, will you?"

Bryce knew Superintendent Todd was cleared by the Trail Hikers for any operation his officers were assigned to. Claudia kept Colt informed.

"Will do."

Todd nodded.

"Good man. Now get out of here and stay safe."

Bryce left the office with a feeling he'd never had at work before—the sense that maybe he wasn't being completely honest with his boss.

Zora couldn't have gotten under his skin, not this quickly.

Could she?

Chapter 10

Crystal chandeliers glittered in the marble-floored foyer as Zora's heels clicked on the hard surface. She'd opted for practical but still-pretty shoes, not wanting to look as if she was ready to run the distance in her heels but needing to be able to. The rhinestone-encrusted shoes set off her dress perfectly. As she'd thought, Claudia agreed to Zora ditching her Kevlar "only if Bryce is with you each step of the way, including getting you safely back into your home."

She pulled up her crystal-sequined bodice. It felt almost as heavy as her vest, albeit much more sparkly and feminine. Soft navy organza flowed from the bodice's waist to the floor, making Zora feel like a floating fairy princess.

"The lights are reflecting off your dress. You look like an angel." At Bryce's whispered observation near her left

ear, Zora sputtered the tiny sip of champagne she'd tried
all over the marble floor.

"Careful." His hand kept her grounded as it remained
on her bare skin, his arm draped casually over her shoulders and upper back.

"It's a little difficult to feel like a heavenly vision
with this wig and these glasses." Instead, she figured she
looked like a spinster librarian sprung loose for a night
of revelry. And the reassuring pressure of his hand on
her back and shoulders was in direct opposition to their
mission and her need to keep her heart safe.

"I see past that."

Did he feel the delicious shiver his reply sent through
her?

"You must be Reverend Hammermill." A strange
voice boomed into their intimate space.

"Yes. And you're Chuck Wainright, I believe?" At the
newscaster's nod, Zora turned toward Bryce.

"Allow me to introduce my fiancé, Bryce Campbell."

"We've met—many moons and cases ago, right, Detective Campbell? How are you doing?"

Bryce and Chuck shook hands, and they all chatted
for a bit about the gala and the beautiful surroundings.
The newscaster was a reporter at heart, however, and
couldn't let the opportunity to dig go by.

"It must make you feel safer to have Bryce around
with a serial killer on the loose, Colleen. Especially one
targeting female ministers."

Zora braced herself and issued her practiced reply.

"My vocation is to help others with their faith, so
what good am I if don't practice it myself? Having Bryce
nearby is certainly a comfort to me and the entire Silver Valley Community Church congregation, but it's my

faith that allows me to go to the office each day, and to continue with our Christmas schedule. And I have faith in SVPD, too. They'll catch the killer."

"Still, it has to be frightening."

"I noticed you said 'serial' killer, Chuck. Technically we don't know who we're dealing with yet." Bryce's voice was low and he maintained a casual stance but the challenge in his tone was unmistakable.

"Come on, Bryce, you and I have known each other long enough. You mean to tell me you don't think the Female Preacher Killer isn't a sociopath, a serial killer?"

"I didn't say any of that. I'm just stating the facts, Chuck."

"The facts are all I'm going by, too." Chuck looked at Zora as if expecting her to intercede and placate their sparring. Zora kept her smile in place and simply nodded as if they were all having a grand time.

"Oh, I see someone we must speak to. It was so nice seeing you, Chuck."

"You, too."

Zora didn't miss Bryce's tight smile or the way it quickly disappeared once Chuck was out of sight. "Let me guess, you hate the press in all forms."

Bryce looked surprised. "Not at all. They have their job to do, and in Silver Valley they usually do it very well."

"But?"

"But I don't appreciate the sensationalism that can overshadow otherwise solid reporting. When we're trying to solve a major case, the last thing we need is a fear-frenzied public trying to take matters in their own hands."

"The public needs to know if they should take safety measures."

"Of course. That's why I do this job, why you're doing yours, I assume. But it's not license to give out crime scene details that could compromise our objectives."

"What details have they given out?"

"None, but only because I spoke to Chuck one-on-one last week. I asked him and the station to withhold the fact that the shooter left flowers with each minister right before he killed her."

"Are we sure it's a he?"

"Yes. You don't think the man you saw at the football field was a woman in disguise, do you? The profiler is all but certain it's a man."

"No, it was a man. But he was too far away and I had these awful glasses on. He could have been wearing a wig, I suppose. I do agree, everything suggests it's a man." She stopped abruptly and Bryce's hand moved from her shoulder to her elbow. He gently squeezed.

"What, Zora?"

"It's Colleen, remember? Nothing's the matter, except… the day I went to see Claudia, when you were…" She didn't want to mention the Trail Hikers or Claudia in public, no matter they were in a corner of the lobby off by themselves.

"Yes?"

"I stopped in to tell her something, and it's a long shot, but…" She shook her head as she saw the governor approach them. "I can't talk now. We'll go over it later."

The newly elected governor paid no notice to Zora as he zeroed in on Bryce.

"Governor."

"Bryce."

Bryce knew the governor?

Of course he did. Bryce seemed to know everyone.

"I can't thank you enough for all you did for us with the interstate road rage case."

"It's my job, sir. Glad SVPD could help."

Sharp eyes met Zora's and a broad smile lit up the politician's face.

"And who is this lovely lady?"

"Governor Paxton, this is Colleen Hammermill, my fiancée. She's the new minister at Silver Valley Community Church."

"Wonderful to meet you, Colleen." The governor's grasp was firm and warm. "My family went there when I was a boy. I have such good memories of Sunday school—well, the cupcakes and other treats are what I remember most—and of picnics and Boy Scout meetings. It's not the church it was then, but it's so nice that it's still thriving and here for the community."

"What do you mean it's not what it was, Governor?"

"That's right, you're the interim. Are you from the area?"

"More or less. But I don't know the whole history of my church, if that's what you mean."

The governor paused as if gathering his thoughts.

"It was originally a place where pioneers seeking to head west stopped for a last-minute prayer before they faced the wilds of western Pennsylvania. Then it was a Civil War interim church, put up as a place for the Union Army to have some respite and say a prayer or two before they had to go into battle. After the war they built a real church on the spot, where it remained for over a hundred and fifty years. When I was in high school—I imagine I'm at least twenty years older than both of you—they made it into the bigger complex it is now, with the intent for it to be nondenominational so that the entire Silver Valley population would feel comfortable there. It was never meant to compete with other churches but to act more as a meeting center for all."

"They've had a series of ministers of different denominations for as long as I remember." Bryce nodded in agreement with the governor.

"I have to admit I've been worried about Katherine, and now you know you need to take extra precautions, Colleen." The governor looked at her with concern.

She nodded and smiled. "I have the best protection I could hope for." She turned to Bryce and gave him a smile she imagined a fiancée would offer the man she loved.

Bryce smiled back and her breath lodged somewhere in her throat.

The governor coughed, not unlike Shirley Mae had, with a little extra emphasis, and they turned to him.

"I'm glad to see it. I've got to go give the opening remarks, but please, Bryce, call my secretary and get you and Colleen on the docket for dinner with Elaine and me."

Dinner with the governor and his wife?

"Will do, sir."

He cut a trim figure as he walked across the lobby toward the dais.

"I didn't realize you were friends with the governor."

"Neither did I. We met and worked together when he was still a state senator. I was a rookie on SVPD and helped with security on several public events. Sometimes they got a little rowdy and he always remembered to thank the force for our work. Once he was elected governor last year, he called me and asked if I was happy on SVPD, which I am."

"Did he offer you a job?"

"Maybe." Bryce's lips twitched. She was so intent on looking at his mouth, she wasn't prepared when he quickly leaned over and placed it on hers in a brief but warm kiss. "We have to play the part, remember?"

How could she forget?

"You're doing a good job of it."

"Let's keep it going—they're about to start the orchestra."

"We're not going to dance!" She wasn't the best at ballroom moves.

"Oh, yes, we are. We have our 'future marriage' to celebrate, and you have to raise some money for Silver Valley Community Church, don't you, Reverend Hammermill?"

Without outward protest, she allowed him to grasp her hand and walk her toward the ballroom.

Bryce never stopped being a cop. He knew that much about himself. It was second nature to check for all the exits in any building or room he entered, noting when and if he saw someone or something out of place for the particular event.

But damn it, he was having a hard time focusing on anything but Zora when he held her in his arms. Her dress and the way she carried herself drew the admiring glances of their fellow gala-goers, but he knew the men were drawn by her figure. She was all curves and elegant sex appeal in the holiday ball gown she wore with confidence born of a woman who'd served in the navy all over the planet as she had.

"What were you going to tell me earlier?" Keeping it on business would help him focus.

"Not here."

"Is it relevant to the case?"

"Probably not, no. But you should know, just in case. How long do you think we have to stay here?"

"Why, Reverend Hammermill, are you propositioning your fiancé?"

She pulled back and looked up at him. Even with the ugly wig and ridiculous glasses her beauty was evident. As was her agitation.

"Trying for an acting award, are you?"

"I always do my job to the best of my ability." The fact that his job included having her breasts pressed to his chest didn't hurt, either.

"You're wearing your Kevlar, Bryce, aren't you?"

"I'm your bodyguard. One of us needs to."

Her expression was too grave, too serious.

"Do you ever relax, Zora?"

"I'm relaxed now. Why, I'm dancing around with five hundred of my closest friends. And you should talk, Mr. I'm-the-Best-Cop-on-SVPD-and-the-Governor-Knows-Me."

He laughed. "All circumstantial. The Harrisburg area is big, but it's got a small-town feel. And Silver Valley is a tiny part of it."

"Okay, I'll let you be modest." She glanced around. "Bryce, don't you think it's creepy to think the shooter could be in this room with us?"

The thought of another bullet hitting Zora made him want to put her in the precinct until they caught the killer.

She's your work partner.

Problem was, his instincts didn't agree.

* * *

True to his word, Bryce didn't leave Zora's side all night. What surprised her wasn't how she reacted to his nearness—their chemistry constantly simmered and was something they'd have to ignore if they were going to stay focused on finding the killer. The surprise was that she didn't care that he was treating her like she imagined he'd treat someone he cared about.

She was letting herself enjoy the thought of Bryce wanting to be her love interest.

He knew as well as she did that they'd be depending on each other when the killer came after her. She knew he trusted her abilities. She didn't have anything to prove to him.

"What do you want to bid on?" They perused an assortment of gift baskets, gift certificates and travel packages that had been donated to the silent auction.

"The knitting basket from the local yarn shop looks fun."

"You're being facetious, right?"

"Not at all. Did you notice the afghan on my sofa? Or this shawl?" She held up the beaded navy blue lace stole she'd knit last winter when they'd had the worst cold snap in years. Never in a million years had she thought she'd be using it while posing as a minister with Bryce Campbell at her side.

"You made this?" His large hands reached for the frothy alpaca creation.

"Careful—it's not made of steel."

His fingers touched the wrap, and as big and muscular as they were, he handled it with grace and care.

"You're quite the talented woman, Zor…" He swore quietly.

"I know you meant Colleen."

She saw him inhale deeply as he pulled back and took in the room.

"Go ahead and write in your bid. Then we should get back to our seats."

"Aye, aye, sir," she murmured under her breath as she penciled in a fair amount for the basket of assorted fibers.

"I heard that."

Straightening, she put her arm around him and leaned into him, knowing they needed to look like the enamored couple they weren't.

"What were you saying about needing to play the part?"

On their way back to the table, a tall woman with what Zora thought was overdone hair and makeup came up to her, smiling a full-voltage smile. She looked familiar and it took Zora a beat to recognize the newly elected mayor of Silver Valley.

"Mayor Lemmon."

"You must be Reverend Hammermill. I heard they were getting an interim at Silver Valley Community Church for the holidays. It's a delight to meet you."

Zora introduced Bryce.

"Yes, Detective Campbell's reputation precedes him." The mayor offered Bryce a curt nod before she resumed her conversation with Zora. "I'm not sure if Reverend Pearson was able to leave you detailed notes, but I was planning on giving a little bit of a sermon myself at the children's pageant."

"Oh?" Zora hadn't seen the mayor's name in any of Katherine's notes. And judging by how the hair on the back of her neck stood on end, she thought she might understand why Katherine would have overlooked the mayor's request. A politician delivering a sermon? Really?

"Well, yes, it's so important to me that the people of Silver Valley who elected me understand that I share the same traditional values that they do."

"And what, exactly, are those values, Mayor Lemmon?"

Bryce's hand increased its pressure on her lower back and she got his message: cool it. She chose to ignore him.

"Well, we don't know each other well, Reverend Hammermill, but I'm sure we share some of the same views on how our current culture is ripping apart the fabric of what Silver Valley stands for. Family, community."

"I'm not sure we do, Mayor, but if you'd kindly send my secretary an email with your request we'll be sure to consider it."

"But Reverend Pearson already told me I'd have a chance to speak."

"There's so much going on with Katherine having to go home to her mother, and during such a busy season. Plus the concerns about the Female Preacher Killer. We have to keep security as our number one concern, I'm afraid. I'm sure you understand."

"Oh, I'm not worried about security. Detective Campbell will guarantee that, won't you?" Zora swore the woman glowered at Bryce.

"It's not your security I'm worried about, Mayor. It's my congregation. If you come in for a service, and do so publicly, that might encourage the shooter to show up, for more publicity."

"I wouldn't tell more than one or two of the local news stations, believe me."

Bryce smiled. "I'm sure you won't, Mayor. As my fiancée said, she'll take full consideration of your request, and see what kind of security detail SVPD can provide if your request is approved."

"Well, I must say I'll be very disappointed if it doesn't work out. I know so many families in the congregation and they were counting on getting photos with me for their Christmas cards."

"That can still be arranged, Mayor. If you don't mind, Bryce and I must go in. They're getting ready to close the silent auction."

Bryce followed her lead and turned with her away from the mayor.

As soon as they were out of earshot, Zora covered her mouth with her gloved hand. "What is with that woman?"

"She's an interesting character, and a politician all the way."

"I got the impression she's not a fan of yours. Any reason?"

"Several, including SVPD tickets for not licensing her dogs, and her penchant for illegally parking downtown."

"It's her town—why can't she use the mayor's parking spot?"

"This was before she was elected. The election was a huge fiasco, with both sides accusing the other of foul play."

"I remember that. I was in the middle of a short op for…you know, but caught some of it on the news. She got elected after all."

"She did. And whether I'm a fan of hers or not is irrelevant. I support all elected officials equally. And as for your comment that Silver Valley is her town, I beg to differ."

"Oh?"

"Silver Valley is *our* town. She's an elected official, period."

"Why don't you tell me how you really feel?"

"You'll never get me on your counseling couch." Bryce's expression was playful.

"I don't recall asking you."

"You don't have to. Your eyes give it away. Seriously, though? I've never given it much thought."

"It's okay if you're not a fan of psychology. You're entitled to your opinion." It didn't surprise her that he might have an issue with counselors, since first responders were required to receive counseling at regular intervals and after particularly grueling ops. They were often fearful that they'd be put on administrative or medical leave because of a counselor's findings.

"It's not personal. I'm ambivalent. I know you help a lot of folks." He pulled out her chair and took her elbow, allowing her to sit with minimal discomfort. "It's nice to see you moving without wincing."

"It feels pretty good, too."

She accepted his change of subject. They turned their attention back to the gala.

At the table, Zora remembered why she didn't miss the social requirements that navy life demanded. It was getting closer to midnight and she wanted nothing more than to crawl between her covers and sleep.

Of course there was the small issue of a killer being after her.

They'd made small talk with the three other couples at the table. There was another minister and his wife, the mayor of Silver Valley—who pointedly ignored them—

and her husband, as well as the superintendent of the Silver Valley School District and her husband.

"Do you think you won the yarn basket?"

"Doubtful."

"Why so grumpy? Are you an early-to-bed kind of girl?"

She turned to give him a scathing retort when her cell phone vibrated in her clutch. Bryce's phone lit up at the same time. Zora kept the phone just inside her opened clutch but both she and Bryce could read it.

Another minister attacked. Get home ASAP.

Bryce looked at her and she watched his expression go from neutral to grim.

"You got the same message?"

"Yes. Time to roll, partner."

They made quick excuses to their table mates and worked their way out of the ballroom in short order. Once outside, they stood away from the valet as they waited for Bryce's SUV to pull up.

"He didn't wait long. It's not even officially the fourth Sunday of Advent."

"No."

"He's going to try something at the children's pageant on Christmas Eve. That's the big showstopper, isn't it?"

"We can't know for sure, but yes, you could be right. No matter what, you're not doing this alone, Zora. That's how it is with local law enforcement—no one is a loner. We are a team."

"So you've mentioned. It was like that in the navy. I get it."

"Good." Judging by his determined tone, she knew he'd do whatever it took to protect her.

"Bryce, we're partners and we have each other's backs, one hundred percent. But you wouldn't put my safety over catching the killer, would you?"

"Of course I would."

She shook her head. "This is where my military training conflicts with our mission. Sometimes you have to keep the mission first. Above all else. I can handle my own safety."

"Like you did in your driveway?"

"My Kevlar saved me. I'm the one who put it on."

"If the shooter had aimed at your head we wouldn't be having this conversation."

"Unless the shooter didn't meant to hurt me, not seriously. Maybe it was just a warning."

"Doubtful. You got lucky, Zora. Let's leave it at that."

She didn't totally disagree with him but she didn't believe in luck so much as in being prepared and doing your best with whatever was beyond your control.

They remained silent as they drove the I-83 South Bridge across the Susquehanna River. Zora looked at Bryce. His profile revealed nothing, but she couldn't stop watching as the bright highway lamps shone through the windshield, spotlighting his face. "Stop staring at me."

"I'm not staring, I'm looking. I'm trying to relate the Bryce I knew back then with who you are today."

"Forget it, Zora. We've got a job to do and the kids we were wouldn't have the first inkling of how to handle it. We do."

"Right." Of course he was right. He was an expert

at what he did. She still felt like such a newbie when it came to law enforcement, even with the exceptional training of the Trail Hikers.

Chapter 11

Claudia was waiting in her car in Zora's wide driveway when they pulled up.

"Does she ever sleep?" Bryce cut the engine after he parked next to the small black sedan. Low-profile enough to be unremarkable but Zora bet Claudia had the car outfitted with every technological gadget available. And probably those not available to the general public yet.

"I've determined that she sleeps less than two hours per day in order to get her job done."

"You didn't get a lot of sleep when you were on a ship, did you?"

"It wasn't that bad. Watch schedules can be grueling, especially during wartime operations, whether they're shipboard or at a remote location. There was always a spot here or there to get a power nap. That's what I learned to get by with."

"It's the same with SVPD. Most days are routine and I

get a decent night's sleep. But then there are other times when sleep can't be a priority."

"Other times" applied to finding the Female Preacher Killer, she assumed.

As they opened both car doors, they could hear Butternut's frantic barking. Rounding the hoods of both cars, Zora noted how much they steamed. The temperature had dropped several degrees since they'd left for the gala earlier this evening.

"Claudia." Bryce spoke first, remembering to stick to first names.

"Let's get into the house before Butternut has a stroke." Zora waved her hand in dismissal.

"She knows it's us out here—that's her friendly bark. When there's a stranger she mostly growls with shorter, sharper barks."

"Good to know." Bryce fell into step behind her and Claudia. A gentleman even when working an op.

"Butternut, it's okay." She flicked on the hall light and bent down to scratch the worked-up dog.

"Why don't you two make yourselves comfortable at the table while I let Butternut out for a few minutes."

She took the dog back to the mudroom and opened the door to allow Butternut access to the large area she'd fenced off. The electric fence sent a warning beep to Butternut's collar to let her know if she was getting too close to the perimeter. Zora had hated the idea of a shock collar of any type, but Butternut had been trained quickly and only ever received a light shock when the fence was first installed. She never went out of her area, even for the many deer and rabbits that frequented the area.

But if Butternut felt that Zora was in danger, she'd break the barrier without a second's hesitation.

As Zora surveyed the frozen ground, her eyes adjusted to the dim light, the glow from the house windows and the moonlight the only illumination. Butternut sniffed furiously all around the small porch and on the ground next to the house.

"What do you smell, girl, a rabbit?"

Please don't let it be a skunk. Butternut had been sprayed last year by a local black-and-white furry beauty, and the scent took weeks to fade.

Shivering in her wrap, she peered at the ground and abruptly stopped shaking.

Footprints. Deep, the tread most likely from boots. Imprinted on the muddy, recently frozen ground around her home.

She bent closer and ran her fingers over one of the prints—it was frozen with crystal drops of frost on each tread mark. Zora tiptoed off the porch in her heels and quickly followed the path made by the visitor. He'd gone up to the porch, and around the house to her bedroom window. The prints then went toward the woods, where she was unable to ascertain which direction they took— and she doubted there'd be definite tracks there, with the leaves carpeting the forest floor.

Even with the bright moonlight she felt she'd been plunged into a darker version of Silver Valley. Someone was awfully interested in her and her house. And had avoided the police security detail.

Back inside, Zora was relieved to see that Bryce and Claudia had made themselves at home with a steaming-hot carafe of fresh coffee. Half-and-half, sugar and Stevia were placed neatly next to the mugs they'd found.

"Someone was here tonight."

Claudia and Bryce stopped their conversation and stared at her.

"When?" Bryce was on full alert. If he were a dog she swore she'd see his hackles rise.

"I'm not sure, but there are footprints out back that indicate he was interested in the back door and my bedroom window. I always leave the light in my master bathroom on, to give me a chance to see when I get in."

"Call in forensics." Claudia directed her order at Bryce, who was already texting furiously on his smartphone.

"They're on their way."

"They're going to start to despise coming to my place." Zora poured herself a half cup of coffee, not needing a lot of caffeine to stimulate her mind. It was already racing with the stark reality that the killer could have stopped by to kill her.

"He knew the police were out front, and took advantage of the woods," she mused aloud.

"Bryce, isn't the security detail doing regular walk arounds?"

"Up to the end of the driveway, where they can see the back of the house. They're not walking through the yard."

"Butternut would have alerted if she heard anything."

"But the security team is down at the base of the driveway, in the car for most of the time. They wouldn't hear her right away." Bryce spoke as he dialed a number.

"Campbell… Yeah. What have you seen tonight?" He listened as Claudia and Zora waited. "Did you happen to hear the dog barking in the house?…No, it wasn't at you guys. We had another visitor who came up to the house. The prints are fresh."

He looked at Zora for confirmation. She nodded, grateful the Trail Hikers training had included imprints as evidence. Those prints couldn't have been made earlier as the ground had been solid until the deluge of rain had fallen that afternoon. The ground had refrozen that evening in the quickly dropping temperatures that heralded Silver Valley's first cold snap of the winter.

"Right. Forensics will be here within sixty minutes. It'll take them a while longer to get everyone up and out the door at this hour....Right." He put his phone down.

"They never heard Butternut?"

"They did, but they thought she was barking at a herd of deer they saw milling around at dusk. Those woods are thick and lead to nowhere that would allow someone quick access to a highway. I have to admit it was a smart way to come in."

"Unless he was on a scooter, motorcycle or horse." Zora had seen all three conveyances since living in the farmhouse.

"A horse is too conspicuous." Claudia had a faraway look in her eyes as she mulled over the situation, but she didn't miss a bit of the conversation.

"Wouldn't they want to kill me—I mean, Reverend Hammermill—closer to the church?" That was what the profiler had suggested.

"He's killed three ministers, all in their church parking lots."

"The third—it's why we're here. Who was she?" Bryce brought them back to the case.

"Reverend Elizabeth Bissell. She was getting ready to retire from the Methodist church just on the edge of town next month."

"I know her. She's a major player at the community helping-hands shelter." Bryce referred to the clearinghouse of sorts for everything from household and clothing donations to Meals on Wheels for Silver Valley.

Every church, synagogue and mosque in the area was involved, and it never turned away anyone in need.

"Her visibility is what got her killed. She was shot in the parking lot of the soup kitchen, two hours after the last bowl of soup had been served."

Anger surged through Zora.

"How dare they! She was a living angel. If not for her, our community wouldn't have a place for domestic-violence victims to go." She'd had several of her counseling clients make use of the secret women's shelter while they transitioned from living in abject fear and danger to a normal life. It was so gratifying to counsel them through their pain and watch them heal as they moved on to live meaningful lives, free from fear. And to see the perpetrators brought to justice.

"Yes." Claudia's one-word response weighed heavily in the room, lingering between them.

"She's gone," Bryce said. "But her work remains, and no loser like this killer is going to stop the good work she was doing. Not for long, not if we have anything to say about it."

"Correct, Bryce. I'm here for two reasons. First, to go over what I foresee as the much larger burden the community faces and that you are part of. Second, to let you know, Zora, that you're not crazy. That *was* your biological mother in Walmart a few days ago."

Bryce watched Zora as Claudia delivered her verbal missive. Instinct told him that Claudia wasn't referring to Anna, but wasn't Zora's mother somewhere in upstate New York? Why would she be in Silver Valley?

"I knew it. How are you so certain?" Zora's face was a stony mask.

"We used the security camera footage and compared it with photos of your mother that are on file. As you might have guessed, she never left New York State, and only moved one town over from where you'd lived with the True Believers." Claudia paused and studied Zora intently before she looked at Bryce.

"She's told you, right?"

"Yes."

"Yes, I filled him in." They answered simultaneously.

"From what we could ascertain, she moved down here about a month ago."

"When one of Wise's cronies was let out of jail." Bryce couldn't ignore the timing.

"Is she looking for me?"

"It appears so."

"How did she find you? You said you were relocated here with WSP." Bryce wasn't about to let Zora's past haunt her if he could help it.

"There was a clause in the legal proceedings that she'd be allowed to know if I was alive and well. I never gave permission to the WSP to let her know my new name, though, or where I lived."

"She's been looking for you for years, Zora. You're her only child and she was devastated over losing you." Claudia spoke with compassion.

"She should've thought about that before she took up with Leonard Wise."

Bryce and Claudia remained quiet at her outburst. Frustration boiled in Zora's belly and she suddenly longed for a hard run through rough terrain.

"I've had a good life—and I've never spoken about the events of my childhood as much as I have this past week. Please tell me it's a coincidence that she's in Silver Valley, Claudia."

"I've checked out your mother's background since you left the True Believers, Zora." Claudia's tone got her attention. If anyone had the resources to dig into a federal case that had been sealed, it would be the Trail Hikers.

"Tell me."

Claudia waved at the chair across from her.

"Sit down first. We don't have long but you need to know this."

"I can leave if you want." Bryce gave her the way out she thought she'd want.

She surprised both of them as she placed her hand on his forearm. "No, stay. I've got nothing to hide, and like you said, we're partners."

"Your mother stayed in touch with some of the True Believers only because she didn't have the cash to move away right after the trials sent the leaders to prison. As soon as she saved enough by working at a diner—a different one than the one you remember—she left for Buffalo. She lived there and put herself through Erie Community College to get her certification to work as a medical aide. She moved around a couple of times, with no apparent reason, until she settled down in the small town I mentioned. But then with no explanation, she moved here. Her most recent employment is at the Silver Valley hospital. She works there and lives in the apartments off Silver Pike."

"Silver Pike?" Zora held on to her coffee mug to steady her hands. "But that's only a few miles away. And the hospital... She could have known I was a patient there after the shooting."

"Yes." Claudia stared at her. "Zora, I think she's found

out where you grew up and maybe hoped you'd still be here."

"I don't want anything to do with her." Guilt clawed at her. She had to tell Claudia her biggest secret.

"That's up to you, but she's here in Silver Valley. If you ever decide to talk to her, not that I'm saying you should, she's here."

"It's odd that she's shown up here and hasn't contacted you." Bryce didn't fully buy the story Claudia presented.

Claudia didn't respond, inspecting her hands as they rested on her desk.

Zora sighed. "It's my bust." She used the navy slang to confess her guilt. "I put out some feelers for her when I was still in the navy. I just wanted to make sure she was all right. The PI I hired must have leaked my information somehow."

"That could have led you right back to the bastards who held you hostage in that godforsaken compound!" Bryce couldn't hold back.

"I know. But I'm not an innocent twelve-year-old any longer. I have resources and I wasn't trying to start a relationship with my mother again. It's just that…" She didn't want to get into it, not now. "Claudia already knows everything. I had to tell her when I was approached by the Trail Hikers."

Claudia cleared her throat.

"There's something else I think you should know, Zora."

"Now what?"

"It's not that bad, but we already knew who you were when you came to us. The US Marshals have never failed a protected witness, and because of that we have ties to them as needed. Your name is flagged."

"It never came up when I got my security clearances in the navy." She'd worried that it would preclude her from her top secret/SBI clearance as an ensign. It would have been the death of her intelligence career.

"No, it wouldn't. You truly were given an entirely new identity. But having a PI investigate your mother, even under your new name and not telling the PI it was your mother…"

"I knew it was a risk, but I figured even if she found out she wouldn't say anything. All of the big players were in jail, are still in jail."

"Except for the two who got out last year."

"And one more last month." Bryce added the grim detail.

Silence settled again on the three of them.

"My mother showing up in Silver Valley has nothing to do with the Female Preacher Killer case, right? So let's get our focus back where it needs to be. For heaven's sake, a woman was killed in cold blood tonight."

Claudia and Bryce exchanged a look and Zora rolled her eyes.

"Come on, folks, I know you're thinking I'm in denial, or not wanting to face my past. That's not it. I hold nothing against my mother. She was brainwashed, pure and simple. I hated her for it for years, until I reached the age she was when she turned to the cult. I had the good fortune of a wonderful education behind me, and a world of options for my future. She never had any of that. How can I blame her for taking the best meal ticket she could grab?"

Again Claudia and Bryce looked at her with compassion but she couldn't see past what she felt was their pity.

"Do *not* feel sorry for me."

"No one's throwing a pity party here, Zora. You're capable of handling life-or-death situations and have survived being shot. You don't need anyone's pity." Bryce's words were matter-of-fact but his compassionate manner made her want to lean her head on his shoulder and sit while he stroked her back, like he had at the gala.

Claudia's eyes sparked with understanding and Zora wanted to scream from frustration. Working with the Trail Hikers was turning into a freak show. It was as if her entire life were under a microscope.

And she wasn't the criminal!

Now Claudia was seeing things between her and Bryce that didn't, well, *couldn't*, exist.

"So tell us, Claudia. Reverend Bissell. Was it one shot or more that took her out? Bryce is convinced the killer's a hunter. What do you think?"

"I think you don't have to be the best shot to kill, although he's obviously used these weapons before. All you need is a working weapon and a motive."

They hashed through the case as they knew it so far. Seven victims in total, all female. Four near misses including Zora. Three deceased, all ministers at local churches. All killed by gunshot wounds to their chests. Their hearts.

Zora voiced her thoughts. "He probably *is* a hunter. He's been able to pull off three lethal heart shots with a hunting rifle. Four, if you count the shot to my vest, using a different weapon, of course." The killer had used a handgun instead of a rifle in her driveway.

"He's using a caliber that could stop a bear in its tracks." Bryce's dry response annoyed her because it was true.

"I think he's planned for this for a long time. And he has a whopping resentment against women in the ministry. Probably in other traditionally male roles, as well." Claudia stood up and walked to the coffeepot where she poured herself another oversize mug of coffee.

"Claudia, do you ever sleep?" She voiced what Bryce had asked less than an hour earlier, though it felt like days ago.

"When I need to, yes." Claudia didn't stop at the personal query. "Our killer is probably very habitual in his routine, and possibly a boring person otherwise. The profiler thinks it's a local, and I concur. Especially now that we know he was in your yard."

"We don't know it was him, for sure. We can't. Let's see what forensics tells us." Zora tried to sound more detached than she felt.

"It's going to tell us what you already figured out, Zora. This bastard thinks you're Reverend Hammermill, and you're his next target." Bryce's protective feelings were clear in his tone.

Claudia interrupted them. "No. She's his last target."

They both looked at her.

"Claudia?" Bryce's voice had that gruff challenge in it again.

"Think about it. He's upping his game, losing any nervousness he had. He took three shots to kill the first victim, until he got in the heart shot. Then he killed your client, and he only needed two shots. This time he did it in one."

"You're right, Claudia. His accuracy is improving. He's also collecting information on his victims before he kills them. That's obvious, since he's sending them flowers beforehand." Bryce spoke the words Zora had already thought.

"He's more confident, wants to make sure he gets to the big bang. Um, sorry." She felt herself blush at the awful pun.

"All he has to do is watch the local news to understand that his chances of getting out of this alive are small," Bryce continued. "We will do everything to take him in alive, of course, but this is an all-or-nothing mentality we're dealing with. He's planning for the contingency that either he'll go down, too, when the big episode happens. As long as he proves his point." Bryce's comment showed that he'd been doing more than dancing at the gala. He never stopped analyzing.

"Well done, Bryce. You're in alignment with the profiler and with my thinking, too. Zora, do you have anything to add?"

"Hey, I'm the rookie here as far as law enforcement goes. Just tell me what you need me to do next and I'm there. We have to stop him."

"Be observant while you're at work. Assume nothing is regular. Don't trust anyone. Bryce, your marching orders remain the same."

"What are *your* 'marching orders'?" Zora didn't realize Claudia had given them separate orders.

"To keep you alive."

"I'm staying here tonight, Zora. Go get your wig and dress off and get into bed. I'll bunk on the sofa. Butternut will guard the door."

His stance was wider than normal and with his hands on his hips he looked as though he could single-handedly take out the killer.

"I'm not refusing your help, Bryce. I just wouldn't want you to get hurt because you stayed."

"No one's after me. And he's not going to come back, not tonight. But if he does we'll be ready for him." An additional security detail was patrolling the woods behind her home all night.

She glanced at the digital clock on the microwave. Four hours of sleep was the most she could hope for. Even feeling this wired from the stress of the case, this exhausted, she had a hard time keeping her mind off her body's desire for Bryce.

When she met his eyes, she saw the same struggle reflected there.

"This is hard work, isn't it?" Her voice squeaked from exhaustion.

"Just stay focused on how good it's going to feel when… we catch the killer." What he left unsaid was clear in his tone, his stance, the fire in his eyes.

She closed her eyes and gave her head a little shake.

"I have to be at the church office by eight. What's your reason for being there tomorrow going to be?" The next day was the Saturday before Christmas. Then it would be Sunday—the last Sunday of Advent.

Bryce smiled.

"Why, didn't you know I'm training to be a youth minister?"

Chapter 12

After she made sure Bryce had enough blankets, a pillow and a towel, Zora got herself ready for bed in record time. She didn't think she'd be able to sleep. Too much had happened and even Butternut wasn't at her usual place of honor at the foot of Zora's bed. Instead, she lay in the hall between the master bedroom and the top of the stairs. Bryce was downstairs, but because of the age and solid walls of the house Zora couldn't hear anything but the quiet tick of her alarm clock.

And the wind. It had picked up from the start of the gala and was close to gale force. No wonder it was so cold. She got up and tiptoed to the thermostat, which was on the wall in the upstairs corridor.

It said forty-five degrees Fahrenheit, even though it was set to kick on at sixty-five. No wonder she was shivering.

The pilot light was probably out.

She went back into her room to get a throw to drape

over her robe and flannel pj's, along with her warmest slippers. Moving quietly through the house as Butternut followed her, she made it to the bottom of the stairs and headed toward the basement door.

"You okay?" Bryce's voice sounded from the living room, making her all but jump out of her fuzzy slippers.

"I'm fine, but aren't you freezing? The pilot light on the heater went out. I'm going to restart it."

"Do you need a hand?"

"No, no, I've got it. Butternut's helping me."

Bryce grunted and she made out a bulky shape under several blankets on the sofa, turning over.

"There's a guest room, Bryce. You'd be more comfortable there."

"I'd never sleep. I'd be listening too hard."

"Whatever," she muttered more to herself than him and opened the basement door. Once down on the cellar floor she could see that the pilot light was out on the heater. She struck the small lighter she kept on a shelf nearby for just such occasions.

No flame.

"C'mon." The chill of the approaching winter seeped up through the hard floor and made her toes numb. Her fingers were sure to follow. She tried to light the pilot light three more times before stopping, as the directions suggested. She sat back and rubbed Butternut's warm body as the dog lay next to her.

Footsteps shuffled on the landing at the top of the stairs.

"No luck?"

"No, but it'll go on. Sometimes it's tricky."

Stairs squeaked as Bryce's feet appeared. "How old is your furnace?"

"No idea. It came with the house."

Bryce's face looked gaunt in the harsh glare of the bare bulb that hung from the ceiling.

"You've got a much nicer upstairs than this basement indicates."

"This house is almost two hundred years old. It's solid, just a little unfinished around the edges."

Bryce didn't reply. He was on all fours, inspecting the spot where the gas came through to fuel the heater. He depressed the ignition key.

"I'm not hearing the gas when I press on the button."

"I didn't, either, but I hoped it was because my teeth were chattering so much."

"It's not your teeth. Your gas isn't coming in here. What about upstairs? You have a gas stove, don't you?"

"Yes."

"Where's your water heater?"

"Over there." She motioned across the basement to a modern water heater, which looked incongruous against the aged wall and dirt floor.

Bryce walked over to the water heater and felt it.

"This is barely room temperature." He bent down and checked where the flame should be. "Its pilot is out, too."

"Sometimes a wicked draft can blow out the pilot lights."

"At the same time?"

"Once, two years ago, we had a hurricane come through and the winds took out the electricity as well as the pilot lights."

"You were back here for that?" Heat forgotten, Bryce's eyes seemed…hurt, confused?

"I didn't try to contact anyone when I came back, Bryce. I wasn't ready." He was the only friend she'd ever considered keeping from high school, and she'd forced herself to let go of him before they even graduated. Didn't he realize what a loner she was?

"Huh." He bit his lower lip and looked back at the water heater as if taking the time to think through the mechanics of it all.

"Let's go check your gas line. Where's the main shut-off?"

"There's one here." She looked at the space between the heater and the wall. "It's still open."

"Then it's involving the main. Shut off the valve here and let's go look outside for the turnoff."

They huddled with a flashlight over the gas meter as high winds lashed at their backs.

"Here, use the wrench. I'll hold the flashlight." She handed him the heavy tool.

His hands were so strong, so capable. She couldn't keep her mind from wandering and thinking about what else those hands could do besides handle a tool.

With one deft move Bryce restored the valve to the open position.

"Hand me the flashlight."

She did and watched as he swung the beam around the meter, and then down on the ground.

More footprints. Similar to the booted prints that she'd discovered alongside her house earlier.

"Did Forensics tell you they'd found these?" She asked the question even though she knew with certain dread what his answer would be.

"No."

"I guess there's no reason they would have. They were focused on the back of the house." She spoke the words like a professional but inside she felt the raw edges of fear. Fear unlike anything she'd known since breaking free from the True Believers.

"Damn it." Bryce stood in front of the meter, his head up toward the moonlit sky as if seeking an answer from above.

"He wanted to send a message. We got it. Let's go back in, Bryce." She placed her hand on his arm and realized with a start how comfortable, natural, automatic the gesture was.

His hand covered hers with a tight squeeze.

"Thanks."

"For what?"

"For not railing at me like you should. I was sleeping on the other side of this wall. There's no excuse for me to have missed him if he came back."

"I don't think he came back, Bryce. And if he did, this wall is almost a foot thick. It's not a modern home, and we're not in the middle of a quickly slapped-up development. This house has been here a lot longer than any of us, and it's solid. On a still summer night you wouldn't necessarily hear an intruder. Butternut never sensed any danger or I'm sure she would have alerted us." She tugged on his sleeve. "Let's go in. I'm freezing."

Chapter 13

"Good morning, Reverend Hammermill." Shirley Mae greeted Zora from her desk that doubled as a reception area for the church offices. "How was the gala last night?"

Had it only been last night? Zora felt as though weeks had passed since she'd danced in Bryce's arms. And endured another forensics team visit to her home.

"Absolutely lovely. I had no idea the ballroom at the Hilton was so large. It was a much larger crowd than I'd expected."

"So it was a nice date for you and Detective Campbell, as well?" Shirley Mae's head tilted at just the angle to tell Zora that she was wondering what no doubt a lot of people were—how did a nondescript woman with huge glasses and mousy, outdated hair land a man like Bryce?

She wanted to laugh but Shirley definitely wouldn't get the joke.

"It was. How about you, Shirley Mae, what did you do last night?"

"Oh, nothing more than the usual. Curled up on the sofa with my two kitties and watched *Modern Family* reruns."

"Sounds relaxing."

"Would you like a cup of coffee, Reverend?"

"Yes, but let's get a few things clear. First, I pour my own coffee. Second, call me Colleen. It's silly to be so formal."

"Works for me, Colleen." Shirley Mae's peony-pink lipsticked mouth stretched wide in a grin.

"I'll be in my office again this morning, and I'll take appointments after lunch. I have two scheduled—feel free to pencil in anyone else who calls."

"Will do."

Zora poured herself an extralarge mug of coffee from the communal carafe on the station just outside her office and liberally added nondairy powdered creamer. Usually she preferred almond milk when she wasn't at home, but today she needed the extra luxury.

After she'd studied the sermon and the Christmas pageant program, she got up from the desk and stretched. She wandered out of her office and found Shirley Mae at her station.

"I'll be in the sanctuary if anyone needs me, Shirley Mae."

"Uh-huh." Shirley Mae's gaze never left her computer screen, where Zora caught a glimpse of the week's bulletin. She'd read that it usually went to the printer by ten in the morning on Friday, but due to the Christmas season's rush they were printing it in-house this week.

The administrative offices were part of a huge, circular addition that had been added to the main church building in the mideighties. An enormous theater and audiovisual entertainment center had been added only ten years ago, and it was where most of the Sunday services were held since the congregation had grown so quickly after the church opened its doors to the entire Silver Valley community. It was truly ecumenical in both form and function.

Exactly what the Female Preacher Killer detested, she was sure.

The outer buildings were beautiful and highly functional, including a coffee bar that served a variety of hot beverages, doughnuts and soup, all of which were also available for takeout. If a church member ran a business, he or she could advertise in the church bulletin. Many offered their services at a discount to the church community.

It was hard for Zora to see a church so open and welcoming to the public and not think back to the True Believers and how it had been exactly the opposite. Closed, not open to other beliefs or practices and downright hostile to anything or anyone who threatened Leonard Wise's gospel of hate and control.

She shoved the unwanted memories aside with an ease learned from years of practice. This was now, and she was safe. From the True Believers, at any rate.

The Female Preacher Killer. That was a different story.

She came to the end of the long, modern corridor and turned to walk through two sets of double doors. The second set was original to the first church. Each one was eight feet tall and made of a thick slab of oak, simply carved with a cross and a small window in its center.

The spirits of many Christmases past surrounded her as she walked into the sanctuary where the Sunday school teachers and youth minister's team had been busy bringing in props for the Christmas Eve pageant. A large crèche was on the altar, as was a very large papier-mâché star, which rested against the rustic wooden structure. She looked up at the ceiling above the altar and could make out a small hook, which no doubt needed some fishing wire strung from it to hold the star aloft.

"We have a lot of work to do yet."

She shrieked and spun around, her hand at her back, reaching for a weapon that wasn't there. She'd left it in her purse in the office.

"Whoa, I'm sorry to startle you." A man of medium build and in his early twenties stood in front of her, hands up in a "calm down" gesture.

"Well, you did."

"I'm Peter Hoffman, the youth minister. You must be Reverend Hammermill." He held out his hand, which Zora shook. Firm and straightforward. His grasp didn't elicit any panic.

"It's Colleen, and I'm pleased to meet you, Peter." She cast her gaze around the sanctuary. "How on earth are we going to fit three thousand people in here?"

He smiled, revealing deep dimples that she found adorable.

"We're not. Only the families of the children in the pageant will be in here, along with you and me, and the choir. Everyone else will catch the action on the wide screens in the auditorium. The entire pageant will parade through the auditorium at the end."

"Even the llamas?"

"Ah, I see you've read the schedule and script. Yes,

along with three dogs, a sheep and maybe an alpaca or two—they haven't confirmed yet."

"I can't wait to see how the llamas look, dressed as camels."

"They look like furry camels. Last year our biggest worry was the cleanup after the animals but we were blessed—none of them took a bathroom break while they were in the sanctuary."

"We'll still have a plastic runner put down, right?"

"Absolutely."

Relief eased some of the tension in her shoulders. She might be a fake minister but her appreciation for the historical and spiritual significance of the original church building was real.

"Have you thought about what you'll say?" Peter's frank gaze was relieved only by the slight twinkle in his eyes.

"I haven't written the sermon for Christmas Eve yet, no. I tend to write notes all week and then put them together by Friday night. I have tomorrow's sermon done. I'll squeeze in the Christmas words before the big day next week!" How she was managing to lie so smoothly she wasn't sure. It was a bit unnerving to do it so easily.

"The parents love it when you mention their kids by name, but if I may, I'd like to suggest that the service is for the children. They're more interested in hearing about how each of the roles they're playing had a part in the Christmas story. It gives them more of a stake in the presentation."

"Thank you, I'll keep that in mind. Dress rehearsal is still on for tonight?"

He nodded. "Yes, and fair warning, the kids are going to be cranky. They all still had school yesterday and they have it again on Monday before they break for the holidays. They're sugared out from all of the goodies at school and here, and they can't think about anything besides Santa Claus."

She laughed.

"Well, I'm not going to dress up as Santa Claus."

"That would be pretty funny, to have Santa Claus show up bearing gifts for the infant."

"This is a forward-thinking, open-minded congregation, but I don't want to push it that far, especially as an interim pastor."

"I hear you. I've only been here for a year myself, and I'm hoping to get a promotion to another church when this assignment is over. I need a decent reference!"

"Where do you want to go?"

Peter's expression was hopeful.

"I'm not sure yet, but it probably will be out of state."

"Are you from here, Peter?"

"Yeah. I grew up in Harrisburg. But it's not the same place it used to be. I'm looking for something different."

When he didn't elaborate, she let it go. Adolescents were entitled to their wanderlust; she'd had it herself.

"I'm sure you'll get a great reference, from everything I've heard about you."

"I hope so. Well, I've got to run a few errands. We're missing some costume material from last year and I promised the parent volunteers I'd have everything ready for the last-minute fixes tonight."

"Nice meeting you."

She watched him exit the old building and rubbed the tops of her arms. Zora didn't believe in the bogeyman but it sure felt as if she was living in a haunted world between the footprints in her yard, filling in for a minister undercover and, oh, yeah, being shot in her own driveway.

And now waiting for the killer to aim at her again.

Maybe the Trail Hikers would be a temporary job for her. She couldn't imagine doing this kind of work as her body aged.

The pews were wooden, old and massive. She sat in one and looked at the altar for a bit, trying to imagine the pageant as she'd read in the script.

Peter was right. It was going to be very crowded and no doubt overheated. Maybe she could ask Ernie the custodian about turning down the thermostat so that none of the children got too hot with their costumes on.

A creak sounded in the hushed room and she looked to her right. As if summoned by her thoughts, Ernie stood next to a utilitarian waste bin on wheels, his hand resting on the canvas container.

"Ernie! You startled me."

He tipped his cap to her.

"Sorry, Miz Hammermill."

"How long have you worked here, Ernie?"

"Since I was a teenager, really." His tone was noncommittal.

Zora pressed on. "Was that before or after the newer buildings were added?"

He shifted on his feet. "The office building and classrooms were added while I was growing up. Then the big showpiece came in." He jerked his thumb in the direction of the auditorium.

"I take it you don't like the modern touches?"

"It's not for me." Simple words, but said with such conviction Zora stood and tried to appear casual while she watched him for any tells, any indication he was more than a janitor.

"What do you mean?"

He shrugged and took off his cap, scratching at his shaved head. His janitor's uniform consisted of a green flannel work shirt, white T-shirt and dark, worn cargo pants. He wasn't skinny but he wasn't overweight, either. Very much an average male.

"I don't mean anything, not really. It's just that I've seen a lot of changes since I've been here. Newer ways of doing things."

"You don't like the newer ways?"

"I'm not saying that. If folks want things all modern, good for them. I'm more of an old-fashioned type."

"Do you go to this church, Ernie, or just work here?"

His eyes widened and his head jerked back as if she'd slapped him. "I've gone here since my mother brought me as a little boy. I'm one of the longest-standing members of this church."

"I didn't know. Thank you for your service, Ernie. That's the picture of dedication, for sure."

"It's what I know. Now, if you don't mind, Ms. Hammermill, I need to get this place shipshape before the parents come in tonight and complain that their little ones got their socks filthy black from the floor."

"Please don't let me keep you. I do have one request. Do you think we can keep the heat turned down during the pageant?"

"Yes, ma'am, I always do. It's going to get very hot in here, mark my words."

"Thank you, Ernie." She had the distinct impression that she'd stepped on his ego, implying he wouldn't turn the heat down.

As she walked away she noted that he didn't stop watching her until she was clear of the doors.

The members of Silver Valley Community Church were awfully protective of their domain.

"That smells so good." She sniffed with gusto at the aroma emanating from the white paper sack Bryce held. He looked even more delicious in a white collared shirt with a red tie under a formfitting V-neck pullover. It was the exact shade of his eyes, and accentuated his powerful build. She allowed her gaze to drift lower and couldn't ignore the delicious desire at the sight of his slim hips and powerful thighs.

"Pleasing to you, ma'am?"

His eyes brimmed with humor and...desire. He'd caught her but wasn't holding it against her. He didn't have to.

"Sorry. I don't get many visitors in here through the day. They're all afraid of the 'interim.'"

"Uh-huh." He let it slide but she knew that he hadn't fallen for her weak excuse. Not at all. He took a seat across the desk from her and opened the bag.

"One ham-cheddar melt for you." His fingers brushed hers as he handed it to her and she knew he was watching her face for her reaction.

"Nice try, Bryce. You're not going to make me blush again. I have nothing to be embarrassed about."

"So *that's* why you just turned red. You're attracted to me. I figured you were too young for hot flashes."

"I am, and you're barking up the wrong tree."

"Perhaps." He pulled out a sandwich for himself, along with two iced teas.

"You've gone all out today."

"Hey, I'm doing my part to keep the minister well fed and ready to roll."

"I've met some interesting people this week." She unwrapped her sandwich and let out a high squeal. "You got me pretzel bread!"

"Don't you like it? Are you gluten-free or something?"

"No, no, I absolutely love it. It's my favorite. I don't do it all the time. Too many carbs. But for today, it's just what I needed."

"Yeah, I figured. Last night wasn't the most peaceful. The gala turned into a long night, didn't it?"

"Yes. But it's part of the deal right now." She bit into the soft bread and savored the dough and fresh ham.

"Aah, this is like Christmas morning when everything tastes so delicious."

"Mmm." Bryce ate his own meal, his gaze on her face. Making her blush. Again.

"Stop it, Bryce. Now you're the one staring."

"Sorry," he mumbled with his mouth full. She couldn't help it; she giggled. Which turned into an all-out gale of laughter.

Bryce didn't respond except by raising his brows and taking a long drink of his iced tea. "I've met the youth minister. Is he aware that he'll be 'training' you yet?"

Bryce nodded. "I stopped in to see him earlier. I asked him if he'll train the 'new youth minister' for a few months before he leaves for his next position."

"I'll bet he was thrilled by that." She watched Bryce for his reaction.

"He wasn't overjoyed, no, but he wasn't rude about it, either. It'll be over soon and he'll be able to follow his original plans." Bryce put his sandwich down on her desk, his expression neutral.

"You know, things would go smoother between us if you just spit it out. Tell me what you think about folks, about what's going on."

"But you need the space to make up your own mind."

"We don't have time for that, Zora. This isn't the navy and you're not analyzing an enemy who *might* strike. We're in the middle of the war here. Don't worry about telling me something that ends up not being relevant. I'm entirely capable of separating the chaff from the wheat, so to speak. I'll be damned if we let this killer ruin Christmas for even one child." His voice was low to avoid being heard by eavesdroppers.

"Sounds as though the holiday atmosphere has gone to your head."

"Maybe it has. I used to love the Christmas pageant as a kid. I kept helping with it through high school. Remember the time I roped you into joining me on the tech crew?"

She smiled. "You mean the time Mary got chicken pox?" It was her classmate who'd contracted the illness, and the role of Mary had been in jeopardy. Zora had been plucked out of the stage crew to act as Mary.

"Yes. You were a wonderful Mary."

"I was hoodwinked."

They chuckled and Zora loved the sound of their laughter together. It sounded as if they harmonized. Like an old Christmas hymn that you immediately recognize when the first chord is played.

She shook her head and took a big gulp of her tea. "I was so afraid I'd drop that little baby. I'd never held one since…"

She froze, realizing she'd been about to say "since I moved here, away from the True Believers." There, on the compound, child rearing had been considered an exalted science, one that women needed to take seriously and learn as early as possible. Which meant that by eight years old, Zora had known how to bottle-feed, diaper and bathe an infant. There'd been plenty of babies to practice her skills on with the number of young women Wise impregnated. She still couldn't believe the authorities weren't able to do a damn thing until she'd broken her silence and told a hospital nurse what was going on after the security guard had taken her to the police.

She rubbed her elbow, a comforting gesture she'd adopted there in the compound.

"Does your elbow hurt?"

She blinked. "Not anymore. But it did when I got hit by Wise for not knowing one of the babies' names. He'd had seven in three months at one point. I was only eleven and I'd been up all night taking care of the infants so their mothers could rest. You know, so that getting pregnant again wouldn't be a problem. When he hit me he knocked me onto the concrete floor and I fell directly on my elbow. It was a small fracture, a chip, really. But sometimes it still aches."

It was more like the *memory* ached, reminding her of all she'd lost as a child. When the dark thoughts came she used it as a reminder of how far she'd come. How much she'd gained and been blessed with by leaving and living her own life. Free of the past.

Until last week when she had seen Edith in Walmart.

"Are you going to go see your mother, Zora?"

"You must mean Anna, right? Because the woman I saw in Walmart was nothing more than an incubator to me." She knew it was a lie as she said it, but damn it, so much time had passed and she'd suffered for so long under her mother's distorted thinking.

Bryce remained silent.

"Why would I want to see her ever again?"

"To have closure." He spoke the words quietly, yet they seemed to have the power of a thousand men shouting them.

Closure.

Could she ever truly have closure from a cult that had all but ruined her childhood? "Zora." His voice brought her back.

"No. Not happening."

"This isn't the time, with this case on our shoulders. But once we have the killer... It is Christmas, Zora."

"No."

"You're playing the part of a minister. Isn't atoning for the past part of preparing for Christmas? Advent? Maybe Edith wants to atone for her sins."

"You're a detective, a very good one from what everyone says. Why don't you stick to that and leave the counseling to me? Besides, she can't take back what she did. Ever."

"O-kay." She recognized Bryce's concern in his careful reply.

"I've heard you, Bryce. And it's not as if I don't have thoughts about my mother from time to time. It's why I hired the PI. As I've gotten older, I realize that she had no one to lean on. She was ripe for an addiction of some type. Hers happened to be bad religion. There's good religion out there, and I hope she's found it, or whatever else she needed. But I couldn't be with her anymore, Bryce. Living with her was unbearable. She was complicit in the abuse that went on."

"Did she know about all of it?"

"No, no one did. I didn't even. But I knew enough."

"And you did the right thing. You put away a lot of terrible men."

"Some good it did if they're all getting out over the next several months."

"Not all of them." Bryce's voice maintained a neutral tone.

"Do you have any idea what I lived through, Bryce?"

"What you've told me, and what I read in the case study. Have I lived through it? No. But I knew you right after." It was his turn to drift off, and as she watched his expression she thought she could almost see the memories playing across his mind.

"I must have looked pretty lost to you." She remembered the first time she saw him. He'd been washing his family's station wagon with his father in the blacktop driveway. They had a mixed-breed dog that was barking and begging them to squirt him with the garden hose. She'd been fascinated by the sight, since she'd never known her father, and the men at the compound had never played with the children. Playing was only allowed with other children and only up to a certain age. Once the girls were ten, they were expected to take up their mothers' chores as helpers. Playtime went by the wayside.

"You were quiet, and you were too clean in all the new dresses and outfits Anna bought you." Bryce smiled. "But you weren't afraid to get them dirty. You joined every game and sport with as much gusto as any of the guys in the neighborhood."

"My favorite was when we played flashlight tag all night."

"Yeah, but you wouldn't play it right away. It took until the end of that first summer."

"With the fireflies."

"The fireflies, yes."

The warmth of that summer night was unforgettable, as had been the sight of what seemed to be thousands of blinking lights floating above their yards and the distant farm fields. In upstate New York fireflies came out only on the rarest of nights. But in the depths of the Central Pennsylvania countryside they sparkled in midair like the stars in her favorite cartoon films.

Anna and Adam had allowed her to play flashlight tag as long as she stayed near the houses their friends lived in. Now, of course, she realized Anna and Adam had been on the front porch the entire time, as had the other parents, looking out for them. But when she was running across the lawn, the glittering backdrop of fireflies all around, she'd felt like the star of her very own fairy tale. She'd felt her first taste of freedom.

With Bryce.

She looked at him and wondered how she'd been able to walk away from him all those years ago. After all the time they'd spent sharing long afternoons and deep confidences as easily as if they'd grown up together from birth.

Fear of allowing him to see her too well, to know her too deeply, had driven her to escape Silver Valley without looking back.

Until now.

"Thank you for lunch, Bryce. I think I'd better get ready for the pageant practice. Will I see you there?"

"Yes, later. I need to stop in and see my parents. I

haven't had a chance to spend any of the holiday season with them yet."

"It's hard to believe Christmas is less than a week away."

And they still hadn't caught the killer.

Chapter 14

Bryce pulled into the town house community where his parents had moved two years ago and smiled to himself. It always seemed like Mayberry here—the neatly trimmed lawns and shrubbery, and the traditional yet contemporary design of the river-stone fronts. The best part of the deal was that his parents didn't have to do any of the garden work as it was all handled by the community.

The same community that would provide assisted living care, if needed, for his parents, who at the moment showed no signs of slowing down. His father had retired last year from a long career as a police officer and then superintendent of police for Silver Valley. His mother was still teaching music at the high school but was eligible to retire in two years.

He parked the car and walked up to their door, noting that his mother had been at it again with her decorative touches. Fir garlands framed the door and a large wreath with red berries gave off the aroma that can only be described as "Christmas."

The door burst open before he finished ringing the bell and he was enveloped in his mother's arms, the scent of her favorite perfume, Chanel No. 5, wafting through the small entryway.

"Bryce! Great to see you, honey. Come on in, it's too cold to stand here with the door open."

He walked over to his father, Ed, whose blue eyes assessed him steadily. "You doing okay, son?"

"Yes, Dad."

Ed Campbell nodded and opened his arms to give Bryce his trademark bear hug.

Never short on affection, his parents.

A tiny yipping caught his attention and he laughed.

"That is the sorriest excuse for a dog, you guys."

"Hey, watch it. This here's my baby." Ed bent his huge frame to reach the little white ball of fluff and brought the dog to his chest. "Don't listen to him, Itsy Bitsy. He's just jealous that he's not living with us anymore." Ed's gruff voice was at odds with his silly words for the dog.

"She's the light in his day, let me tell you." Fran Campbell headed down the hall toward the kitchen. "Come on back and talk to me while I finish up our dinner. It's your favorite!"

His "favorite" was absolutely anything his parents made him. As the three of them made their way to the kitchen he felt what he always did in the presence of his immediate family—love, lots of it, and a little bit of sadness.

The sadness had been there ever since his sister had died of cancer at age three. He'd been ten years old and it had all but broken his parents. Somehow they'd rallied, for him, and gone on to live a meaningful life together and individually. Only now as an adult could he appreciate it.

"Smells good, Mom. What is it?"

"Chicken potpie—you know, a healthier version for your dad. And I'm making up a nice bowl of salad. You can pick your own dressing."

"I like yours best, Mom."

"Suck-up." His father stood next to his mother with that froufrou dog in his bulky arms, frowning at Bryce. The brightness of his eyes, the same shade of gray-blue as Bryce's, gave away his mirth.

"I don't get Mom's cooking as much as you do."

"Lucky for you. She's gone all no fat, no salt, no taste on us."

"That's not true. Bryce, don't listen to him."

"Dad, Mom tells me you've got to watch your blood pressure."

"Humph. Let me tell you, it was a lot higher when I was on SVPD. The doctors... Sometimes I think they're just looking for ways to keep us alive past our expiration date. We're not supposed to live forever, you know."

"We want you nice and healthy while you're here." Fran chopped a carrot as she spoke, her deft hands as good with a chef's knife as they were on the piano keyboard.

"How's the musical going, Mom?"

She waved her knife in the air, at which Ed, still holding the dog, made exaggerated dodging motions.

"Whoa, woman! Put down your weapon."

"Take that beast out of my cooking space and go sit next to your son."

Fran waited until Ed was seated on the counter stool next to Bryce before she answered.

"The stage mothers are in a tizzy because there weren't enough roles for the girls. The boys are stretched to the limit, believe me, but after having so many female-focused productions, we needed something more suited to the talents of the high school boys."

"You could've picked a girl for Peter Pan."

"We could have, yes, but none of the girls fit the part as well as Jeremy. That kid's going to be on Broadway someday, trust me." She pointed her knife at Bryce.

"I trust you, Mom. What about the flying apparatus?"

"That's where the angst all started. The stage moms raised the money for the equipment, and then most of their girls got cast in the ensemble. A few of them were none too pleased."

"They're not supposed to be raising money just so their daughters can have time onstage. It's a group effort, right? And aren't the kids the ones who should be upset?"

"You know how it goes, honey. Most of the kids are absolutely fine with it all. There's one mother who'd love to tear my heart out, but her daughter is the sweetest thing. She's just not the best singer in the world. It's a shame, really, when her parents have paid for so much training."

Bryce bit his cheek, trying not to laugh. The Silver Valley High School musical was a Big Deal each year and his mother had borne the brunt of stage mothers and their helicopter-parenting styles for ages.

"I'm involved with the Silver Valley Community Church's Christmas pageant this week. I hope we don't have any stage moms like you do."

Of course, if they did, Zora would be dealing with them, in her role as interim pastor.

"Since when do you go to church?" Ed's query was typical of his father: direct, honest and always looking for the next joke.

"Since there's a killer murdering female ministers in town, or have you forgotten?"

Ed shook his head. "I saw the reports on the news, and put a call in to Colt. If you need me…"

"Dad, we can always use your experience and opinion. But we've got it, honest."

"I don't like you working in a church with such a crazy sick bastard on the loose," Fran cursed as she chopped.

"Mom! Language." He had to tease her; it was his job. His mother was the picture of the perfect high school music teacher—sweet, pretty, animated. But she could cuss like a sailor when she needed to. Speaking of sailors…

"Hey, do you guys remember Zora Krasny?"

"Remember? We play golf with Anna and Adam whenever the weather cooperates. This winter has been brutal so far, hasn't it? We've been trying to convince them to move into Serenity Springs with us."

"So you know Zora's been back in Silver Valley for a while?"

"Hmm, I may."

"Mom, why didn't you say anything? Dad?"

"Son, your mother told me to stay quiet about it."

"Bryce, honey, I know it was a painful time for you when Zora didn't go to the prom with you."

Bryce had to struggle to not roll his eyes. He couldn't, not at his mom.

"Mom, I was a kid. And I still went."

"With that cheerleader who turned out to be so shy, but, at least, thanks to you, she had a date."

Sometimes having a mother who taught at the same high school he'd attended had its drawbacks.

"Mom, I'm almost thirty-four. I left high school a long time ago."

"You'll always be that handsome senior to me. Remember how excited you were when you found out you got into Penn State?"

"And he studied criminal justice, just like his old man." Ed never missed an opportunity to emphasize what he considered the genetic gifts he'd given Bryce.

"I've inherited the best of both of you. You raised me in the best possible home." He'd always trusted his parents. Even in the darkest days when Karen was sick and then died, he'd known his parents loved him with all their hearts. That he was safe.

Zora hadn't had that.

"Why are you asking about Zora now, Bryce?" His mother's quiet tone didn't fool him, nor did the fact that she appeared not to be particularly interested in his response. She continued to roll out the crust for the potpie. Fran Campbell was 100 percent mother hen when it came to his love life, or what she perceived it to be.

Not that Zora was in *that* category.

"Oh, I've run into her. Mutual acquaintances and all. She's a counselor now that she's left the navy."

"Yes, I think Anna mentioned that. Any chance you'll be seeing more of her, honey?" Mom was blinking rapidly. Her eyes must have something in them. Or… "Spill it, Mom."

Fran frowned for a split second—long enough that

he knew she'd been keeping information from him on purpose.

"Anna asked me to not tell you she was back, because Zora swore her to secrecy. Zora wanted to get reacquainted with her old school friends on her own terms, if at all."

"Most of us aren't even in the area anymore." The crowd they'd run with had all been the "geeks," with many going to Ivy League and comparable schools that took them across the country and globe.

Fran assessed him. "No, you're not. And I can't help but thinking that maybe you were supposed to go out there, too. Find something bigger than what our town has to offer."

"Now, Fran, the boy's doing what he wants to do."

"Mom, Dad, I'm in Silver Valley because this is where I belong. I love it here. It's not as if I don't travel enough on my own."

"You planning another big trip for your vacation time this year?" Pride boomed in Ed's voice. He'd told Bryce he thought he was crazy for taking a trip on his own through Southeast Asia, but he knew his dad had been proud of him for doing it, too.

"Vacation is the farthest thing from my mind."

"Why are you asking about Zora, honey?" His mother had her bone and wasn't going to let go.

"Actually, we're working together on a case. She was the counselor for the first minister who was murdered."

"Oh, dear."

"Has she given you any insight into why that particular reverend was targeted?" Ed's detective face was back on.

"No, nothing yet. But we keep hashing it over, hoping something will come through before…before…" He glanced at his mother to see if she was still listening as she opened the oven door and put the potpie on the rack.

"Before he gets the next one." His father spoke low and quiet, and Bryce met his gaze. Dad understood.

"Yes."

Ed's huge hand squeezed Bryce's shoulder. "You've got the smarts for it, Bryce. You'll get him. Just don't let him get you first."

"I'm doing my best not to, Dad." He meant it, too, except his priorities had changed. Somehow, in less than two weeks, his number one priority had become to keep Zora safe.

Holy hell.

The day before Christmas Eve, Zora took a two-hour break in the late morning before the last big dress rehearsal. She had a newfound respect and compassion for cancer patients and anyone else who had to wear a wig all day. She couldn't wait to get rid of her disguise.

Being undercover had its own challenges as far as making sure she didn't let any details from her real life slip out in conversation, and having to make certain she didn't spend too long with any of the church members, in case someone looked at her for too long.

"Come on, Butternut. Let's get a walk in." She was grateful for the chance to escape the house in no more than workout clothes and her winter coat. The cover story they'd agreed on, that Reverend Hammermill was staying with her as they'd been college roommates, had been genius. As long as no one expected to see them together.

The police car at the foot of her drive was too familiar. She knew it took time to lure out a killer, and the

Female Preacher Killer was no exception. Still, the long days made the almost two weeks they'd been working the case feel more like a year. She waved at the lone officer who sat in the car but didn't stop to chat as she usually would. She'd left a dozen doughnuts with the detail this morning and hoped there were some left for the afternoon crew.

Snow fell in huge, fat flakes and she wondered if they might need to cancel the rehearsal. She'd been stationed in colder climates and of course had grown up here, so she wasn't a stranger to snow and it rarely deterred her from her objectives. But the parents of little children didn't need to take risks on the road for a simple church play.

"Over here, girl." She gave a short tug on Butternut's leash to keep the dog in sync with her own steps as she led them into the woods. It was a route they took regularly, one that allowed for a good hour's cardio, covering well over three miles through the surrounding forest.

Butternut growled as if she'd detected Godzilla, and Zora laughed when she saw the reason—a squirrel raiding her bird feeder.

"That's where all the seed is going." The feisty gray ball of fur switched its tail in annoyance at her and Butternut's interruption.

"Don't worry, we're not going to bother you." Good thing the congregation couldn't see her talking to a squirrel.

Once at the edge of the woods Zora paused to adjust her hat and enjoy the way the snow blanketed even the tiniest branches. She loved how the holly berries looked as if they were frosted with sugar.

Christmas.

She hadn't thought much about the holidays, except for the church services, since the Female Preacher Killer case had taken over her life. Last year by this time she'd finished three operations in a month for the Trail Hikers and was counseling eight clients. Her father had helped her chop down a tree on her land, which of course was too big once they'd brought it up on the porch. With his judicious use of the saw on the bigger branches, and a lot of muscle, they'd wrestled it through the front door, and she'd decorated it with the ornaments she'd collected in her navy travels.

This year she yearned for something…different for Christmas. She wasn't sure what, but the prospect of only having her parents over didn't seem enough.

Bryce would fit in well.

"Come on, girl." Butternut immediately broke into a casual trot, keeping pace with Zora's moderate run. The dog had abandoned her constant sniffing of the ground to breathe in the air around them instead, pointy ears flat against her head in true doggy concentration mode.

Bryce's reappearance in her life had stirred up a lot of old memories. She had to keep that in mind. The case would end, and so would their collaboration. Silver Valley was a big enough place that the odds of working together on another Trail Hikers mission weren't great. Plus the Trail Hikers often sent her to places far from Silver Valley. They hadn't sent her overseas yet but she had an inkling that every once in a while she'd be called in to help with international cases.

It took everyone working together these days to keep the world a civil place. And a safe one…

The sweat from her exertion soaked through her first layer and she relaxed into her stride.

"Good, good girl, Butternut, baby." She'd trained the dog since she was a pup to mind orders and stay in stride whether Zora was walking, running or at an all-out sprint. Butternut rarely ran in front of her, and when she did it was for a valid reason like an approaching stranger or vehicle.

The snowfall wasn't as heavy in the woods under the thick layer of branches but the wind still made it through the trunks, stirring up whorls of snow in miniclearings.

It was her first run since the shooting and it felt good. Some stiffness still lingered in her rib cage but nothing she couldn't handle, as long as she kept her exertion reasonable. They easily passed the halfway mark and she wondered if maybe she should slow it to a brisk walk. Getting loosened up was one thing but she couldn't afford to have sore or tight muscles when she faced the killer.

Without warning, Butternut bolted across her path and she went sprawling as the leash wrapped around her legs. "Butternut!"

The dog tucked in her tail and sat, her expression contrite.

"Zora!"

She peered through the veil of snow toward the source of the familiar voice. "Bryce?"

Brushing snow off her pants, she stood up and waited. In a few more seconds he was at her side, affectionately patting Butternut on the head.

"Damn dog," she grumbled as she unwrapped the leash from her legs.

"What did this princess do?"

"She decided you were friendlier than me apparently."

He wore workout gear, gloves and a blue ski cap that brought out the intensity of his eyes.

Desire warmed her insides and she had to fight the urge to jump him.

She laughed at the thought.

"What's so funny?"

"Nothing. And how did you find me here? Wait— let me guess. Officer Samuel called it in when I left the house. You drove up to the back of the woods."

"Excellent deduction. You know, if you ever decide you don't want to be a counselor, I'll bet you could find a position with SVPD."

"I feel as though I'm part of SVPD already. You're all so professional and such a strong team." As she said the words, she realized how true they were. No one at SVPD ever made her feel excluded or like an outsider, including Bryce. Especially Bryce.

"Well, none of the other officers know who you really work for. And we all have enough training to know not to ask. As long as the superintendent approves you, you're in."

"You never had an inkling about the Trail Hikers before you were asked to join them, Bryce?"

"No." He motioned toward the trail. "Want to keep going? I'm here to join you if you're okay with it, not slow you down."

"I was just thinking it's time to walk. It felt so good running the past mile but I don't want to push it."

They walked along the narrow path, where he allowed her to go first.

"Smart of you. Although I'm astonished that you're already out here like this. You took an awful hit."

"Have you ever taken a bullet?"

"Once or twice."

"So then you know. It's better to move than to sit around and ache."

"Sometimes." His hand touched her elbow and she stopped. He drew level with her and looked into her eyes.

"I also know that sometimes it's okay to slow down and allow things to heal. To let things happen as they need to."

She grasped his upper arms through his light ski jacket as his mouth lowered to hers. It was the most romantic setting she could think of—country woods, first snowfall, silence except for the twitter of birds foraging for seeds and berries.

But Bryce's kiss wasn't romantic; it was pure heat and she didn't bother to decipher her body's response or wonder at the sanity of their kissing. The past didn't matter and she couldn't put any energy toward the future. All that mattered was this moment, this time, this kiss.

A solid weight pressed against her leg and Zora broke the kiss, looking down at Butternut's snow-covered head.

"She's keeping me from freezing."

"I want to keep you hot and bothered." Bryce's voice rumbled next to her ear as he brought her hips to his. He obviously needed her to understand that he was as affected by their kiss as she was.

"It's probably not the most mature or professional thing we could do. Working as partners and all."

"No." His pupils were dilated as he leaned his forehead against hers and she watched their breath form a single cloud.

"And we're both professionals."

"Yes."

They stood like that for what felt like a long time but could only have been a few minutes.

"I have to get to the church." She took a step back, reluctant to break away but needing distance before she really did try to take the embrace further. The snow would cushion his fall, and his body would cushion *hers*…

"Yes. We both do. And you need time to get back undercover." He had her cap in his gloved hands and he placed it back on her head. "Nothing can hide your beauty, Zora, even that god-awful wig and old-lady glasses. But it's a delight to see your real hair."

"How about the frumpy suit over my Kevlar? Now, that, you have to admit, is sexy."

Bryce didn't respond and they fell into silence as they walked back toward her house. The clearing to her yard came up and she turned back.

"Bryce…"

"Not now, Zora. You need to get dressed, and we both need to get our heads on straight for the next few days."

"You think the killer is going to strike soon, don't you?"

"Didn't his poem say as much? And he's threatened to kill at least one, if not two, more." Bryce's face was set in grim lines that she understood all too well.

"I want to catch him so badly I can taste it."

"Your job is to lure him out. Let me and my team do the catching."

"You're not my bodyguard, Bryce. We're a team, remember?"

"We are. But I'm not apologizing for my tactics."

"Okay, don't. I won't apologize for mine, either." She

placed her mittened hands on his chest, reached up and planted a firm kiss on his warm lips.

"Zora, this is going to have to wait until after the case..."

"Too late, Detective."

Chapter 15

Zora put the last bobby pin in her wig, tugged to make sure it was secure and stepped back to take in her overall appearance in the full-length mirror. Dowdy and nerdy, all in one package.

"See you later, Butternut." She took her handbag and water bottle. Her phone vibrated as she reached to take it from the counter.

"Hi, Claudia."

"Zora, I need you to come into the office. Are you able to leave church at the moment?"

"I'm actually finishing up an early lunch break before a long evening with the Christmas pageant practice."

"Come straight here."

Claudia clicked off and Zora stood still, shocked by the reaction her boss's brusque demand inspired in her.

She wanted to call Bryce.

* * *

Bryce wasn't looking forward to watching Zora take another emotional blow. First she'd found out that her mother was living in Silver Valley, and now this. He'd reported what he'd discovered when he got back to the station to Claudia, who sat across from him as they waited for Zora.

Good thing he hadn't followed his instincts and taken Zora to bed after their walk. It would've been awkward to get calls from Rio and Superintendent Todd and for Zora to get the summons from Claudia while they lay in bed. Naked. Satisfied.

He shifted in his seat and bit his inner cheek.

"She'll be here in a few minutes, Bryce. Stop fretting."

"Yes, ma—Claudia."

"Chill out, Detective. I'm not your drill sergeant. We're a team here."

He didn't reply. He couldn't, not without sounding like a lackey.

The door behind him opened and he felt the air electrify with Zora's presence. He wondered if Claudia felt it, too, or if it was just his sixth sense where Zora was concerned.

"Claudia." She walked to Bryce's side. "Detective Campbell is here, too. Great. What's the good news this time?"

"Sit down, Zora."

Zora did and Bryce's abs tightened with apprehension.

"We've learned some more details that are crucial to this case and of personal interest to you."

"Okay, shoot." Zora nodded. Hell, she thought it was just another navy intel brief, didn't she?

"Bryce, fill her in."

"We've been watching a trailer park on the edge of

Silver Valley that has a history of transient-related crime. Unpaid rent, domestic violence, drunk and disorderly. Over the past six months, it's cleaned up."

"And that's a problem?"

"Well, yes. A single owner has purchased the property. It has five hundred units—quite a substantial rental income potential. The previous owner sold it without advertising, for an amount that's far more than market value. He retired to Florida with his family at the end of the summer."

"Okay."

"This has taken a lot of work on the part of SVPD. We've been working with the FBI on this. The buyer— we think it's a pseudonym for Leonard Wise."

"Impossible. He's not even out of prison yet."

"Actually, he was released earlier this month." Claudia took the reins. "The appearance of your mother in the area doesn't look so coincidental any longer. We don't think she's here to only be near you."

"I could have told you that." Zora's professional demeanor continued but Bryce saw how her hands clenched on her skirt. As if to keep herself from any kind of emotional outburst.

"It's not that simple, Zora. Now we're going to need you to meet your mother again. We have to determine if and what she knows about the former cult members showing up in Silver Valley."

"We have to stop a killer. Doesn't that take precedence?"

Claudia nodded. "Yes, and that's the catch. There's a chance the cult is somehow involved in the killings. A slim chance, but we can't ignore anything at this point." Claudia slid a file across her desk.

Zora opened the file and Bryce saw that her expression remained neutral until she came to the same devastating conclusion he had. "They already have children living there?"

"Two families who are registered church members at Silver Valley Community Church, in fact. They're not living with the cult members per se, but in the same trailer park."

"Too close for comfort."

Bryce ached for her. He saw she was trying to keep the reality out, to somehow force the harsh fact that the cult continued its sick actions out of her awareness.

"Yes." Claudia paused, waiting for Zora's expression to look a little less haunted, he assumed. "Do any of the names look familiar to you yet?"

"Rebecca and Jess. I met with them. I told you about it." She looked at Bryce.

"Yes, you did. And I told you I knew the neighborhood. I didn't know this about it, however. Not until today. We're concerned that the cult might be interested in moving to Silver Valley. Making contact with a vulnerable church member, especially a teenager, at one of the largest churches in Central Pennsylvania fits Wise's previous behavior."

Zora nodded. "He always excelled at finding the darkness in even the nicest person." Edith came to mind. "Even if the cult isn't involved in these murders, I want to help break them up before they set roots down in Silver Valley."

Zora's hands were still and she didn't feel as though she wanted to kill anyone.

Yet.

She turned the pages of the report Claudia had given

her and read it carefully, not allowing Claudia or Bryce to rush her absorption of the facts.

"Wise didn't waste any time, did he?"

"No. As soon as the first of his cronies were released last year he had them set about finding a new place to bring the True Believers all back together again."

"But why Silver Valley?" Zora asked the question as she read on, expecting to see what she feared. What she already knew.

"The private investigator you hired was legit, from Virginia. But he in turn contacted two unsavory PIs back in your old hometown. One of them was a True Believer."

"For all the education I've received I'm pretty stupid, aren't I?" The weight of her mistake was unbearable. She'd just wanted to see if her mother was okay.

Yet she had to face her error in judgment if she was going to help clean up Silver Valley before the cult took hold.

"You didn't know, Zora. And you used your new name, Zora Krasny."

"Yes, I did. But they still put it together and figured out who I used to be."

"Daisy Simms."

"Yes."

"You want me to meet with my mother, don't you?"

Claudia's eyes were full of knowing and compassion. Were those unshed tears in the retired general's eyes?

"You don't have to, Zora. But it would help us, yes. If you don't, we can still watch these suspects and see if they have plans to abduct any girls from the community, or brainwash their parents to turn them over to Wise. It would be a lot easier if you can find out if Edith Simms knows anything. Names of all the cult members in Silver Valley would be helpful."

"Wise wasn't due out of prison for another few months." Zora said the words by rote, remembering what she'd read online in national news outlets. But even the press didn't know everything. They didn't know the horrors that had struck too many of the girls in that compound.

The thought of the True Believers setting up shop in Silver Valley made her want to throw up.

"The plan was probably to have things ready for him when he got here. He got out a month or two early. It happens."

"I would've thought he'd go to a different part of the country. Pennsylvania's still close to New York. Unless… unless he's coming back to get revenge on me. That's what you're afraid of, isn't it?"

Bryce spoke. "It's all too slick. And no, I don't think it's a coincidence that he's chosen the same place that you live. He convinced the parole board that he's a new man, and he got out on good behavior. He obtained permission to leave the state, as well. He reports to a parole officer locally."

Bryce's hand was on her forearm and she looked at it. Strong, warm, reassuring. She met his gaze. "What I suggested to you about meeting with her before, for closure—I was wrong, Zora. You don't have to meet with her if it's too painful. You've been through enough."

"I'll meet with her. But I want you to feel free to wire me. She's nothing more than a suspect to me, an accessory to a crime."

Claudia and Bryce exchanged a glance Zora wasn't inclined to interpret. It didn't matter what they thought of her. She'd survived the True Believers and was stronger for it. The least she could do was give it her all to keep them from ever harming another child.

"Is Edith living in the trailer park yet?"

Claudia shook her head. "No, she's still in the development I told you about. She came here ahead of Wise's purchase of the trailer park."

Zora felt stupid for not suspecting any of this sooner, but at least it wasn't too late to make a difference. "One thing, though. We need to get moving and get this finished before I have to be back at church."

If Zora thought the wig and ugly suits were a pain to go undercover in, getting wired was worse. Not physically, but emotionally and mentally, knowing that Bryce and Claudia were privy to everything her mother would say to her.

That didn't frighten her. She was afraid of what she herself might say.

"When she answers the door, stay calm and don't take no for an answer. Remember, she came here to track you down, in all likelihood."

Claudia spoke to her as the SVPD sound tech officer did last-minute checks on the microphones. Zora wore one wireless mic and one wired to a battery and transmission pack that was strapped against her lower back, concealed under her leather coat. Both microphones were no bigger than the end of a pencil eraser and virtually undetectable under her blouse and jacket collar.

"I'm ready." Zora was relieved to have Claudia and Bryce with her in the police van. She wasn't afraid of conducting any mission asked of her but she was nervous about seeing her mother again. In Walmart she'd been able to walk away and go into denial. She could pretend she'd never seen her mother, that the woman had been only a doppelganger. Some kind of distorted mental image Zora had conjured up while being weakened from the gunshot.

Now she was about to knock on the door of a woman who'd all but sold her young daughter into sex slavery, even if Zora had escaped before it happened.

"We're right here, Zora. And the backup team is on standby at the station." Bryce went over what they'd already discussed. Because of the sedate neighborhood Edith lived in and the potential for unwanted witnesses, they'd have to play it easy going in. Nothing too overt or overpowering. Just Zora, wired, and the van a block away. If she found more than they bargained for in her mother's apartment, she only had to say the code word they'd all agreed on.

She felt a familiar sense of reassurance when Bryce wrapped his hand around her upper arm and leaned in close.

"I've got your back, Zora. You're not the little girl who was under her control anymore. You're safe."

She turned to look him in the eye. "I know. Thanks."

He squeezed her upper arms before he released her.

She turned to Claudia. "I'm ready. Let's go."

The van followed her as she drove her sedan to Edith's street. They continued on the parkway while Zora turned left and parked in front of the correct townhome.

She assessed the property as she walked up the sidewalk.

It was a nicer place than she and Edith had ever lived in back in New York. Images of the cheap carpets, torn linoleum, mice, cockroaches and cold beds threatened her composure.

"Don't think about it." She was a trained counselor, damn it. These images were no longer real. She wasn't there.

As soon as she rang the doorbell she felt "on." Time to go to work.

"Can I help you?"

If the green eyes looking at her from the wide crack in the door didn't tell her, the voice confirmed her suspicions. This was indeed Edith.

"Do you know who I am, Edith?"

Edith stared at her as if she could see straight through her. Zora imagined the judgment of her long, fashionably styled hair, sexy yet classy clothing and makeup, including fuchsia lipstick. She'd hurried home to change out of her Colleen Hammermill outfit.

Stop.

"Shouldn't you be calling me Mother?" Edith opened the door wider. "How did you find me?"

"It wasn't hard. You're listed, and after I saw you in Walmart last week I looked you up. The real question is how did you find me?" She wasn't going to reveal that Claudia had tracked Edith down.

"I wasn't looking for you. It was divine guidance. Can you come in?" Edith had always said everything was "divine guidance." But Zora knew Edith had sought her out.

Edith held the door open and Zora stepped inside, even though she wanted to turn and run. Not from the mission but from the memories of who she had been, where she'd been headed, before she'd broken from Edith.

"Thank you. You have a nice place here." It was a lie, she realized once she walked farther inside. The building was nice enough but Edith had no furniture in the front room.

"Let's go back to the kitchen. I've got tea."

Ah, yes, tea. Or some weak idea of tea. Edith had been making herbal concoctions for Wise from the minute they moved into the compound.

"That sounds nice." It didn't, but she held Claudia's guidance close to her heart.

Keep Edith talking.

"So how long have you been in Silver Valley?"

Edith ignored her as she put a pan of water on the electric stove and pulled two plain white mugs from the cabinet.

"Do you still like chamomile? It was always your favorite."

"It was never my favorite. You forced it on me to make me sleep."

"Oh, Daisy, don't be so ugly. You were the sweetest child. I can't believe you've allowed yourself to take on so much of the ways of the world."

"What have you done these past twenty years, Edith?"

"Can you find it in your heart to call me Mother?"

She couldn't, but she could find it in the Trail Hikers' best interest.

"Mother. Have you been living here, or in New York?"

Edith clapped her hands together as if in prayer and smiled.

"That's better. Let's see, I moved here a bit ago. I've lived a little here, a little there. Got some training so that I could get a better job. Until..." Edith turned away and busied herself with the hot water at the stove.

"Until what, Mother?"

Edith turned toward her, and her face was animated. Zora tried to stop the bile from rising in her throat as Edith's expression threw her right back into the little girl she'd been, the child who'd had no recourse from Edith's sickness.

Think like a therapist.

Studying Edith with the detachment of a professional, she no longer looked so powerful or scary. She looked like the patients Zora had to observe in the hospital psychiatric unit as part of her degree program. Except Edith wasn't medicated—unless you counted chamomile tea and a sick sense of religion.

"Are you working?" She already knew the answer but needed to keep Edith talking.

"I have a job at the medical center. I got certified as a medical assistant."

"That's wonderful. It must feel good to not have to work as a waitress anymore."

"I'm not going to have to work at the hospital for too long, either."

"Why not?"

Edith brought the cups of tea to the card table that sat in the middle of the otherwise empty kitchen. She motioned for Zora to sit on one of the folding chairs while she sank into the other.

Edith was thinner, frailer than Zora remembered. Her mother had always at least looked strong and healthy, even though her mental and emotional state contradicted that.

"How's your health?"

Edith raised her tired gaze to her and shrugged. "As good as ever. I give my aches up to the angels and I trust I'll be healed. You know we all will, Daisy, don't you?"

Zora gritted her teeth against the scream that threatened to erupt from the deep well of regret that was her childhood.

"I'm more interested in the here and now, Mother."

She prayed the microphones were picking everything up.

"This isn't all there is, Daisy. We have so much more waiting for us. One day all of our suffering will cease and if we've been righteous we'll get our rewards."

"That's nice." She risked a sip of the tea. Good grief, it still stank like cat poop and made her gag.

"What's in this tea?"

"The chamomile you used to love, and some extra herbs and treatments that will help your digestion and clarity."

"Do you still grow your own herbs?" At the compound her mother had huge gardens that she'd harvest. Then she'd dry the herbs and try to sell them to the local town from a sorry wooden shack she'd built herself. Leonard Wise believed in free enterprise, as he called it. As long as it didn't interfere with his plans for the young girls.

"I don't have time to do as much as I used to but I've started a few pots of mint and echinacea out back. The winters are milder here so it's a longer growing season."

"What are you waiting for, Mother? You said you're waiting."

"Just for things to be right again." Edith's hands shook as she put her mug on the table with a *thump*. She started to fidget with the edge of the awful apron she wore over her plain clothes.

"What do you mean by 'right,' Mother?" Zora wished she could wash her mouth out on the spot. Calling this woman "Mother" tasted like poison on her tongue.

"You know, Daisy. You left behind the way God wants us to live and because of your lies, perfectly good men went to jail."

"Do you still believe that? That they were good men?"

"Maybe not completely. But they didn't mean harm. And you were never touched, Daisy."

"I wasn't touched because I was still only twelve. It was a matter of time."

"I wouldn't have let them touch you. I won't *ever* let them touch you." She spoke with the conviction of a comrade in arms. Zora questioned Edith's measure of sanity. With a degree in counseling she didn't have the expertise to diagnose her biological mother, but she'd long suspected Edith suffered from a multitude of mental illnesses.

Gratitude for her own health empowered her and she sat straighter in the chair. Bryce and Claudia were waiting for some answers.

"I've heard that some of the people we knew are being released from prison."

"Many already have been, Daisy. They've served their time. Their sins are wiped away. That's what justice is, my daughter."

She cringed at "my daughter" but kept going.

"Where do you think they'll end up, Mother?"

Edith stirred her tea with the cheap spoon that had nicks and was slightly bent in the middle. Apparently she still shopped at thrift shops and in garbage bins.

"We were all a family. Family belongs together."

"How so?" She made a point of looking around Edith's barren kitchen and townhome. "You live alone."

"I'm never alone. God provides what I need. I won't be here much longer. We'll all be together again."

Zora agreed with her about God, but would bet her life savings that her God was a lot more loving and forgiving than the one Edith envisioned.

"Do you keep in touch with any of them, from before, in New York?"

"You know I do or you wouldn't have come here. I know you're somehow involved with the authorities, Daisy. I didn't raise a stupid girl. Ever since you betrayed me and told that store guard what you thought was happening, you've put your belief in the police."

Thank God she had.

"I didn't betray you. I was trying to save both of us."

"You betrayed me when you didn't trust me to keep you safe from the ultimate sacrifice. I would have, you know. I'd still do whatever it takes to protect you, my daughter, from harm."

Zora had no doubt her mother believed her own words but all Zora felt was…flat. She faced a strange woman she'd known once, who'd loved her like a real mother. Once. Long ago.

Anna was her real mother and had been ever since Zora came to Silver Valley.

Even as a young girl approaching adolescence she'd sensed her mother was getting sicker. She hadn't had the words for it back then. Only after being in the navy for several years and then going to school for her counseling degree did she realize her mother had sunk into a mental illness of some kind.

You can't save them all.

The words of her first professor echoed as she looked at Edith. Edith's gaze was on the window, but Zora suspected her mind had wandered to wherever it went when reality tried to creep in.

"Are they coming here, Mother? To Silver Valley? Why?"

Edith turned to her, although her eyes seemed to be looking at something else, something past Zora. "We'll all be together again. It is right."

Chapter 16

"She's not going to get any more out of her. We should pull her out. She can leave now." Bryce's muscles hadn't relaxed since Zora walked up to her mother's front door. He fought the urge to run up to the house, kick in the door and grab Zora away from that crazy lady and run. Far away where Zora would never be hurt again.

"Wait, Bryce. I know this is difficult to listen to, but it's probably harder on you than Zora." Claudia's hushed tones reminded him that their job was to listen, to keep Zora safe while she gathered the intel they needed.

Harder on him? He cast Claudia a sidelong glance. Her profile revealed nothing. But somehow she knew he cared for Zora, probably before he did.

Hell, did Claudia miss *nothing*?

They continued to listen as Edith babbled on in her monotone. It was so damned annoying to have to sit in the van while Zora faced down the woman who'd essentially sold her.

Again, he marveled at Zora's strength. As a young girl she'd been bright and avid. As a woman, she was unstoppable.

He really hated how Edith kept saying she'd "protect" Zora. Like she had twenty years ago?

He must have been fidgeting because Claudia shot him a "chill out" glance and tapped her headset.

"When are they coming here, Mother?"

"They already are here, Daisy. I'll be moving to the home myself, once Leonard is back. I promised him I'd always wait for him."

"Don't you see that he's only ever used you? That you'll never be his wife or even girlfriend?"

"It's not for me to judge that, Daisy. It's for me to follow and serve where needed."

Edith's education and new job didn't appear to have done her any good. She was still caught in the vile web of the cult leader. Even while serving time, he'd held her spellbound from his prison cell.

A cell he'd been sprung from.

"If you decide you want help, you can find me at my counseling office. I can get you the best treatment options available. You don't have to suffer like this, Mother."

"I'm not suffering, Daisy. I get the shakes sometimes, but nothing my teas and prayers won't cure. You should drink yours, Daisy. You'll feel better."

"I feel fine without it, trust me."

Bryce wondered if Edith had made Zora drink some kind of drug-laced tea when she was young.

"Thank you for seeing me, Mother. I wish you the

best." Zora's tone indicated she didn't expect Edith to ever realize her wish.

"We're not done, Daisy. I promise I won't let any harm come to you."

"So you've said. Take care."

"She's out!" Their plainclothes officer who sat in an unmarked car across from the town house reported on the wireless system.

Bryce took off his headset. "I'm going to get her."

"No, you're not." Claudia's hand was on his forearm. "Wait. Let Zora drive to the station. She needs the time by herself to decompress." Her reasonable tone did nothing to calm the tension in his gut. Zora was hurting. How could she not be, after facing down what had to be her worst nightmare?

"I'm sorry I couldn't get more out of her." Zora's red hair flamed around her pale face as she sat with a hot cup of coffee, untouched, in front of her on the conference table.

"You did great, trust me. We have what we need to keep an official eye on the trailer park. We'll make sure it doesn't turn into another True Believers compound." Bryce wished they were alone so he could pull her close and comfort her. He suspected Superintendent Todd and Claudia knew it, too, judging by their stern glances.

"Bryce is right. SVPD can start to keep an eye out for any wrongdoing, and we can do our best to make sure Jess and the other children in that neighborhood are safe."

"I did it for her. I can't let them hurt one more girl." A shudder passed over her shoulders and Bryce slammed his hand on the table.

"They won't, not if we can help it."

Superintendent Todd sat in a relaxed pose but he didn't fool Bryce. His boss was as angry as he was that a cult thought they'd stand a chance in Silver Valley. Taking advantage of the citizens.

"What can we do to get Jess and her mother out of there?"

"Right now, nothing. If you can keep an eye on them at the Christmas pageant practice and then on Christmas Eve when you do the full event, that would be helpful. Her mother hasn't fully committed to the True Believers who've moved into the park, not yet. But she's incredibly vulnerable and has been seen having coffee with one of the men several times over the past week."

"That's how they got Edith. Leonard Wise did the country equivalent of wining and dining her. Buying us both the most expensive meals on the diner menu, taking my mother out for coffee at all hours."

Bryce stilled. It was the first time he'd heard Zora refer to Edith as "my mother."

He wanted to help her stop running from her past. He knew it was her favorite way out of the pain. Running from anything as painful as Zora's memories only acted as a temporary bandage on a deep wound. It bled through too often to work permanently.

"They'll stick to their modus operandi, if it worked for them before." Claudia tilted her head. "Colt, how many SVPD officers can you spare to monitor the trailer park, undercover?"

"Not many. But I'll make it part of the training schedule and rotate all our officers through it. We can't have eyes on the place 24/7 without probable cause, but we can have someone drive or walk through there every day and night. I'll have them split it up."

"We don't want to advertise that a cult is moving in." Bryce preferred to err on the side of caution when it came to squirrely criminal types. They could run at the slightest provocation and he wanted to nail this group once and for all. Send them all back to prison where they couldn't hurt the public.

"I'll handle who we inform, Detective." Superintendent Todd smiled but his meaning was no less decisive. He wanted Bryce focused on the op.

"Keep me in the loop, too, Colt, would you?" Claudia's question was posed exactly as the superintendent's had been. As an order.

"Will do, ma'am." Bryce noticed the flare of anger in Claudia's eyes at the way Superintendent Todd addressed her and had a revelation. Did they know each other outside of work? They were both single, to the best of his knowledge, married to their jobs.

He shook his head. None of his business. Since Zora had shown up in his life he was seeing relationships and romance where he hadn't before.

"You okay, Bryce?" Zora hadn't missed a thing.

"I'm fine. Why don't we have a late lunch before you get dressed for church?"

She smiled. Her discomfort in the undercover getup was an inside joke for them.

"Do you dress up to go to the office?" Claudia's incredulous tone made Zora's smile deepen and her dimples emerge.

She was breathtaking when she smiled.

"No, no, Bryce is yanking my chain about how much I whine over the heinous wig and ugly suits I have to wear."

"I see." Claudia looked like the wise woman she was,

but Bryce hadn't missed that moment of vulnerability between her and Superintendent Todd.

It seemed none of them were immune from their emotions.

"You're right. Even if anyone from Silver Valley walked in here, he wouldn't have reason to see us." She was relieved Bryce had suggested the nice Italian tavern restaurant in Hershey. The cozy booths nearest the bar were intimate and private.

"It's about time we got out as just ourselves, isn't it?"

She still wasn't comfortable with the thrill his deep voice triggered in her, but she wasn't hiding from it, either. She was attracted to Bryce. Off the clock, why not go with it?

"Maybe. We do still have a big job ahead of us."

His hand grasped hers across the table and she lowered her menu. She'd decided what she was having the minute she saw seafood risotto on their daily-lunch-special board, but the leather folder had kept her from facing Bryce's unnerving gaze.

"And we're going to finish it. After that, I don't intend to stop seeing you, Zora."

The thrill turned into all-out want. She wanted to be with Bryce, too.

"With our history, Bryce…"

"Our history is just that—history. May I say we both had a lot of childhood sadness to overcome? Mine wasn't as long-lived as yours, and I had loving parents the entire time. But it still wasn't a cakewalk."

"No, I know it wasn't. Anna and Adam have given me the family others only dream of. And I never had to go through losing a sister like you did. That's just plain awful, Bryce."

"I appreciated it that you never seemed to feel sorry for me when I told you back then. You just acted like it was sad, and we all have sad times, and let's go play!" He smiled.

"I think in a sick way I was relieved that you'd had hard times, too. It made you approachable. I was so threatened by the other kids who seemed as though their families were perfect. They had two parents, and even the ones who had single parents were happier and better adjusted than I was."

"You get it all now, don't you? After going through your counselor's training?"

"Most of it. But it's like the shoemaker cliché. I can analyze the most difficult cases and family dynamics, except when it comes to my own."

"Have you ever gone to counseling yourself?"

She laughed. Bryce's concern was so genuine, so honest.

"Yes, it's part of the training to become certified. But my mom and dad had me seeing a therapist for most of junior and the beginning of senior high school. I worked hard to deal with it all and then let it go so I could look forward to the rest of my life."

"You never told me any of that."

"I couldn't. Even the counselor had to be screened and pass a clearance background check. My parents knew about what I'd been through, of course, and the counselor was told I'd suffered a trauma from living with criminals. She wasn't given the full scoop, to protect both of us."

He nodded. "Sounds as if you had a prosecuting team who looked out for you."

"They did. The system worked for me, mostly due to a US Marshal who took a special interest in the case. She made sure I was safe, that I was never alone throughout the trial, that I was placed where I'd have the best chance to thrive."

"You're an amazing woman, Zora."

His gruff observation made her want to move over to his bench and hide her blushing face in his shoulder.

"Have you folks decided what your pleasure will be today?" Their waiter stood with his notepad and they both laughed.

Their "pleasure" was going to have to wait.

"You like seafood, I take it?" Bryce had felt a deep satisfaction watching Zora polish off an entire bowl of risotto laden with mussels, scallops, clams and crabs. Her love of food made him wonder how she stayed so thin.

"Mmm. Love it." She sipped her sparkling water with a look of pure enjoyment. "I'm lucky that I've been blessed with a fast metabolism, so far anyway. I was always able to put away the huge meals at the academy with no problem."

"You work out a lot. And your running helps."

"I suppose so. What about you?"

"I have to watch it. I lay off the sweets except for the holidays, and I work out as much as I can. My schedule makes it tough at times."

"I imagine it does, with all the cases you work on. That other SVPD detective—Rio Ortego—talked to me when the forensics team was there for the second set of footprints. He said he's helping you out while you work on this case."

"Yes, Rio's solid. We could use another detective or

two at SVPD, but it takes time for the officers to get the experience that lets Superintendent Todd promote them with confidence."

"He seems like the best boss."

"He is."

"I haven't had a real boss since I left the navy. Now I have Claudia, for these jobs." He liked the way she looked at their mission and the Trail Hikers as long-term employment. It meant she might stay around. "Do you see yourself staying in Silver Valley?"

She blinked. "Yes. At least I did. I have to admit I don't like the thought that the same cult I escaped is reappearing here, though. I don't want to live in the shadow of that kind of insanity ever again."

"You want to run."

"Instinctively, yes. But I know in my head, and even my heart, that will never work. I'll just be looking over my shoulder to see who's followed me to the next place. And while I always have the option of asking for a new identity, I can't. I am where I hope to stay, yes."

Her dedication and forthrightness was enviable.

"Even if it puts your life at risk?"

"It's at risk now, isn't it? The Female Preacher Killer could pick me off in the next few days between the pageant dress rehearsal and Christmas Eve services. Or I could get into a car accident on I-81, or some loon could wander off the interstate and decide to pull a weapon in the same convenience store I happen to be in."

"You didn't answer the question, Zora."

"Yes, even if it puts my life at risk. I'm done with running, Bryce."

He hoped it meant she was done with running from him, from their attraction. But they had work to do first.

"I've got the check. You need to go home and get dressed up as Reverend Hammermill. Why don't you head out and I'll meet you at church in an hour or so?"

She eased herself from the booth, and when he thought she'd walk by and out of the restaurant, she surprised him by placing her hands on his shoulders and leaning in close.

"When this job is through, let's see what we have here, shall we?" Her lips met his as they had in the woods, and if they hadn't been in a public restaurant he knew they'd be in bed for the rest of the afternoon. The kiss was too brief, too chaste, for his liking, but it was Zora's kiss. He'd take whatever he could get.

She pushed back and walked away, leaving him enveloped in the unmistakable scent of her perfume, his mind abuzz from the kiss she'd given him.

Chapter 17

Zora did a quick head count of the children as they lined up for their last practice. The youth minister was running the show, aided by several parents who might as well have been wearing T-shirts with the words *helicopter parent* on them. As loving as Anna and Adam had been to her, they'd never suffocated her with their concern, nor intruded on her social and school functions.

Relief washed over her when she saw Jess. The girl was dressed in black, as were the other members of the technical crew, and she looked animated, enjoying the hubbub.

Scanning the pews for Rebecca, she came up with nothing but didn't let that concern her. It was a good sign if Rebecca allowed Jess to be here without her supervision. Less chance that Rebecca was being sucked into a cult and bringing Jess in with her. If indeed one was forming again.

She had no doubt the previous True Believers would start up where they'd left off. She understood now that those men didn't know any better, and women like Edith didn't know anything other than to drift from one obsessive system to another. It was surprising that her biological mother had completed her college courses. Her attempts at self-improvement made it even sadder that she couldn't break away from her predictable robotic existence.

Zora pinched herself and focused on her gratitude for her own wonderful life, even with the possibility of a serial killer aiming his sights on her. She had a choice—a choice to fight, a choice to help law enforcement bring someone to justice.

As a child in the True Believers, choice had been taken from her.

Forcing her attention on the action, she was drawn into the timeless story portrayed by the kids, with the expected silliness and hilarity added in. A long shadow caught her gaze and she saw Bryce walking through the sanctuary, "learning" about being a youth minister from Peter, who for the most part ignored him. Peter was focused on his job.

The old choir loft was hot but it gave her too good a vantage point to pass up.

Besides, they were almost finished with the last run-through before Christmas Eve.

She was so stupid, sitting up there like a lame duck. It gave him so many ways to take her out. The obvious, with a bullet, of course, would be so easy. But it could be more interesting to set fire to the tinderbox and let the whole damned building go down.

Because the building and the believers in it were all damned. They'd let a female come into their fold for the second time, a female serving as their minister.

If only Mama was here to see this. He was glad she wasn't. She'd be so angered and dismayed by the blatant disrespect of the same churchgoers she'd sat next to for over forty years of her life.

"What are you doing, Mr. Ernie?"

A short figure dressed as a donkey looked at him, head tilted back to see him fully.

He didn't want any kids ruining his plans, that was for sure.

"I'm cleaning up everything so that it's nice and pretty for your play."

Go away, brat.

"Why do you have to clean these stairs? Nobody goes up them. And it's a *pageant*, not a *play*."

"Aren't you a smart little one? I think you'd better get back to the practice or you'll miss your turn to go up the aisle."

The donkey shook its head. "I don't want to go back down the aisle. This costume is hot and sweaty."

Stupid little kid.

"I heard they're giving away candy canes and hot chocolate after the practice, but you have to be good to get it."

The donkey kid paused, as if he was weighing the odds that Ernie was telling the truth. In this case he was. He'd be the one to mop up the sticky floor after the kids and their parents messed up the place. Not to mention the live farm animals they brought in each year at the Christmas service.

"Okay. Have fun and Merry Christmas!"

Ernie stared after the much-used gray costume.

"Donkey, where's my donkey?" Peter, the youth minister, approached Ernie and the little boy.

"I'm coming, Mr. Peter!"

"Well, hurry up now. The infant is about to be born and you need to be there with the Holy Family."

The kid ran up the aisle as if Santa Claus were on the altar.

"Hey, Ernie. Everything going as planned?"

"You tell me. I'm ready for whatever you give me."

Peter nodded. "That's why you're here, Ernie. You can be counted on. You'll never let the small stuff keep you from doing your job."

Ernie's gaze followed Peter as he went back to his charges, and his glance fell again on the rumpled donkey.

He'd be a horse's ass himself if he let some kid stop his plans for the Silver Valley Community Church's most memorable Christmas yet.

"It's going to be tomorrow or on Christmas Day. You know that," Rio said as he walked next to Bryce. They made their way up and down the overcrowded aisles of Silver Valley's Last Minute Christmas Bazaar. A popular event locally, it had gained national attention a few years earlier during a cable television network broadcast from the fair. What made it unique was that most Christmas hand-craft sales were over by now; this was exclusively for the discerning but last-minute Silver Valley shoppers.

Which, judging by tonight's crowd, included the entire Susquehanna metropolitan area.

"You're right. I agree. It's tomorrow or Christmas Day." His concern needed to be as focused as Rio's on the Silver Valley Community Church and the threat to the civilians. It was, but it was also on Zora.

"She's safe, Bryce. We have the best officers on security patrol at her place and I had them double it for tonight."

"That was a good call. We can't be too safe." And it was a call he should've thought of. Problem was, he knew in his gut he'd go by there tonight to check on her anyway.

You want to do more than that.

He did. He wanted to be with Zora in every way a man could be with a woman. She was as professional as he was, and as such their relationship wasn't going to the next level until the op was done.

Unless…they changed their minds.

It wasn't as though keeping their relationship out of the bedroom was a hard and fast rule. It was his rule, and hers, too. She felt the same attraction he did. Her whispered words to him in the restaurant in Hershey proved it.

Rio knocked into him and Bryce reflexively grabbed his shoulders.

"Sorry, man. Those tote bags are lethal." Rio grumbled at the huge shopping bag that hung from the shoulder of a woman who was oblivious that she'd jostled another shopper, much less tipped Rio into Bryce.

"It's nuts. I'm only here to get that night-light for my mother. My dad can't do it because he's working with her at our church's table."

"The angel table?" Rio started to laugh.

"How did you guess?" His parents' church had a group of women who were talented painters. Bryce's dad was a woodworker at heart and had every saw and tool imaginable in his garage, so he was a natural target for their charity project. From August through November, his dad produced angels of all sizes, and the paint team, headed up by his mother, gathered in the basement of the church hall to bring the wooden figures to life with hand-painted faces and embellished wings.

"There are the night-lights." Bryce picked out the one his father had asked him. It was decorated with a music sheet that included the notes for the song "Love Me Tender," which had been their wedding song.

"Your parents are still this…romantic?"

"Always. You sound a little bitter about the four-letter word."

"You say bitter, I say realistic."

Bryce studied his friend. They didn't often discuss their personal lives. "You dating anyone, Rio?"

Rio grunted. "You know I'm not, man. SVPD keeps me too busy."

They continued down the aisle.

"Okay, can we get those doughnuts my family wants and get out of here?" Rio had clearly had enough of the crowd.

"There's the doughnut stand," Bryce said, handing him a ten-dollar bill. "Buy me a dozen of the doughnuts, will you? I want to check out a table."

"Traitor. You don't want to wait in that long line."

Bryce eyed the lines waiting for cinnamon rolls, potato doughnuts, sand-tart cookies and other sweets native to central Pennsylvania. "Bingo."

"Okay, meet me outside in ten." Rio had driven them from the station, where Bryce had left his car. The crowds meant parking was a premium at the bazaar.

As they'd walked around, the light reflecting off a table of gold and silver jewelry had caught his eye. He'd planned to take some sweets, namely the potato dough-nuts, to Zora either tonight or in the morning. And he wasn't getting her a Christmas gift, per se. It was more of a memento.

"Can I help you?"

"Yes, I— Kayla. Well, hi." Shit. Not again.

"This is interesting. Two times in less than a week, and when we dated I never saw you." Her smile didn't lessen the sting of her barb.

"Yeah, well…"

She gently punched his upper arm.

"I'm teasing you, Bryce. I don't have hard feelings. We weren't supposed to be together. It's okay. I'll bet you're busy with this awful killer on the loose and all."

"We'll get him."

"I don't doubt it. All of Silver Valley will be cheering when you do. How's Zora?"

"Fine, just fine. In fact, I'm looking for a little some-thing for her. I didn't realize this was your table."

"It's not, it's my friend's. I'm helping her sell these." She waved her hand to encompass the collection of sil-ver and gold jewelry that glittered under the auditorium lights.

"I thought I saw a nativity scene when I walked by earlier."

"This?" She plucked a silver and gold piece and handed it to him for his inspection.

It was a work of art, very finely detailed and yet large and bold in its design. The simple portrayal of the manger with the Holy Family—mother, father and infant—struck him as very fitting for the woman who was portraying a minister for the sake of the community's safety during the Christmas season.

"Zora would love this," Kayla said sincerely.

"Do you think so?"

"Oh, yes. She wears a lot of larger pieces. The great thing about this is that it can be a pin on a jacket or coat, or it can be worn on a necklace. Zora likes choker necklaces and this would be perfect on a silver choker. It looks like her."

"It does." He looked at Kayla and his regret must have shown in his eyes.

"Stop it, Bryce. You don't have to feel bad about it anymore. Really."

"Have you met anyone, Kayla?"

"Yes. But it's not going to work out, either." Her eyes misted and he wondered who had gotten to the sturdy woman he'd "barely dated."

"I'm sorry."

"Don't be. My choice, not his. Here, let me wrap that up for you. You're buying it, aren't you?"

"Yes."

He couldn't pretend to regret that he and Kayla hadn't worked out. There was one woman for him, probably had only ever been one woman since they were twelve years old. But he'd like to know Kayla had found happiness, too.

It seemed she still had some struggles along those lines. He was certainly familiar with the concept that the path to love wasn't always smooth.

"Here you go. There's a card with the jeweler's information on it in the box, but Zora knows her. She buys a lot of her pieces from her shop."

Doubt made him pause. "What if she has already this one?"

"She doesn't. This is the first year Lori has made a Christmas line."

"Thanks. Merry Christmas, Kayla."

"Merry Christmas, Bryce."

"Allow your body to flow from your strong plank position to downward dog. Don't be afraid to let your bottom reach for the sky."

Zora followed along to the yoga class she was streaming on her laptop, trying to let the stress of the case and the worries of the tomorrow's services stay at the church. Butternut lay on the sofa nearby, ever vigilant for an intruder.

She wasn't expecting anyone, not with the double security detail surrounding her land 24/7. Bryce thought the killer would strike tomorrow, as did Claudia. The murderer's poem wasn't dependable as far as timing was concerned. He'd murdered before the last Sunday of Advent, and he could murder before Christmas Day. That left Christmas Eve, either during the children's service when the Christmas pageant took place, or the later evening service that was attended mostly by adults.

Playing Reverend Colleen Hammermill was getting tiresome, she had to admit. It would be worth it when they caught the sick bastard.

"Ease into your cobra position and remember to breathe."

As she exhaled she tried to visualize her life when it got back to normal. No more wigs or heavy suits or ugly shoes.

No more seeing Bryce every day, either. Unless...

She tried to clear her mind, as yoga required, but her thoughts kept interfering.

Bryce wouldn't go away. Would he?

That didn't have to be how things went, did it? He'd said he wanted to move forward once the case was closed.

They didn't have to leave their desires unfulfilled. Unless one of them decided to. Unless Bryce realized he could never trust her after all.

Twenty minutes and six yoga poses later she sat in lotus position with her legs crossed and her hands on her knees. She'd needed the stretching after such a long day.

The stillness of the living room was broken only by the soft crackling of the fire she'd started when she'd returned from the church.

Heavy footsteps sounded on her porch at the same instant Butternut alerted. Her heart felt as if it lunged forward in its own downward dog and she jolted in her sitting position.

"Easy, girl. We're safe."

Were they?

As soon as she spotted the familiar figure on the porch steps through the window she knew they were more than safe. But was her heart?

Enough. Bryce might really need something from her.

She yanked open the door. "Bryce! Has something happened?"

Snowflakes glistened on his hair and his face was flushed from the cold. A nor'easter had started its slow move up the coast and it was predicted to bring up to six inches to central Pennsylvania.

"Nothing's happened, and it probably won't until at least tomorrow. I thought I'd bring you a treat and we could talk over our working strategy for the next few days."

"Strategy?" She couldn't keep from teasing him; he was so transparent.

"Can I come in first? It's a little chilly out here, and the patrol is going to wonder why you're being so mean to me, keeping me exposed to the elements."

She opened the door and he strode in, handing her a large gift bag.

"What on earth?"

"The appropriate response is 'Thank you, Bryce.'"

"Thank you, Bryce. You know where to hang your coat." She motioned to the coatrack that stood behind her door and walked into the kitchen, where she placed the bag on the table.

"Can I open it now?" she hollered to Bryce down the hall.

"Hang on."

He was back at her side in a few seconds. Clad in a thermal shirt under a flannel plaid, jeans and what looked like hand-knit socks, his appearance screamed *boyfriend*.

"Did someone knit those socks for you?"

"Huh?" He looked at his feet and held one up for her closer inspection. "Actually, yes. My aunt. Do you remember her? She lives up on the hill, not far from here."

"Your aunt Henrietta? The one who made me matching scarves and hats all through high school because you wouldn't wear anything she'd knit for you?"

"Yup, that's the one. And her skills have greatly improved. I don't mind wearing these socks at all."

"Socks are fun, but they do take a lot of time. She used good wool for you with those." She recognized the green hue as one of the colors in her favorite sock fiber blend, and named the company.

"I don't know if that's it, but you're probably right.

She told my mother the socks cost more than if she'd bought me a sweater."

"That's about right."

"I don't get it. Why would you spend so much money on yarn?"

"Why do you spend so much money on the best weapon? So it won't fail when you need it, right? Quality, performance, durability."

"You are the only woman in the world who could draw a parallel between yarn and a deadly weapon."

"Don't be so sure about that. Can I see what's in the bag now? Wait—what's in the other bag, the one you put on the counter?"

"Those are potato doughnuts, for later. I wasn't sure if you liked them or not but they're a Christmas favorite of mine, along with sand-tart cookies."

Christmas Eve was tomorrow. Was he planning on staying through the night?

"Go ahead, open your gift."

Eagerly she removed the layers of purple tissue paper to reveal a bottle of red wine, a box of local Santa-shaped dark chocolates and a small box.

"What's in the box, Bryce?"

"Open it and find out. Don't worry, it's not something crazy."

Tell her heart that. It pumped in triple time as she wondered what it would be like to get *that* kind of jewelry from Bryce.

Stop it.

She popped open the dark green velveteen box to reveal a contemporary Christmas broach. It was a primitive outline in silver of the Nativity scene with a sparkling crystal jewel at the top of the stable to give an overall impression of the Christmas spirit without being gaudy.

"It's beautiful! This is just like the kind of jewelry I wear."

"I know. It turns out the designer is someone you know. She only started doing Christmas styles this year. Kayla was working the table at the bazaar where they sold them. I thought you'd like it to dress up those ugly suits you're so fond of. And after we solve this, you'll have it as a reminder of how you helped take down your first bad guy for Silver Valley."

Tears flooded her eyes and no amount of blinking could stem a couple from streaking down her cheeks. She wiped them away and tried to smile at him.

"Thank you so much, Bryce. I'll treasure it."

"It's not worth the tears, Zora. Save them for something really special."

He'd started his reply on a humorous note but when he stopped talking they both grew quiet. They stared at each other, hands at their sides, unblinking.

Was this going to be a special Christmas for them?

Chapter 18

"Want some hot cocoa?"

"I'd rather have a dram of Scotch, but not while we're working this case. Hot chocolate sounds good."

"I can add a shot of reinforcement to it if you change your mind."

He grasped her hand before she could escape to the stove.

"We have something remarkable here, Zora."

She stared at their hands. They felt as if they'd held hands their entire lives.

"How can we be so sure? Sometimes it feels like the past never ended. That I'll never be free to live a normal life."

"Your time at the compound is over, Zora. You're free now. And you're going above and beyond to keep our town safe from the same kind of people—not to mention a serial killer."

Their eyes met.

"You're doing it, too. You do it every day. I'm just a part-time Trail Hiker." More tears rolled down her cheeks and she went to swipe at them but he held her other hand, too, and drew her close.

This close, with her bare feet against his wool socks, the warmth they shared wasn't from the radiantly heated floor. Big flashy snowflakes fell outside, illuminated in the motion detector light she'd repaired over the kitchen window after she'd been shot. A portent of the nor'easter to come.

Here she felt safe, at home. It was the most at home she'd felt since she'd moved into the farmhouse over two years ago.

"I promised myself I wouldn't make love to you until we caught the bad guys and all was well in Silver Valley again." His breath caressed her face as his fingers—Bryce was shaking, too—traced her forehead and curled a lock of her hair around his finger, his expression childlike in wonder.

But his eyes sparked with purely adult emotion.

As adult as the erection she felt against her midriff.

"Bryce, did it occur to you that I might say no?"

Her attempt at teasing him fell flat. She knew, and knew that *he* knew, she'd never deny the chemistry they shared. Not when they'd built up a newfound trust with each other.

He continued to trace her features, and when his fingers landed on her lips, he smiled.

"Maybe for a split second. Are you, Zora? Are you going to say no?"

She didn't answer and he replaced his fingers with his lips on hers, giving them what they both wanted.

What she needed.

* * *

Bryce had been kidding himself up until the moment he knocked on Zora's door. He'd thought he was going to come in, present her with the broach to show her he believed she'd have a happy family of her own some day and leave.

Once he'd seen her, rosy and relaxed from her yoga, all bets were off.

Her skin warmed under his tongue as he licked her neck, the hollow at the base of her throat. His breath came in gasps but he was so turned on it didn't scare him that he had no control over his reaction to her.

"Come here." She pressed her pelvis into his at the same moment he pulled her to him, and he cursed the weight of his denim jeans between them. Her yoga pants left nothing to his imagination as he let the fullness of her ass fill his hands, his fingers wandering around to her front, closer to her center.

She cried out when he touched her at her most intimate spot.

"It's been a while for me, Bryce."

"Good." He didn't want to compete with any more memories. If he had his way, Zora would forget about the pain of her past and the worries of their next few days.

Everything would be okay, at least for right now.

He sought her mouth with a hunger he knew at some level he'd never fully satisfy. This was more than a roll in the sack to ease the tension of their hours of working together. More than a casual hookup for old times' sake. More than a step toward the possibility of a future relationship.

He and Zora shared the kind of bond that would never

be broken, regardless of what either of them chose to do about it.

Her lips met his with the same hunger and need. When he reached under her sweat top and pulled aside her athletic bra, it felt as if this was the first time he'd touched a woman's breast. Her skin was so soft… Zora resisted none of his caresses, only encouraged him by placing her hands over his and showing him what pleased her most.

He backed into her kitchen counter and reached around her thighs to lift her onto the hard surface. Her yoga had remarkable benefits as her flexibility and strength made it a natural movement. She wrapped her legs around his waist, her arms around his neck, and savored how his tongue felt against hers.

She reached between them and stroked him through his jeans. He pulled back from their kiss.

"Heck, Zora, you're going to finish this before either of us gets what we want."

Throaty and full, her laughter was warm in his ear.

"Let's go to the bedroom," she whispered.

Zora walked first into her room and opted to leave the lights off. Not because she was afraid of Bryce seeing her naked, but because she didn't want to see her undercover getup where she'd hung it on the outside of the master bedroom's closet door. She didn't want any reminders of their mission.

This was their time to be alone together as Zora and Bryce. Not as a fake minister or the detective assigned to protect her.

Before she got to the bed, Bryce's arms were around her waist, pressing her against his chest, his hips. She leaned her head to the side so she could reach his lips and kiss him. The need to show him how much she wanted this blocked out any concerns about how they'd deal with having taken their relationship to this level before they caught the Female Preacher Killer.

Danger would always be part of their lives as long as they were both in the Trail Hikers, as long as Bryce was SVPD. This moment, this chance to express what had occupied so much room in her heart since she returned to Silver Valley, was the chance of a lifetime.

Her lifetime—was it too risky to picture it with Bryce?

"Stop thinking." He turned her around and drew up her yoga top, waiting for her to lift her arms over her head, which she did without hesitation. Freed of the shelf-style bra that was part of the top, her breasts were bare to his gaze, her nipples throbbing with the need for his touch.

He didn't tease as his hands gently cupped her breasts while he strummed her nipples. When he pressed harder into her, Zora's thinking stopped, and all she could do was hold on to his shoulders.

"Kiss me again, Bryce."

He kissed her and lowered her yoga pants past her hips, taking her tiny lace panties with them.

"Let me." She pushed his hands from the bottom of his sweater and repeated the same steps he'd taken with her. Their breathing grew more ragged as each article of clothing was removed. When she got to his button-fly jeans she struggled a bit with the stiffer denim material.

"Are these new jeans, or what?"

"Just for your pleasure." He grunted. She could have laughed, too, but her arousal kept her focus on getting his pants off and getting Bryce inside her as quickly as possible.

They finally stood in front of each other completely naked.

Bryce caressed the side of her face and kissed her deeply as he held her hand. There was a tiny chasm between them but she felt the heat roiling off his skin. Heat for her.

He desired her as much as she craved him.

"I've wanted to be like this with you since I saw you in the patrol car in that awful getup."

His enlarged pupils almost obliterated his gray-blue irises as sincerity flickered in their depths.

"I avoided running into you when I moved back on purpose. I was afraid this would happen."

"And now?" He rubbed her bottom lip with his thumb.

"There's no place I'd rather be."

"I hate to ask this at the last minute, but do you have…"

"Protection? Yes."

"If you didn't, I brought some."

"You were a Boy Scout. I wouldn't expect any less."

This time they laughed together. She allowed relief to wash away her fear that he'd change his mind. That he'd decide it wasn't worth it, getting so close to her. The look he gave her was not that of a man who was going to reconsider his current situation.

"Stop." He kissed her. "Thinking." He kissed her again, this time allowing his hands to wander to her most private places, making the act of standing an athletic feat.

When her knees gave out, she pulled him with her onto the bed. She stretched to tug back the thick down comforter but Bryce stopped her. "Don't. We don't need it, not yet."

With two more kisses Bryce was poised above her,

running his fingers through her hair as he bore his weight on his forearms.

She looked up into his eyes and he smiled.

He entered her in one quick stroke that nearly sent her to her climax. She brought his mouth to hers and they set a rhythm pleasing to both.

Like the team they'd become, they didn't need words as they let touch and feel be their guide to each other's pleasure. By the time they both cried out in complete surrender, Zora knew that she'd never be satisfied with just one time with Bryce.

Before they separated enough to be able to spoon under her down comforter, she knew she wanted more.

Much later the wind still hadn't subsided and the farmhouse's eaves shuddered with each gust. Bryce didn't know the last time he'd felt more relaxed.

It wasn't just the exceptional sex, although an argument could be made for that. No, it was the woman who was curled into his arms, her skin soft and supple wherever it touched his. He'd never tire of the feel of her.

He could live a hundred years and he'd never forget how good it felt to be with Zora.

"What are you thinking?" Her voice, soft after their lovemaking, drifted across his forearm.

"Not thinking. Just feeling."

She stretched and turned to face him. "We need to get our game back on."

"Oh, I'd say that's already in the works."

"Not that. You know what I mean. The case."

He took a lock of her hair and played with it. Her bathroom night-light allowed him to see glimmers of red in the silky strands.

"Cases will always be there, Zora. They never go away. Once we get this bad guy, another will show up. I wish it weren't true, but we've both seen enough to know how it works."

"Yes. I'm not used to being in the midst of one, that's all. In the navy we had ops that were intense, especially in the war zone. But my job was support. I made sure my aircrews or whoever I was working for had the information they needed to do their job and not let the bad guy stop them. Here, I'm in the middle of it. I know I can handle it—I am…we are—but I'll feel a lot better when it's over."

"I know."

"You think it'll be tomorrow, don't you? That he'll try to kill me during the Christmas Eve service?"

"He'll try to kill Reverend Colleen Hammermill."

Her fingers touched his jawline and he nipped at them.

"That's me, Bryce. I'll get through it. *We'll* get through it."

He didn't want to think about the cold reality facing them tomorrow. Forcing the killer's hand at the church or near it was part of the plan. A plan he'd executed in previous ops without a second thought.

Before he'd made love to the one woman he'd never forgotten.

Chapter 19

At work early on the afternoon of Christmas Eve Bryce's touch still lingered on Zora's skin, under the dreaded Kevlar vest and wool suit. She made a silent vow to burn the duds once this was over.

"Chaplain Hammermill?"

Rebecca stood at the entry to the minister's office. Lines of exhaustion splayed from the corners of her eyes and she looked ten pounds lighter than when Zora had spoken to her and Jess a few days ago.

"Come on in, Rebecca. It's Colleen, please. How are you doing? Are you ready for Christmas?"

"Jess is missing."

"What do you mean 'missing'?"

"She was supposed to catch a ride here with me and wait the extra hour before the service while I practice with the bell choir. She was at a sleepover with some girls from school last night, and the older sister of one of her friends dropped her at the entrance to our trailer park earlier this morning. When I got home from the grocery store to pick her up, she wasn't there. No note, either. It's not like her."

"Could she be with other friends?"

Rebecca shook her head. "No. I called her father and he swears she's not with him, either. He's worried, too."

"What about neighbors?" She didn't want to reveal just how much she knew about Rebecca's trailer park. Alarm zinged over her skin and she managed to acknowledge that part of her would always have a core fear of the True Believers. But they were no longer running the show. SVPD and the Trail Hikers were. And she was a trained Trail Hiker, not an innocent young girl.

"Yes, but she's not there. I went back to check. This isn't like her."

"Does she have a friend in the trailer park she could be with?"

"No. I'm worried, Colleen. There are some new men who moved into our park and they seem nice enough, but they're pushy. I don't know them at all, and Jess told me that one of them has made it a point to say hello to her each day when she gets off the bus."

"Have a seat. Let me see if my fiancé can help."

She hit the speed-dial number for Bryce and was relieved when he picked up immediately.

"It's me."

"I know." His tone went from sexy to serious as he must have sensed her tension. "What's wrong?"

"I have Jess's mother here, Rebecca, and she's concerned because Jess didn't show up at home after school. She's not at home now and she was supposed to be there to get a ride from her mother. Jess is on the technical crew for the pageant."

"As the youth minister understudy, I actually worked with her yesterday. She's not the type to just disappear, especially seeing how excited she was to be working on the pageant."

"I agree."

"Did Rebecca say anything about the new neighbors? The True Believers losers?"

"Yes, but I have no idea if that's what's going on."

"I'm on it." Bryce disconnected.

She put the phone down and looked at Rebecca. "I can't tell you not to worry, because you're a mother and you love Jess. We all do. But if anyone can find her, Bryce will."

"Thank God you're engaged to a detective! I don't know if the police would have listened to just me, calling them. Don't they usually make you wait twenty-four hours to file a missing-persons report?"

"Not with juveniles. It doesn't matter. Bryce will get back to us. We have to rely on our faith until then." Zora realized she meant it. Faith that all of this would work out okay.

"I need you to come with me, just in case we run into any trouble." Bryce addressed Rio as they confirmed the addresses of the two new tenants at the trailer park where Rebecca and Jess lived.

"They're not just tenants. Leonard Wise owns the place. They're his buds. I was able to trace them back to the original group that was put in prison in New York." Rio pulled up the property-title document receipt on his screen. He let out a low whistle. "The sale was closed only a month ago by his attorney."

"And the new trailer occupants are former cult members."

"You got it."

Rio's dark gaze never wavered from his computer screen as he clicked from one file to the next, absorbing all he could.

Bryce had street experience, but when it came to pulling information and intel together, Rio was SVPD's best.

Rio finally leaned back and looked at Bryce. "We ready to go now?"

"Yes. I'm telling you, Rio, the only thing that's kept me from storming over there sooner is that if they do have Jess, I don't think they want to hurt her."

Rio grabbed his cover and weapon. He was in his officer's uniform, Bryce in a shirt and tie, his usual detective "uniform."

"Not hurt her? Maybe not, but they want to brainwash her, man. Let's get the girl out of there."

Bryce had already called in the report to Claudia but for now he was acting as an SVPD detective, not so much a Trail Hiker. He let Rio drive one of the station's marked vehicles as they buckled up and headed south toward the outskirts of town.

Taking the main pike they passed the high school, it hit Bryce how much his life had changed since the night two weeks ago when he and Zora had met again, after so many years. After a lifetime, really.

Last night had been a game changer. Zora might be a woman of the world who could handle the "friends with benefits" idea but Bryce was done with that kind of relationship. He wanted what he'd only find with Zora.

First, they had a few things to take care of.

"You're quiet, Detective."

"A lot's been going on. I don't need to tell you that."

The starkness of Rio's expression highlighted what they were up against. "It's always busy this time of year. Between the DUIs, shoplifting and domestic violence it's nonstop. You know it. But this Female Preacher Killer's got us all uptight. We'll all sleep better when he's caught."

"We will." Bryce couldn't keep from reliving last night and longing for more time with Zora.

"I'm not going to let him kill one more person," Bryce vowed, knowing Rio understood his conviction.

"None of us are. We're a good team at SVPD but even we can't stop all the crazies. You're still pretty certain you'll lure him into Silver Valley Community Church?"

"Yeah. You saw the flowers. He's after the woman he thinks is the new minister."

"Sure looks like it. I saw her—Zora—in the conference room with you and the boss, and that other lady who shows up from time to time. Her name's Claudia. Anything I need to know about?" Rio asked the right question in the right way. Casually, as if he hadn't noticed too much.

"Nope. Nada."

Rio laughed. "Right. Okay, I get it. If and when I need to know more, you'll tell me."

Bryce didn't respond. He'd been in Rio's place only a week earlier, before he'd been signed by the Trail Hikers. Come to think of it, Rio would make an excellent Trail Hiker himself. Hell, all of SVPD would. They were that good and Bryce trusted each of the other officers, including Superintendent Colt Todd, implicitly.

Maybe they'd all quit SVPD and become Trail Hikers. No way.

"What's so funny?"

"Did I laugh out loud?"

"No, but you got a stupid grin on your face." Rio teased him he way they used to tease each other when they were partners.

"I miss doing patrols with you, man."

"Sure you do. Right up until you get to be the big sexy detective with a certain redhead."

"What I do in my personal life is my business."

Rio snorted. "I knew it."

They swung into the trailer park and Bryce took note of the entrance sign, which had been cleaned up from its usual dingy state. Christmas lights framed it, blinking through the early dusk.

"We'll both go up to the door, and I'll do the talking. Keep your eyes peeled for the girl. She's twelve, about five feet tall, long dark hair. Skinny kid."

"Will do."

The door opened after the second knock. A man who could easily be mistaken for any elderly gent peered at Bryce and his badge, then took in Rio's uniform and badge.

Bryce recognized him immediately as one of the released felons from the cult.

"What can I do you for, gentlemen?" Bryce saw the intelligence in his eyes. The cunning.

"We're looking for a young girl, about so high." Bryce held his hand to his chest. "We're wondering if you've seen her."

The man took a step back but didn't invite them in.

"Nope."

"You haven't noticed any children out here, maybe walking home from school?"

"No, officers, I pretty much keep to myself." Sure he did. Just like he did as Leonard Wise's number two in the True Believers.

"Her mother's really concerned. It's not like the girl to go off with friends and such."

"In my experience, kids that age know what they want and do things maybe their parents wouldn't like." The man's eyes were on Bryce, challenging him.

"Not this girl. Anyone else in the area you think we should talk to? Any of your neighbors outside a lot? Do you have a neighborhood busybody we should speak to?"

"I'm new here, as I'm sure you know, Detective." The gloves were off. "I have to report my location weekly. Do you honestly think I'd get out of jail and risk going back in?"

"I have no idea, sir. But I will tell you that if I get even a whiff that you've had any contact with any underage children in the area, you'll be back behind bars so quickly your head will spin."

The ex-con stared at him, and Bryce watched as the consequences of not cooperating registered on his face. "Sometimes kids just like to play video games and such. I heard that there's a neighbor over in number 33 has a brand-new video game. The one all the kids want for Christmas."

Bryce's anger surged. The bastard knew how to work around the system.

"We'll check that out. Meanwhile, you see anything strange, you call SVPD immediately."

"Will do."

The man closed the door and Bryce glanced at Rio. No words were needed. Two minutes later they knocked on trailer number 33. The door opened wide, a short woman smiling at them.

"Good afternoon, officers. Is something wrong?"

"You tell us. Do you know the whereabouts of a young twelve-year-old girl named Jess?"

"Gosh, I see a lot of kids get on and off the school bus here. I don't know their names, though."

Bryce heard the blare of a television in another room. "Mind if we come in?"

"Actually, I do. I haven't cleaned up, you see." Behind the drab woman, the trailer looked as if it had been scrubbed bare. The woman knew the law, too, and knew they didn't have a search warrant or they would've shown it.

"We don't mind a little mess. What's that noise? You watching a Christmas cartoon?"

"I don't watch television. I don't believe in it."

Quick footsteps sounded through the thin walls and the blare of the television became clear as a door opened. Gunshots and explosions sounded from the room, but not from weapons.

From a video game.

Jess appeared at the edge of the tiny hallway.

"Mr. Campbell!" She looked shaken, but none the worse for wear.

"Hi, Jess." Keeping it casual was important. "Did you know your mom's been looking for you?"

Jess shot a quick glance behind her as if fearful of something or someone.

"I didn't know. I just came here and got sucked into the new game." She spoke in a fear-induced monotone.

They weren't Jess's words—someone had told her to say them.

"Do you want to come back with us now, Jess?"

She nodded quickly. "I need my backpack. It's in the bedroom."

When she said *bedroom*, Bryce clenched his jaw so tightly, his teeth hurt. If the bastard had touched her...

"Let's get it, shall we?" He drew his weapon slowly, walking toward the shaking Jess.

As he walked into the trailer he ignored the woman's ridiculous protestations.

"Jess, go outside. Wait for us in the squad car. I'll get your backpack."

Jess didn't have to be told twice as she bolted past him toward the front door.

He looked at the woman. "You need to sit down in that chair right there, please. Who's in that room?"

She complied, but not without one last effort. "Bill Brown's in there. He told me not to bother him."

The blaring television was silenced.

"Mr. Brown, SVPD. Please come out with your hands up." Bryce waited with the bedroom door in his sight.

The door clicked open and Bill Brown walked into the hallway, a lopsided grin on his face. "What's all the fuss about?"

"You're going to tell us what it's all about down at the station. You can either come willingly or I'm sure I can figure out a reason to arrest you."

"I doubt it. The girl wanted to play the video game. I didn't bring her here under any force, and I didn't touch her. You've got nothing."

"Your choice. You and your girlfriend can come willingly or risk going back inside." At the reference to prison, the man's shoulders dropped.

"Fine. I'll come in. But you've got nothing."

Bryce was willing to take the chance.

The backup unit they'd had on standby came in and drove Bill Brown and his girlfriend to the station while Bryce and Rio took Jess with them.

"We'll be lucky if we can get you back in time to do the pageant, Jess. We have to take a statement at the station from you."

Tears slipped down her cheeks and she nodded.

"You're safe now, it's okay."

"I didn't want to stay there. I didn't even want to go in, but they said they had puppies and that I could play with them, maybe convince my mother to take one. But when I went in, there weren't any puppies and then he showed me the video console."

"We'll talk about it in the station. Then I'll do my best to get you to church in time for the pageant."

He'd already called Zora, who told Rebecca to meet Jess at the station.

Some Christmas Eve this was turning into.

The main corridor leading to the original sanctuary was stuffed to the gills with almost fifty children in their nativity costumes. Parents corralled the youngest, adjusting halos and wings on angels while Zora and Shirley Mae helped with the larger animal costumes.

Peter was giving last-minute directions.

"It's crazy in the sanctuary. Did you see the guards there?" Shirley Mae kept her voice below the din, so that only Zora would hear her.

"Yes. It's a necessary evil, I'm afraid. Until they catch the…you know." She wasn't going to have this conversation with so many underage ears about. Nor with all the parents, whose hysteria could be even worse. While they all banded together in a show of solidarity for their church, everyone was happy to have SVPD provide extra security. Since the Silver Valley Community Church was so large and blessed with a robust operating fund, they'd also hired additional contract security for other, smaller churches that might not be able to afford their own. While it was impossible to police and secure every church with a female minister in the area, SVPD was going to do its best to make sure there wasn't a Christmas murder in Silver Valley.

"Okay, everybody." Peter clapped his hands and walked to the front of the line. The voices hushed and only the rustle of fabrics and papier-mâché from the costumes could be heard. Some of the sheep baaed and a child giggled when an alpaca spit.

"We're going to do it just like we did in practice. If you forget a line or miss your mark, don't worry. Someone else will say it for you. Older kids, I need you to help keep the angels and shepherd boys in their spots. Let's take a deep breath, blow it out. Okay, now, let's say a prayer. Reverend?"

He looked at Zora and nodded.

Sometimes, even with the constant reminder of the scratchy wig and ridiculous suits, she forgot she was here as a minister. The counseling role came naturally, and protecting everyone was part of her duties as a Trail Hiker, but the ministering part, the prayers, weren't as natural a fit for her.

"Sure. Yes."

Stop it. Just say the damn prayer.

"May we all remember why we're here and have fun. Thank you for this time together. Amen."

She finished and smiled triumphantly at the group. The kids were the first to look back up, but it took the adults a bit longer. When they did, she saw some puzzled expressions.

"Did I do something wrong?" she queried Shirley Mae, who stood next to her, a sly grin on her face.

"No, nothing wrong. It's just that Pastor Katherine tends to go on and on. We're not used to such a contemporary prayer, is all."

"Contemporary?"

"You didn't even mention it's Christmas."

"Oh." She looked back at the group, wondering if she should apologize. But there was no need. They were all in pageant mode, preparing to begin the hour-long show.

Zora ran up to Peter before he disappeared inside the sanctuary to manage the show.

"I'll see you later. I'm going to go watch it from the loft. I'll come down at the end and say the closing prayer and appreciation remarks."

"Thanks, Reverend. Any news on Jess?"

"No, but she's at the police station with Rebecca and Bryce. Hopefully she'll be here in time for most of the show, I mean, pageant."

Peter made a doubtful expression before he smoothed his expression into neutral.

"I hope so."

"Break a leg, boys and girls!" She raised her voice so that the "elephants" in the back would hear, too. A smile tugged at her lips. Silver Valley Community Church had to have the most glorious concept of a Nativity. Not limited to simple farm animals, the entire animal kingdom was arriving to pay respects to the newborn babe. The live llamas, alpaca, sheep and a pony were ready to go, their handlers dressed as shepherds. The more exotic creatures were children in costume.

The strains of the evening's first Christmas hymn vibrated from the massive antique organ. With a final wave at the pageant participants, Zora went to check out the main auditorium. The majority of church members who wanted to attend this earlier service had to view it on the large screens in the modern sanctuary. Only parents and selected friends and family of the participating children were allowed entry into the original sanctuary, due to its limited size and the fire code.

She made her way down the corridor and tried to let the festive oversize garlands and gold ribbon that lined the walls calm her and remind her that it was Christmas Eve.

But no matter how bright the red bows on the sashes or on the singularly giant wreath in front of the main doors, she couldn't forget that she was on a mission and this was its deadliest time. She was trained to handle all contingencies and she'd do whatever was required of her, but she'd sure feel better when Bryce came back.

Hopefully with Jess.

If the SVPD hadn't been so annoying he would've been able to carry through with his plan with no risk to any of the little kids. One bullet could take out Reverend Colleen Hammermill, just like the others. But he'd use buckshot on her, to really make a mess. He'd planned to do it from behind the altar. He'd put a hole in the stained-glass window in the back wall of the old sanctuary. The small mosaic piece had been delicate to remove. He'd had to pick a lighter color so it wouldn't be obvious when the light shone through. All he'd had to do was crank up the heat, and so far no one had noticed the drafts.

The SVPD security detail wasn't something he'd planned on. Bringing a weapon into the building was too risky. He didn't need to bring his rifle in, as he only needed to get to the back wall of the building and fire through the hole. But he'd never escape from the courtyard the windows overlooked after he fired. Not with all those officers around.

No, his original plan wouldn't be the best. Not anymore. Instead, he'd have to sacrifice the entire legacy of the church that had been the very first in Central Pennsylvania, the first in Silver Valley. Its brick walls might not burn but he'd make sure everything inside—pews, lectern and choir loft—were burned to ash.

Because they'd already gutted the spirit of the church with female preachers like Colleen Hammermill. He was just helping them see how evil their new rules were.

"I need you to go through the metal detector, Ernie. Nice Christmas flannel you're sporting there." Officer Nina Valesquez had grown up in this church, as had half of the SVPD. He didn't have a problem with females as cops. They'd wind up dead sooner than the men but that was their problem. Women just didn't have the skills needed to do a man's job properly.

"It's a special night." He left the large wheeled bucket to the side and carried his mop with him.

"I'll take that. The metal's going to set it off."

"Okay."

"Step through."

The alarm went off as he stepped over the threshold with his construction boots.

"Those steel toe?" Nina nodded at his feet.

"Yes, ma'am."

"Let's have Officer Holder wand you, for all our sake's. I know you, Ernie, but we have to do our job."

"No problem." He held out his arms while the officer swept the detection device up and over his limbs, torso and feet, where it reacted again to his boots.

"You're good." Officer Holder looked at Ernie and Ernie didn't like the look he gave him. As if he didn't trust him. The young gun hadn't grown up here like Nina had, and had no respect for tradition.

Being the church custodian was a family tradition, first for his grandfather, then his dad, then him.

"Mind if I go back and get my bucket?"

"No, go right ahead. The pageant's about to start, though, isn't it? You're leaving the Christmas cleaning to the last minute."

"It's always a good idea to keep the mop handy for anything sticky the kids drop. Plus with flu season, sometimes they get sick and it's best to be able to clean it up without delay. You know kids. Not to mention the farm animals."

"Sure thing. Thanks, Ernie, and Merry Christmas."

Merry Christmas indeed.

Chapter 20

It wasn't as stuffy in the choir loft as Zora had expected. The organist had a large bottle of water on the floor next to her stool; no doubt she'd been through more than one long Christmas pageant and Easter service.

There was a minister's seat she could have taken on the altar but she wanted a relative of one of the pageant participants to have the prime spot, and sure enough, a grandmother who had traveled in from Florida was happily seated and would be able to watch her twin granddaughters cavort about as angels.

A familiar sense of knowing hit her and she looked down at the far entryway.

Bryce smiled when their eyes met and nodded toward the stage. As the lights dimmed and the setting backdrop illuminated not only the desert night but the town of Bethlehem, she caught the silhouette of Jess pushing an inn's false front into place.

Her phone buzzed as it was on silent mode and she looked at her message.

Merry Christmas.

She looked up to mouth the words back to Bryce but he was gone. Doing his job, which was what she needed to focus on, too—doing her job as a Trail Hiker. They still had a killer to catch.

As the music swelled to match the onstage drama of the young couple's search for a place of rest, she took her time to account for each child and the parents she'd been able to meet in such a short week working at Silver Valley Community Church. No one in the audience looked out of place or alone.

That was the best thing about Silver Valley. If it was Christmas for one citizen, it was Christmas for all. If a person seemed to be having trouble or was disgruntled, most folks would make a point of being extra nice, or offering help. It was the Silver Valley way of life.

It was what had brought her back here.

And now what was making her stay? Mom and Dad. Her counseling career. Her Trail Hikers assignments.

Was Bryce going to be the biggest reason?

No, this wasn't the time to think about that. She stretched and scratched her collarbone under her vest. Life was going to be so nice when she didn't have to wear the Kevlar.

The taut sense of impending danger wasn't new to Bryce. He felt it before every case broke, some more so than others. It had been hanging over him for the past several days, and he couldn't blame it all on the stress of finding the Female Preacher Killer.

It was more. This case threatened not only Silver Valley but Bryce's peace of mind.

Because Zora's life is at risk.

He worked side by side with female officers and law enforcement agents from many levels of government and had no problem doing so. They were all part of the same team.

Zora was on his team, too, but it was more than that.

You've fallen for her. You love her.

Shit, he couldn't handle this right now. As much as he prided himself on being able to keep a level head during chaos, he wasn't prepared for this storm of emotions.

Their childhood connection made things even harder. Memories fought for his attention. Working the stage crew of his church's pageant, wanting to finish so he could run home to the Krasnys' Christmas Eve dinner. Trading private jokes with Zora about how old-fashioned their parents were.

Her smile hadn't changed.

The church was packed and he took his time surveying the main worship area, which had nearly five hundred people in it, watching the big screens with rapt attention. The organ music was piped in on a state-of-the-art sound system and it felt as if the organ was right behind him instead of five hundred feet away in another room.

The organist was playing in the loft, next to where Zora stood watching the pageant. God, she was breathtaking. She'd never believe his compliments, though, not when she was dressed up like some kind of schoolmarm.

She'd believed him last night, when he'd seen her with

nothing on but the blush their lovemaking had brought to her breasts and throat, up to her cheeks.

The memory warmed him but he stopped it from distracting him from his duty. He caught some questioning looks, some rather prim, as he walked around the aisles. In civilian clothes he looked like any other churchgoer and they probably thought he should just sit down and enjoy the show.

Satisfied that all was well in the huge auditorium, he made sure to make eye contact with each SVPD officer who guarded the doors. Ten in all.

This case was draining their resources. He hated to see the whole team out working on Christmas Eve, but there hadn't been any complaints. They wanted the Female Preacher Killer caught so much that they were willing to do whatever it took to apprehend the bastard.

As quietly as possible he slipped out of the newer sanctuary and headed back for the original church.

SVPD was a pretty good police force, but Officer Nina wasn't the brightest. If she'd taken just a minute to see what was under the towel that covered his bucket, she would've seen the plain clear plastic container that sat in the middle of the sudsy water.

It was full of gasoline.

He'd spent the better part of the morning stuffing the loft with rags soaked in odorless accelerant, cursing Reverend Hammermill the whole time. The stupid bitch had called in all the police and security she could; he knew it had been her. A male minister wouldn't have run scared like Pastor Pearson had, either.

The odorless gas was perfect, and as soon as he saw that the children were all up on the altar toward the end of the pageant, he'd send the loft up as his own Christmas gift to the true church and what it had been when Mama was alive. When it still meant something to be a man. The kids and their families would be able to get out if they weren't too stupid. They could knock out the altar windows and make a run for it.

But anyone toward the back and especially anyone in the loft would be dead. Reverend Hammermill had been bragging to Shirley Mae that she'd watch the whole thing from up there, so that she could appreciate the show without getting in the way. She made his job so easy for him. It still angered him that he couldn't use his gun to take her out. That would be a more poetic way to end it all and make his final statement for the folks in Silver Valley. To make them understand why they had to change their ways.

This would have to do, and maybe it would end up being more fun, too. Plus the fire would be a good reminder of what waited for their souls if they didn't go back to the old ways.

Bryce surveyed the audience and pageant participants. Some of the players onstage were obviously nearing the ends of their good behavior and no wonder. It grew warmer in the wood-paneled sanctuary by the minute, and if he wasn't moving around, he'd be fighting drowsiness, too.

The little ones were overexcited, between the show, the excitement of the after-pageant Christmas Eve party and the anticipation of Santa Claus's gifts tomorrow morning. The Christmas triple whammy.

He looked up to share the moment with Zora.

She wasn't where she'd been before. He took in the

choir loft and tried to silence the alarm bells that blasted off in his mind.

"Mister, I have to go to the bathroom."

A hard tug on his arm forced him to look down at a boy who was dressed as a superhero. Apparently the magi had brought modern friends to greet the infant, too.

"I'm sorry, but you'll have to ask your mom or dad to take you." He scanned the audience, waiting for someone to claim the child. A man hustled up from the third row.

"Sorry. He had a big glass of juice before we left the house. You need to go now, don't you, Ryan?"

The little hero nodded, eyes big.

Bryce smiled. "No problem."

He looked up at the choir loft again, expecting Zora to be back, maybe talking to the organist during the break in the music. Instead, what he saw was a sight he knew would be imprinted on his mind and heart forever.

Thick smoke blanketed the loft and organ, obscuring his view. The flames seared his heart with a fear he'd never known before.

"Evacuate!" He turned to the SVPD officer nearest him. "There's smoke and I just saw flames in the loft. Call it in and get these people out of here."

Before the officer could respond, Bryce was flying up the side aisle, heading for the side stairwell to the loft.

Zora smelled the familiar noxious fumes a heartbeat before she felt the shove in the middle of her back. If not for the high railing, she would have already been on top of the people in the pews below.

Dead.

She turned and grabbed at whoever was pushing her and caught a fistful of wet, cold fabric.

A Christmas red flannel shirt.

"Ernie!" She gasped out his name as his face, contorted in a sick combination of psychosis, rage and purpose, loomed over her.

"You don't belong here, you stupid bitch!" He went for her throat with his hands and she blocked him with moves learned first at the naval academy and most recently in her Trail Hikers training. She used his momentary loss of balance to knee him in the groin while shoving her hand up into his nose. Bones and cartilage crunched under her palm and she didn't stop, allowing instinct to take over. As he bent to grab his injured genitals she shoved him hard and he flipped backward over the antique pew, landing on the one behind him headfirst.

Zora stood shaking as adrenaline pumped through her. Ernie wasn't moving but she couldn't be sure how long he'd be down.

Where the hell was the organist?

Her eyes went quickly to the empty organ bench, next to which lay Eli Jones, his head tilted at an awkward angle. She ran to his side and pressed her hand on his neck.

Thank God, a pulse.

"Zora!"

She heard her name through roar of the…

The flames.

Ugly, white fingers of gasoline-powered flames surrounded her as they climbed up the dry wooden panels. Her eyes teared from the stinging smoke as she looked around, and for the first time since putting Ernie down she realized the church was emptying. The pageant participants were being evacuated.

He'd started the fire before he came for her.

"Zora!" Bryce called for her but the flames were so intense where the stairwell met the loft she couldn't see him.

"Don't come here—you'll never get out!" she yelled as she looked for an escape. She'd never be able to leave via the stairs. Ernie had set both exits on fire.

The loft extended toward the front of the church, near the altar. She could make it there.

Squatting, she spoke to the organist as loudly as she could.

He groaned.

"Can you feel your legs, Eli?"

"Yes." He bent his knees, then moved his feet.

"Great. I'm going to get us out of here. I need you to stand up. I'll hold you as much as I can."

As for Ernie, he was on his own.

Bryce couldn't get past the heat of the flames and had to abandon the stairs. He ran to the most central part of the main floor and his heart threatened to give out when he couldn't see Zora.

"Zora!"

"I'm here!" she answered from the loft. But where the hell was she?

"Where!"

Damn it, where was the fire department?

As if they'd heard his thoughts, the first wail of sirens reached his ears. That was no comfort, though, as he finally saw Zora with—was she dragging someone?

"Zora, get out! You can't take anyone with you."

"It's Eli! Just go to the end of the loft by the altar and help me once I get us there," she yelled in between gasps as she was obviously using every bit of strength she had to help Eli Jones get up and start walking with her.

Relief flooded him. She only had to get to the end of the loft and he'd get her down if he had to catch her in his arms himself.

A huge crack rent the air, and the loft's floor gave way. It seemed to be happening in slow motion as the weight of the organ fell through the wooden planks, bringing down the floor to the very edges of the loft.

He couldn't move as he waited for the flash to subside and shouted when Zora's and Eli's forms reappeared, this time crawling, on the only remaining ledge left.

They had minutes until the entire church went up.

Ernie knew they thought he'd gone down with the loft. One thing about fires—if you stayed low you had a better chance. His flannel shirt was the real trick. He'd soaked it with water before he came up to the loft, allowing him to get through the flames at the entry to the stairs. He practiced earlier today to make sure the red cloth wouldn't look darker when wet and give his plan away. He couldn't take any chances, not this close to his goal.

He made it out of the sanctuary and headed straight for the exit doors. It took him into the snow-covered court-yard, and for a minute he was afraid he'd been caught. But the families were all worried about their little kids and the police were busy with them. The fire trucks would never get here on time.

His balls were on fire thanks to that bitch kneeing him, but it'd be worth it. No way was she getting out of there alive. Neither was that stupid Detective Bryce Campbell, her fiancé. If he was dumb enough to stay and try to save her, let him.

Ernie's nose and entire face hurt like hell and he tried not to look at anyone. They'd think he'd been hit by a falling timber, but he didn't want anyone thinking about him or remembering that they'd seen him here.

Snow had started to fall, and it stung in his one eye that wasn't swollen shut. He lifted his hand to wipe at it and in his momentarily blindness he ran into a wall.

"Going somewhere, Ernie?" He squinted with his good eye into the face of SVPD officer Nina Velasquez. She wasn't smiling.

Chapter 21

Zora saw Bryce standing in the lower pews and she wanted to weep. He couldn't stay there. He couldn't die trying to save her.

"Leave!" The choked plea turned into a harsh wheeze as smoke filled her lungs. Dizziness assaulted her and she was having trouble remembering what she wanted to do with Eli.

"Get down!" Bryce's order reached her and she sank to her belly.

"Can you move?" She couldn't carry Eli if they were both flat on the floor.

"Yes, go, go!" His rasp was weak, too, but audible.

Get low and go.

This scenario wasn't new to her. As a midshipman she'd fought fires in closed trailers at the Philadelphia navy shipyard's firefighting school, thinking it was awful and pointless and praying she'd never have to do it for real. On board ship, an aircraft carrier, she'd participated in countless fire drills and endless fire safety training.

"You can do this, Zora! Remember, stay low, nice and slow, keep moving."

Bryce's words were all she could concentrate on. Her hands fought for purchase on the edges of pews, on the railing. But the wood was so, so hot. The air grew thicker with each breath.

This wasn't how she wanted to go. Not now, not when she'd finally found her purpose.

Bryce.

"Sir, get out. We have it."

Bryce fought against the fireman, panic fighting with logic.

"I'm a detective with SVPD. I have to help. Let me help her."

"This is our job now, Detective. We'll get them."

Ladders entered the sanctuary as Bryce was pulled and shoved out of the building, into the open safety of the courtyard where hundreds of church members and animals huddled for warmth. Foam was being sprayed over the burning blaze.

Never had he felt so completely helpless. Not since Karen had died in his parents' arms over twenty years ago.

"They'll get her out, Bryce." Rio stood next to him, his hand on Bryce's shoulder. Bryce looked at his friend.

"But I couldn't."

"You did, man. You called it in. You worked with her the entire way."

They stood in silence as snow fell from the sky, staring at the doors that the firemen had hoses running in and out of. After what felt like an hour but Bryce knew must have been only minutes, two firemen came out, each carrying a body.

Bryce ran forward to take Zora in his arms.

The fireman handed her to him and she clung to Bryce's neck, gasping and coughing in the clear air. He buried his face in her neck, her hair spilling over both of them.

"Where's your wig?"

"I didn't want it to melt into my scalp."

He knew his practical, tough, fighting Zora was going to be okay.

Zora couldn't remember the last time a shower felt so good. Once the fire department and EMTs had medically cleared her, she'd made sure everyone was accounted for from the church, including the farm animals. Then she'd phoned her parents, letting them know she was fine, that no one had died in the fire, and called it a night.

Bryce had insisted on staying with her, until she'd assured him she'd be fine. He had a lot of paperwork to catch up on and promised to call her in the morning, for which she was grateful. While she'd love nothing more than to lie in his arms tonight and greet Christmas morning together, they both needed to process what had happened.

She certainly needed to figure out what her feelings meant. It still felt like a dream, making love all last night with Bryce. Followed by the nightmare of tonight.

The lavender-and-rosemary soap she'd purchased at Central Pennsylvania's Knitter's Day Out in September made the shower stall smell like a spa. She'd taken a class in Estonian lace knitting from one of the international knitting community's rock stars. As she showered, she thought about the cases she'd handled for the Trail Hikers this autumn. They'd been fairly simple ones, elementary compared to bringing down a serial killer.

Ernie Casio. A janitor. But it didn't matter who he was or what kind of work he did. There'd been enough bitterness in the look he'd given her in the loft to take out an entire town.

But he hadn't. She and Bryce had done their job as Trail Hikers, as had SVPD and the Silver Valley Fire Department. Thank God for Bryce. If she hadn't heard his directives in the midst of the smoke and flames, she wouldn't be here to enjoy the hot shower. Even with all her firefighting courses, when she was faced with the reality of the overpowering smoke and intense heat, she'd needed his help.

The relaxing shower couldn't keep the tremors from shaking her body, though.

She'd survived, just like she had when she was twelve.

Like Jess.

She didn't have the full story from Bryce yet, but Jess had been found and returned to Rebecca. The little she'd gleaned indicated that Jess was okay. SVPD hadn't been able to arrest anyone at this point, but they had the go-ahead to monitor the trailer park. Bill Brown and his girlfriend were free but they'd received a stern warning to stay away from Leonard Wise's activities, if he came to town. The other crony of Wise's hadn't done anything criminal, either.

No one had been hurt.

It was all she could ask for tonight. To keep the True Believers where they belonged—in the past.

All was well.

Butternut's bark broke into her spa experience and she cracked open her shower door.

"Butternut, come."

Nothing.

Usually the dog came when called, unless she sensed someone unfamiliar. Zora reluctantly shut off the shower and stepped out to dry off. The doorbell, followed by Butternut's barks, echoed through the house.

"Not now, Bryce. We said we'd take a night to rest." She spoke to the steamy bathroom. Although she couldn't deny the excitement that rushed through her.

She quickly wrapped her wet hair in a towel and threw on her most comfortable sweats. There was no time or need to dress any more formally. Bryce had already seen her in every kind of clothing. Of course he'd argue that her best look was in bed, naked.

Which they'd both be in short order, regardless of their agreement to give each other a breather from everything they'd been through.

Knocks sounded on the front door as she reached it and she laughed.

"I thought we'd agreed..."

She froze at the sight of the woman at her front door. "Edith."

As soon as Edith walked into the front hallway, Zora knew she was insane in the most textbook sense of the word.

"Can I get you something hot to drink? How about that tea you like?" She didn't have any of the crappy tea Edith drank, but anything would do to keep her distracted until Zora could get help.

Bryce. She had to call Bryce.

"Tea? No, I don't need tea. This is a large place you

have here. Much bigger than it looks like from the outside. I've been here before, you know."

Ignoring the fear that tried to paralyze her, Zora headed for the kitchen as casually as she could.

"I'll put a pot of water on to boil."

Before Edith could react she darted into the kitchen and grabbed her phone.

"I don't want tea." Edith shuffled into the kitchen and Zora lost her chance to text Bryce.

"But I do. It's so cold out."

"Fine, make yourself some tea. We all need sustenance, even at the end."

"The end?"

Edith clammed up, her expression mutinous.

Zora managed to set the teakettle to boil while she was watching Edith. She followed the rule about never turning your back on the enemy. Escaping to the kitchen had been her attempt to reach Bryce.

And it had failed.

Her phone vibrated in her hoodie pocket and she pulled it out.

"Don't answer that, Daisy!"

"Hi." She ignored Edith's shrill demand and kept her responses to Bryce short as Edith watched and listened.

"Okay. Bye." She pretended to disconnect the call and slipped the phone back into her pocket, leaving it on as Bryce had instructed.

Bryce went over the last of the reports that needed to be written up and filed tonight. He'd loathed saying goodbye to Zora but they'd needed time apart. She to heal and rest from the shock of her ordeal, and he to wrap up work as much as possible.

Because when the sun rose, it would be Christmas morning. And he was going to celebrate in style. With Zora. He hoped she'd agree to his festivities, which included chocolate-covered strawberries, champagne and Santa hats.

The papers from his patrol with Rio to find Jess were all he had left to review and enter into the report database. A sticky note was on the file.

Detective,
Compare this with the findings from forensics. Report on top.
Rio

His eyes ached from exhaustion and smoke but he'd be happy he'd done it, come morning. He smiled thinking of how many ways he planned to kiss Zora.

The relaxed atmosphere in the station with the few remaining officers around dissipated when he read over the findings Rio had highlighted. Not only were the footprints next to Zora's gas meter not Ernie Casio's, the lab was certain they belonged to a woman, due to their size and the make of the boots.

Bryce sat back. In the initial interrogation at the hospital tonight, Ernie had insisted he'd had nothing to do with the gas meter. He'd denied ever shooting "Colleen Hammermill," as well.

The hospital staff had asked SVPD to wait until Ernie was more patched up to continue their interrogation. Bryce and Rio had what they needed, however.

Maybe Ernie *had* been telling the truth about the meter.

And maybe his suspicions were correct. Zora's biological mother wasn't here to make amends with the daughter she'd forsaken long ago.

During the wiretap session, Edith had repeatedly told Zora that she'd make sure her daughter was never harmed by Leonard Wise or the cult.

His stomach took a sickening drop.

He picked up his phone and hit speed dial for Zora.

"Hi." Her voice was balm to his worry. Until he heard the other person's voice. Dread threatened his focus.

"You're not alone, are you?"

"No."

"Is it Edith?"

"Yes."

"Has she threatened you?"

"Yes."

"Stay tight. Keep talking and keep the line open. I'm going to transfer this call to our emergency dispatcher."

"Okay. Bye."

Bryce shot up from his desk chair and shouted to the rookie at her desk across the work area as he grabbed his vest, weapon and jacket.

"I'm going to need backup at Zora Krasny's on Cherry Creek and Skyline Drive. Rio, come with me."

No one argued with him. When any of their detectives needed help, that was what they got.

He prayed he'd be in time for Zora.

Butternut stayed at Zora's side, watching Edith with feigned nonchalance, but Zora knew her dog. Butternut's muscles were taut, her senses alert.

Edith took a step closer to Zora and Butternut growled.

"Butternut, no."

"Shut that dog up now."

"She's just shy around strangers, that's all." Actually, she'd never been shy, but one thing Butternut always did was assess a stranger by instinct. Butternut didn't like Edith.

Edith reached into her large coat's side pocket and withdrew a pistol, which she immediately aimed at Butternut.

Son of a puppy.

"Put that dog away in a room now, Daisy."

Funny how being called by her childhood name annoyed her more than the weapon that wavered between her and Butternut. She'd take a bullet for her dog. But not before she brought Edith down.

"Is that pistol really necessary, Edith?" She winced when the name slipped from her. She couldn't call this woman Mother, even in pretense, but using her given name would only rub salt in Edith's wounds. Still, by speaking loudly and describing the situation, she'd let the first responders know they had an armed woman to deal with. "Get that thing away from me."

Edith shuddered and squared her shoulders.

"Butternut's fine. She won't bother you."

Edith's hands shook, but not so much that she had any problem leveling her pistol on Butternut and pulling the safety.

"Do it or I'll put that mutt down myself."

Butternut never fought orders from Zora but she did now, shoving against Zora's legs and doing everything she could to keep from being dragged into the mudroom.

"It's okay, sweetness. Go like a good girl and you can help me out later." When she'd need the comfort only her loyal dog could give her. She kept her murmurs low and for Butternut's ears only.

Butternut finally complied, but once the door was shut she lay down against it with a loud growl.

"Make sure the door is locked and come back in here."

Zora turned to Edith. "I put my dog where you asked. Why don't we sit down and talk this out?" She was grateful to draw on her counseling skills. The earlier events of the evening had left her physically exhausted and even with the adrenaline hitting her bloodstream again, she wasn't sure how much strength she had to spare. Normally she could disarm a woman like Edith with no second thoughts.

"It's too late to talk, Daisy."

"It's never too late to talk." The teakettle whistled. "What kind of tea can I make you?"

Edith's glazed eyes shifted as she looked at the stove and steaming kettle. "None. Pour yours."

It was impossible to make herself a cup of tea without turning her back on Edith and her weapon. Reaching to her side, she clicked off the burner's knob.

"I can have tea later. Why don't we go into the living room? The dog won't bother us as much." Butternut's growls and scratches were escalating, making it hard to hear in the small kitchen.

"You first."

As out of touch with reality as Edith appeared to be, she still had the presence of mind to keep the pistol aimed at Zora and maintain control of the situation.

Zora needed time to figure out the best way to take Edith down. The loaded weapon on her wasn't helping Zora's mental state.

And it wasn't the situation it would have been only a month ago, when she didn't have as much to lose.

"I never understood how you could betray an entire

community of people who loved you, Daisy. How you could betray me, the mother who worked so hard to give you a good life. That's all I ever meant to do, you know. I wanted to give you a good life."

Zora watched Edith's warped thoughts play out through her erratic motions as she paced around the living room, waving the pistol every which way. The room was cold. Zora couldn't bear the thought of lighting a fire when she'd first returned this evening, not after the sanctuary fire. Her skin still felt hot, but her insides were frigid with exhaustion and now fear.

Her heart had been frozen, too, thanks to this woman who had birthed her and lost her mind long ago. Her feelings for Bryce, rediscovered and new, were what had finally managed to thaw it.

"You owe me no explanations…Mother. It was hard to live through all that, no matter whether you were an adult or child."

She'd saved herself and countless other girls all those years ago. But she hadn't been able to save her mother. Edith's mind was still lost.

"After you left, they all wanted to come after me, you know. That's why I had to leave. I couldn't even visit Leonard in prison. It was too risky. One of the other women might see me and then I'd never have any peace. That's all I want, Daisy. Some peace."

Peace. Zora could use a little herself. Between playing the part of Colleen Hammermill for the past couple of weeks and now being addressed by her childhood name, her own mind was reeling from the stress.

But not so much that she didn't see the signs of an imminent mental breakdown in Edith.

Her phone was in her pocket, still on. How much could Bryce or the Emergency Management Service hear?

"Why did you come to Silver Valley, Edith? How did you find my house?"

"Your address was on the books at the hospital. I'm here for the same reason I've been coming since I found out where you live. Since you left the navy."

"What's that?"

"I want to save you from any harm Leonard might do. I know he's free again, and he'll want you, want his revenge. While that's his right, and you deserve it for betraying us, I can't let him hurt you. Not in that way." Even now, Edith couldn't break her denial enough to say the words that described what Leonard Wise did to the young women in his compound. Under his sick control. And in her sick, twisted mind, she believed she was capable of operating separately from the cult leader.

"You think you're saving me from being raped?"

"Don't say that, Daisy!" The pistol was aimed at her again and Zora prepared to hit the floor and take Edith out at the knees. She'd prefer to wait for backup. One of the trained SWAT officers could get a solid lock on Edith through the front window, she was certain.

It depended on when Edith decided she was done talking and wanted to start shooting.

Edith resumed pacing the room, her words rambling, a continuous stream of consciousness, the raving of a madwoman.

"I won't let him get you. I wouldn't have before, either, you know. I would have saved you from it then, too."

"You would have killed me when I was a little girl?"

As Edith paced in front of her Christmas tree, Zora's mind flashed back to the young woman Edith had been before the True Believers, before the cult's teachings had brought her already disturbed mind to its breaking point. They'd had some sweet Christmases in front of a tiny tree with few ornaments, with the basket of rich foods delivered by local churches and community food pantries. Plus the restaurant where Edith worked had always given them a half dozen cinnamon rolls, a luxury they hadn't been able to produce in their small apartment with its almost antique kitchen.

"We had some good Christmases before—we can have more." Maybe a positive appeal would work better with Edith.

Edith stopped in her tracks and looked from Zora to the tree. The lights sparkled on and off, the lively twinkling a contrast to the flat expression on Edith's face.

"Oh, no. No more Christmas for us, Daisy."

Edith's arms lowered and her bottom lip quivered.

"Put the gun down, Mother, and come here." Zora was prepared to tackle Edith if she didn't comply, but thankfully her counseling instincts proved correct. Edith dropped the gun onto the floor.

Where it misfired.

Edith screamed and Zora jumped over the sofa and tackled her, but she needn't have bothered. Edith had put her hands over her head, curled into a fetal position and started chanting.

"We are all going to a better place, we are all going to a better place."

The sound of the gunshot hit Bryce's headset as he drove straight up Zora's driveway and slammed to a stop in front of her porch steps.

"Gunshot. We have a gunshot." The emergency operator narrated back everything she heard, for which he'd been grateful.

Until now.

He and Rio bolted for the front door, weapons drawn.

"Do you hear anything else?" Rio asked.

"Just chanting of some sort. Do you hear it, Detective?"

"Tell me what you hear."

"She's saying, 'We are all going to a better place.'"

"Don't listen to it." Rio ripped Bryce's earpiece out and grasped his shoulder.

Bryce nodded. No words were needed.

Their job was clear, and his training took over.

He crept to the front window and looked carefully inside. The tree sparkled in the corner next to the empty fireplace. One lamp was lit on an end table next to the large overstuffed sofa. No one was in sight. He stood up farther.

Just beyond the sofa, he made out a familiar silhouette. Zora's head. She appeared to be rocking back and forth. The band of dread around his chest lessened but didn't completely release.

He ran up to Rio, who was peering through the side windows of the front door.

Rio's eyes met his.

"Your woman's safe, Bryce."

Bryce looked through the frosted windows, too, and saw why Rio's voice was so quiet, why he hadn't broken the door down once he saw the scene before them.

Zora sat, yoga-style, with Edith in her lap, her arms around her biological mother as she rocked her.

The knock at the door didn't even startle Edith, who seemed to have retreated into the safe space she'd created in her mind.

"Come in." Zora had left the door unlocked, suspecting Edith's arrival meant trouble.

Bryce was on his knees next to her, his arm around her, his face in front of hers. "Are you okay?"

"Yes. We're going to need EMTs. She's had a psychotic break, I think. I'm not a psychiatrist, but…" She didn't have to say any more. One look at the woman's hunched form, her glazed eyes and her barely moving lips was enough for a layperson to know she wasn't in reality.

"On the way."

Zora wept in relief as she accepted that she was okay, that Edith wasn't going to hurt anyone, that she was safe. They were all safe.

Bryce had made it.

"Are you sure you're okay?" It was clear her safety was all Bryce cared about.

"I'm fine. Can you do me a favor and let Butternut out of the mudroom? She's not very happy."

"Why don't I stay here with Edith and you go let her out? She's not going to want anyone but you."

She regarded the most compassionate man she'd ever known. "I can't leave her like this."

"Then, Butternut can wait on the back porch a little longer. We all will." Bryce lowered himself behind her and pulled her against his chest, reaching his arms around to include Edith.

"You're not alone, Zora." His kiss on her temple allowed her to finally relax and release the tension she'd felt since the moment Edith had aimed her weapon at Butternut.

She looked around, taking in Rio's steady gaze on them as he stood waiting for the EMTs and backup patrols at her front door. She noticed the disarray of her shoes and boots that had been knocked off her shoe rack near the doorway. An angry deep scratch on her hardwood floor reminded her of the gunshot.

"Her weapon misfired into the floor."

"Nothing that can't be repaired." His voice was low and more comforting than an angel's touch.

"No." She snuggled farther into him, Edith still murmuring her endless chants.

"I think I hear the sirens. Not much longer."

"Is it midnight yet?"

His arm came up and he held his watch in front of her eyes.

"What does it say?"

"Merry Christmas." She turned as far as she could and he met her the rest of the way, his kiss the best way he knew to tell her she wasn't alone.

For the third time in less than two weeks, SVPD's forensic team swept through Zora's home. She was relieved when they pried the bullet from the hardwood; she didn't want any physical reminders of her mother's breakdown in the house. As for her memories, they would eventually heal.

With Bryce at her side.

When all the emergency responders had finally left, they sat together on her sofa and watched the Christmas-tree lights as night turned into dawn.

"I got a text last night." She rubbed his chest.

"Hmm."

"Not 'hmm.' More like 'yummy.'"

"What do you mean?"

"It seems that the Silver Valley Fire Department has opened its kitchen to the entire Silver Valley Community Church and is offering a free pancake breakfast later this morning. After we have an abbreviated service, also in the fire hall."

"You're not the pastor anymore. You don't have to go."

"Not as Colleen Hammermill, but I can go as myself. Claudia told me to say I was working with SVPD as a civilian volunteer. A shaky explanation, I know, but we're going to say I was using my psychology background to help find the killer. Since you've never been anyone but yourself, you can come, too. What do you say?"

"I say you're unstoppable. First, I'd like to start Christmas with a new tradition of our own. There's one specific activity I'd like to engage in under the Christmas tree with you."

She was exhilarated by the way he said it. As though…

"Stop thinking, Zora. Stay here, today, with me. Just for this morning."

"And after that?"

"We'll talk about it next Christmas."

* * * * *

Don't miss the next thrilling installment in the SILVER VALLEY P.D. *miniseries, coming in early 2016!*

#1875 CONARD COUNTY WITNESS
Conard County: The Next Generation
by Rachel Lee
When his late wife's friend Lacy Devane discovers her bosses' corrupt activity, recovering war veteran Jess McGregor insists on protecting her from possible retribution. As life-threatening danger crosses their paths, neither Jess nor Lacy is immune to peril—and love...

#1876 HIS CHRISTMAS ASSIGNMENT
Bachelor Bodyguards
by Lisa Childs
Ex-cop Candace Baker has never understood other women's weaknesses for bad boys...until she falls for reformed criminal-turned-bodyguard Garek Kozminski. But when Garek takes an undercover assignment to catch a killer, he's risking not only his life, but also Candace's heart.

#1877 AGENT GEMINI
by Lilith Saintcrow
Amnesiac spy Trinity—aka Agent Three—is fleeing the government agency that infected her with a virus. But before she reaches freedom, she must dodge the agent on her tail. Cal knows he and Trinity are two halves of a whole, and he intends to make her realize it—if he can catch her.

#1878 RISK IT ALL
by Anna Perrin
When PI Brooke Rogers is targeted by the Russian mafia, FBI agent Jared Nash rescues her. As the two embark on a mission to search for Jared's missing brother, they fall deeper and deeper into love—and into danger.

---

*When his late wife's best friend comes to Conard County
seeking protection, Jess McGregor can't help but agree.
After all, the former soldier can keep his heart in line as
he guards beautiful Lacy Devane…or can he?*

*Read on for a sneak preview of
CONARD COUNTY WITNESS, the latest book
in Rachel Lee's thrilling miniseries,
CONARD COUNTY: THE NEXT GENERATION.*

Shock rippled through him, but not enough to completely
erase his desire for her. Man, she'd probably have night-
mares if she saw the stump of his leg. It would inevitably
destroy the mood. Then there was Sara, a woman they
had both loved. He'd feel as if he was cheating on her, and
he suspected Lacy might as well, ridiculous as that might
be. Loyalties evidently didn't go to the grave.

Jess sighed and reached down with his free hand to
rub his stump, as if it could free him from the pain he had
never felt when he was hit, pain that his body evidently
refused to forget.

"Can I help?"

"Nah." Oh yeah, she could. With a few touches she
could probably carry him to a place where nothing but the
two of them could exist. But afterward… Hell, he feared
the guilt that might follow. He could ruin a perfectly good
friendship by getting out of line with this woman.

He and Sara had once had a serious discussion about
the possibility that he might not return from one of his

deployments. Just once, but he remembered telling her to move on with life, that he'd never forgive himself if she buried herself with him.

She'd cocked a brow in that humorous way of hers and asked, "Do you really think I'm the type to do that?"

"Just promise me," he'd said.

It was one of those rare occasions where she'd grown utterly serious. "I'll promise if you'll promise me the same thing."

Of course he'd promised. It had never occurred to him he might be the lone survivor. But that didn't mean he wouldn't feel guilty anyway. Maybe he had some more demons to get past.

He realized that Lacy had unexpectedly dozed off against him. Smiling into the empty night, he removed the mug from her loosening grip and put it on the side table. He guessed she felt safe with him, but he wasn't at all sure that was a good idea.

That note. It hung over him like a sword. What the hell did it mean? He stared into the fire, uneasiness joining the pain that crept along his nerve endings and the desire that wouldn't stop humming quietly.

Don't miss
CONARD COUNTY WITNESS
by New York Times *bestselling author Rachel Lee,*
available December 2015 wherever
Harlequin® Romantic Suspense
books and ebooks are sold.

www.Harlequin.com

THE WORLD IS BETTER WITH

Romance

Harlequin has everything from contemporary, passionate and heartwarming to suspenseful and inspirational stories.

Whatever your mood, we have a romance just for you!

Connect with us to find your next great read, special offers and more.

 /HarlequinBooks

 @HarlequinBooks

www.HarlequinBlog.com

www.Harlequin.com/Newsletters

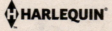

HARLEQUIN®

A *Romance* FOR EVERY MOOD™

www.Harlequin.com